Insignificant Others

ALSO BY SARAH JIO

The Violets of March
The Bungalow
Blackberry Winter
The Last Camellia
Morning Glory
Goodnight June
The Look of Love
Always
All the Flowers in Paris
With Love from London

Insignificant Others

A NOVEL

SARAH JIO

WM
WILLIAM MORROW
An Imprint of HarperCollinsPublishers

INSIGNIFICANT OTHERS. Copyright © 2025 by Sarah Jio & Chris Goldberg. All rights reserved. Printed in the United States of America. No part of this book may be used or reproduced in any manner whatsoever without written permission except in the case of brief quotations embodied in critical articles and reviews. For information, address HarperCollins Publishers, 195 Broadway, New York, NY 10007.

HarperCollins books may be purchased for educational, business, or sales promotional use. For information, please email the Special Markets Department at SPsales@harpercollins.com.

FIRST EDITION

Designed by Nancy Singer

Library of Congress Cataloging-in-Publication Data

Names: Jio, Sarah, author. | Goldberg, Chris, author.
Title: Insignificant others : a novel / Sarah Jio & Chris Goldberg.
Description: First edition. | New York, NY : William Morrow, 2025. |
Identifiers: LCCN 2024021118 | ISBN 9780063371156 (hardcover) | ISBN 9780063371170 (ebk)
Subjects: LCGFT: Romance fiction. | Time-travel fiction. | Novels.
Classification: LCC PS3610.I6 I57 2025 | DDC 813/.6—dc23/eng/20240506
LC record available at https://lccn.loc.gov/2024021118

ISBN 978-0-06-337115-6 (hardcover)
ISBN 978-0-06-344428-7 (international edition)

25 26 27 28 29 LBC 5 4 3 2 1

For Brandon and Viviana

The longest journey

you will ever take is

the 18 inches from

your head to your

heart.

—Thích Nhất Hạnh

PROLOGUE

I hear him snoring before I even open my eyes. His left arm is draped over my side, his breath on my skin. Another day, another lover. As the sun rises, I watch, with curiosity and envy, the shadows dance on the bedroom wall. They flutter unencumbered—free and light—reminding me of how topsy-turvy my life has become.

These past days have been a blur, and, frankly, I'm still making sense of it all, and yet, I don't bother rolling over to size this one up. Is he tall? Short? Does he have a temper? Scratchy stubble on his chin? A foreign accent, maybe? He could be any or all these things. He could be a humanitarian, a con artist, a neurosurgeon, or a philanderer. But I don't care. I just want to understand what is happening and make it stop.

"Morning, sexy," he whispers, inching closer. He kisses my neck, just below my left ear, as I catch a whiff of strong cologne—too strong. His voice sounds familiar, though I can't immediately place it, or where we met.

I close my eyes and hold my body still, pretending to be asleep, relieved when he finally takes the bait, yawning, then rolling over. When the snoring starts again, that's my signal: time to go—and fast.

Fortunately, I'm able to pull away undetected. I take a moment to find my bearings, surveying the spacious loft apartment at the top of some high-rise in some city. This guy's obviously well-to-do. An enormous oil painting hangs on the far wall. It looks like something a six-year-old might create with a canvas and a few jars of paint, though it probably cost six figures. They always do.

Cool air hits my bare skin and I shiver as I catch my reflection in the full-length mirror. I'm not sure whose idea the red lace teddy was, but I cringe nonetheless. *Clothes. I need clothes.* Fortunately, I spy a closet ahead, and *what a closet.*

Divided in half, his belongings encompass the right, hers the left. He must be an executive of some kind, judging by the suits. So many suits. I turn to the other side, wondering about the woman who lives here—well, about her life, anyway. I know who she is, of course, but not really—she's only a sketch, just a scribble on a notepad. Is she happy? Successful? Bored? I glance back at the hallway leading to the bedroom, wondering if she's in love with the snoring man draped in expensive linen sheets. Is he her sun, moon, and stars?

I sigh, running my hand along a shelf of buttery-soft cashmere sweaters, folded in perfect stacks. I select a black one before eyeing her impressive shoe collection. She's got a thing for Jimmy Choos, obviously—and Louis Vuitton bags. I reach for one—might as well— then find a pair of jeans and some flats. *Seven and a half—perfect.*

I tiptoe out to the living room, pausing next to the marble-top kitchen island, where an empty wine bottle and two glasses—one with lipstick on the rim—rest beside a wallet.

I look out the window and spot the Space Needle and the Smith Tower, with its pyramid-shaped rooftop. *Seattle!* My heart surges as I pry the American Express card out of its slot, then grab the rest of the cash in the wallet: a few hundred-dollar bills and some twenties— might as well.

"Lena?" he calls from the bedroom, which sends my pulse racing as I dash for the door, slipping into the hallway, then bolting for the elevator. I feel a little sorry for this one, but I don't have time to go back and explain. Nope. I've got to get out of here—and fast.

Like most of the others before him, I probably won't see this one again. He'll remain a blip on the radar. I sigh as the elevator makes its descent. I do love this cashmere sweater.

The cold air stings my cheeks as I make my way down the hill to Pike Street, picking up my pace as I weave through a crowd of tourists near the Market. I have a ferry to catch and *a lot* of things to sort out. The top priority: FIGURE OUT HOW TO GET MY LIFE BACK.

PART
ONE

EARLIER...

1

"I'm going to need you to open a little wider, please," the dental hygienist says as she scrapes my teeth with what looks like a miniature version of Captain Hook's prosthetic arm. I can't decide if being annoyed is her default, or if my annoyance is contagious. Probably the latter.

Why my twenty-three-year-old assistant, Samantha, scheduled a dentist appointment *today* is beyond me, but I'm here, and I obediently open my mouth wider when told—while holding my phone over my head to read the latest stream of work texts. Earnings are next week, and we're scrambling.

"How many times a day do you floss?" the hygienist asks, her tone suspicious and prosecutorial.

"Two," I lie.

"Hmm," she says, unconvinced. "Well, your gums tell a different story."

I ignore the gum police. My boss, Christina, is calling, and I can't not take her call.

"*Heffow?*" I mumble. The hygienist's hand is still in my mouth.

"Lena?"

"*Fime fat fe fentist.*"

"What the hell are you doing at the *dentist—today*?" As difficult as Christina can be, honestly, I'm impressed. She speaks *Dentist*.

I should explain to her that this is my assistant's fault—the one who spends more time on TikTok than managing my calendar—but I don't. Besides, I can tell by her exasperated tone that our CEO is on the warpath. "Let me guess, Phil's pushing back on the talking points?" I ask when my mouth is momentarily unoccupied.

"To put it lightly," she says with an exaggerated sigh. "But, yes, he has questions. Lots of them. When will you be back at your desk?"

"Soon," I say, glancing at my watch before declining the fluoride treatment. The hygienist looks critically wounded, but I don't have time to play the dental shame game. I have a fire to put out at work, a hair appointment to get to, and a dinner reservation tonight—a very important one.

AN HOUR LATER, I FIND SAMANTHA IN MY OFFICE, BACK TURNED, LINGERING over my desk. She's holding the framed photo of Kevin and me, a selfie we snapped last year on a hike to Alamere Falls, the only waterfall on the West Coast that spills out into the Pacific Ocean. It was beautiful, yes, but hiking isn't my forte—far from it. In fact, I can think of an exhaustive list of things I'd rather do than trudge through muddy hills, out of breath—things like cleaning my toilet. But, for Kevin, I hike. He loves it, and I must admit, the tender moment we shared that day on the bluff overlooking the sea, well, it was worth all the huffing and puffing. He reached for my hand, looked into my eyes, and told me he thought we were "meant to be." That was one year into our relationship, and everything was going according to plan. It still is.

I clear my throat, realizing Samantha hasn't heard me come in.

"Oh," she says, looking up, startled. "I thought you were at the . . . dentist. I was just . . . dusting." She smiles nervously, the corners of her mouth turned upward like the Cheshire cat's.

"You're really lucky, you know," she continues fawningly—a little too fawningly. "Kevin's a catch." She sets the frame back on my desk.

"Yep," I say, repositioning it back in place before sliding into my chair and opening my email. "He is." It's no secret that Samantha has a thing for my boyfriend. I mean, I see the way she lights up when he calls or stops by the office. I don't feel threatened, though. Samantha isn't his type. She dresses her three cats in infant onesies and refers to them as her "children."

"I noticed the dinner reservation on your calendar for tonight," Samantha says, lingering. "Le Rêve—fancy." She pauses, eyes wide. "Do you think he's going to . . . propose?"

My cheeks burn. What's wrong with this generation and their lack of boundaries? Of course Kevin's going to propose, but I don't need to discuss this with Samantha. We've been dating for two years and have checked all the boxes. He brought me home to Nashville to meet his family last Christmas, and tomorrow we're flying to Seattle to visit my aunt Rosie on Bainbridge Island. We've discussed the future, too—travel, the house we'd envisioned in Sausalito, with a little garden, just paces from the shore. But it was that stroll through Tiffany a few months ago that was the culminating moment. I casually pointed to an engagement ring that caught my eye, and he smiled knowingly, then asked the sales associate for her card. Yes, it's all going according to plan. And tonight? The crescendo.

"Are you sure?" my best friend, Frankie, asked me the other night over FaceTime. She was wearing a mud mask and lounging on the sofa in her New York apartment while we shared a glass of wine three thousand miles apart. It's not that she doesn't like Kevin. She adores him, of course. Everyone does—especially my assistant. I nodded my reply to Frankie that evening, but avoided eye contact as I took a long sip of wine. "Hey," she continued. "Sorry. I just want to be sure that . . . *you're* sure."

Sure. Of course I am. In business, my instincts are honed sharper than a double-beveled Japanese knife. I can schmooze the boards of Fortune 500 companies and lead CEOs through corporate minefields like a Pied Piper. I'm decisive, focused, and tough as nails. And love? In my dating life, I've applied the same techniques: assessing pros and strategically analyzing flaws. Like the most ruthless judge on

American Idol, I have zero qualms about giving someone the X. Why waste time with someone who isn't right?

But then came Kevin. His "résumé"? Impeccable. Also, he looks great in a suit, knows how to change a tire, and his apartment is spotless. Hired.

"I'll tell you how *I* was sure," Frankie said, smiling nostalgically as she recounted the night she met her husband, Christian. "It was like he was the missing puzzle piece I'd been searching for my whole life." She paused, staring at me through the screen. "Are you sure you feel that way about Kevin?"

Frankie spoke with such certainty, such knowing, I'll admit her words tugged at my heart: *Is Kevin* my *missing puzzle piece?* Then my sensibilities took over. He's successful, kind, ridiculously handsome. Duh!

"Of course I feel that way about Kevin," I exclaimed, a little miffed. "Now, can you stop giving me anxiety, and can we start talking about what I'm going to wear to Le Rêve?"

Yes, tonight will be the beginning of the rest of our lives—if I can just get through the rest of this workday. I square my shoulders, then open an email from Christina about our CEO's objections to the talking points I prepared earlier. I know the drill—an endless hamster wheel of chest-puffing, appeasing, placating, repeat—and I already know the outcome: Change everything, then change it back. I've got this.

"Oh, I almost forgot," Samantha says, still lingering in the doorway. "You got a few calls while you were out: Jen in accounting, Nick from BlackRock, oh, and—"

"No time," I interject. "I've got to deal with Phil's drama, before I leave for my appointment."

Samantha eyes me with that pinched expression she makes when the copier breaks, or when accounting asks her to send in the expense report early. "You mean your *hair appointment*, right?"

I ignore the tinge of judgment in her voice. "Please get the door on your way out, okay?"

I ARRIVE AT THE SALON OUT OF BREATH AND GREET MY LONGTIME STYLIST, Kristen, with a hug. She scrolls through her phone, proudly showing me the latest photos of her eight-month-old baby daughter, with a pink floral headband adorning her bald scalp.

"Aww, she's so cute," I exclaim, my expression animated, but forced. *Is it just me, or do all babies look the same? Like aliens.*

I slide into Kristen's chair just as Frankie FaceTimes again. "Hey," I say with a sigh.

"What's wrong?" she asks, her eyes narrowing.

"Work's been crazy," I explain. "It's been one fire drill after the next. I swear, one of these days this job is going to be the death of me."

"But not today," Frankie replies with an encouraging smile.

I grin, relieved to be out of the office, but also still going over today's play-by-play. "I'm not going to lie," I continue. "I *am* really jazzed about the tweaks I made to our CEO's call notes for tomorrow. I think I found a more holistic way to diagnose our stockholder issues; you know, drive value to create bottom-line operational efficiency."

Frankie rolls her eyes. "Uh, Lena, English, please?"

"Sorry," I say, laughing, aware of how my corporate lingo makes her cringe. Frankie (Francesca) and I met our freshman year of college when we were paired together as roommates at NYU. Similar enough to connect about the important things in life and different enough keep each other laughing, we bonded over a thousand divergent things: our dislike of cafeteria food and the boy-crazy girls on our floor, our preference for multicolored vs. white Christmas lights, the smell of freshly sharpened pencils, Anne Lamott books, the Strokes, and Zooey Deschanel.

"Anyway, I'm at the hair salon," I continue, smiling at Kristen in the mirror. "I thought I'd go all-out for tonight."

"Just promise me," Frankie says jokingly, "no bangs."

I laugh to myself, remembering that night in college when we decided to cut each other's bangs. I can still picture Frankie, panic-stricken and sobbing as she stood in front of the mirror in our little bathroom after I lopped off a giant chunk of her hair. "I mean," I reply, laughing so hard my sides hurt, "it *was* . . . kind of cute."

"On *you*," she scoffs. "I looked like a poodle, Lena. You should have told me that curly-haired girls can't pull off Zooey bangs!"

"I was eighteen," I counter, still laughing. "What did *I* know?"

After she and I spent several years as post-college roommates in Brooklyn, I got a job offer in San Francisco, while she stayed behind finishing the final semester of her MBA. Despite being at the top of her class at NYU, she passed up lucrative opportunities in Manhattan and instead accepted a position running a nonprofit in Greenpoint serving underprivileged youth. That's Frankie.

When Kristen takes me over to the sink to shampoo my hair, our call ends abruptly, in only the way best friends can.

"Why don't we give you some loose curls," Kristen suggests when I'm scrubbed and deep-conditioned. "Something feminine, romantic."

"Curls?" I hesitate. "I don't know. Do you think that might be . . . too much?"

Kristen shakes her head. "I'm not going to let you walk out of here looking like Shirley Temple—I promise."

What's wrong with curls? I imagine Frankie saying, running her hand through her bouncy dark ringlets, which perfectly match her spirited personality.

I eye my limp, stick-straight, medium-blond hair, remembering a comment Kevin made a few months ago before I left for a haircut. My blunt cut has always been my trademark look, but he'd suggested I change things up a bit, maybe choose a "softer style."

"All right, let's go with *soft* curls," I finally say, biting the bullet. "But nothing too overdone. I don't think I can pull off Frankie's iconic look."

She *is* iconic, in every sense of the word. Smart, funny, down-to-earth—beautiful but not in a showy sort of way. Her mom's a Montessori preschool teacher from Sicily; her dad, a banker from Ohio; but Frankie is uniquely herself. With olive skin and piercing hazel eyes, and those curls, she's beautiful, but effortlessly so—the type of woman who has no clue when people are eyeing her from across the room.

While I'm certainly not *iconic*, I am slim; my eyes are mossy green, which I'm told is rare; and I do have great calves, and I like to think that makes up for my shortcomings in the hair department.

"Let me work my magic," Kristen says, wielding her curling iron this way and that—spritzing and scrunching and tousling my lifeless mane until it looks, well . . . kind of amazing.

"There," she finally says, taking a step back as she smiles at me in the mirror, pleased. "Lena, you look *stunning*."

I swallow hard, taking in my reflection. While I've always been fairly disciplined about my appearance—a touch of makeup, never overdone, a daily three-mile run to keep my 125-pound frame in check, tasteful work attire—this is a whole new *softer* me. Kevin will like it, I know. But do I? I feel a lump rising in my throat.

"Hey," Kristen says, sensing my unease. "What's that face for?"

I bite the edge of my lip.

"It's normal to be a little anxious," she promises. "I was a nervous wreck before I got engaged." She pauses for a long beat. "Is something else going on?"

"I'm fine," I say quickly, squaring my shoulders. "Like you said, it's just nerves."

MY HEART BEATS LOUDLY IN MY CHEST AS I STEP OUT OF THE CAB AND GAZE AT the restaurant ahead. With two Michelin stars, Le Rêve ("The Dream" in French) has a six-month waiting list, a cult following among foodies, and, as evidenced by the smug look on the hostess's face, an unmistakable air of pretentiousness.

I look around the lobby for Kevin, but when I don't see him, I check my phone and find his latest text:

Sorry, crazy day.

Running late.

Get our table for us, and I'll be there in 15–20.

I tell myself not to be annoyed. Kevin works in commercial real estate; his job is just as hectic as mine, perhaps even more so, and today he agreed last-minute to chaperone his six-year-old nephew's field trip.

"Ma'am, your table's ready," Smug Hostess says as I attempt to shake off my disappointment.

I follow a man in starched whites to the center of the dining room. At the table, alone, I feel like I've been thrust into a gigantic fishbowl as nearby diners look over. Fortunately, the approaching waiter's smile calms my nerves—also the glass of champagne he offers. I take a big sip.

"Good evening," he says, one hand placed formally behind his back. "While you're waiting on your guest, may I ask if we're celebrating anything special tonight?"

I down a little more champagne, then crack a smile. "Well," I begin, lowering my voice to a whisper. My black-sequin dress is chafing my underarms, so I sit up straighter. "Just between you and me, I think my boyfriend might *propose* tonight."

"Oh, how wonderful!" the waiter exclaims. "I'll let the violinists know."

As if on cue, the musicians descend—hovering around my table like a mini-symphony for . . . one. I smile awkwardly and nod a few times, then turn back to my phone. Fortunately, they get the hint and meander to another table.

Twenty-five minutes and two champagnes later, Kevin finally

arrives, looking just as handsome as always. "Hey," he says with a sigh as he slides into his chair, declining the waiter's offer of champagne with a dismissive wave. "Bourbon. Double—on the rocks."

"Hi," I say, wondering if he likes my hair.

"Sorry I'm late," he says, rubbing his forehead. "Max refused to leave until we saw the tigers, and then I hit rush-hour traffic."

I smile. "Uncle of the Year."

"As long as it's *once* a year," Kevin replies with a laugh. "I don't know how my brother and sister-in-law do it. Kids are freaking exhausting."

I nod in agreement, reaching for his hand, but he picks up his phone instead. "Hold on, I've got to tie up one last work thing."

"Oh," I say, leaning back in my chair, just as the eager violinists reappear. "Okay."

I watch him as he types, wondering if the ring is in his pants pocket or the inside of his coat. I tell myself that we'll laugh about this someday. We'll tell the story at dinner parties, recounting how he showed up late; that I was overdressed and he, underdressed. Everyone will smile and—

"What's up with the violinists?" Kevin asks, casting an annoyed glance at the hovering musicians.

"Um," I begin as the waiter returns with Kevin's bourbon. "I don't know. Don't you think it's kind of . . . nice?"

He rubs his temples, then continues jabbing his phone screen. "Not when you have a splitting headache."

Our waiter takes the hint and discreetly sends the musicians to another table, while I fish through my purse for a pack of Advil, with no luck.

Finally, Kevin sets down his phone and clears his throat. "Sorry about that." He straightens his cutlery, then glasses—water and bourbon—in parallel lines before patting the lapel of his jacket proudly. "So. I have a surprise for you."

I lean in expectantly, eyes wide.

"I know we've talked about this for a while," he begins, "and that the circumstances weren't right last year, but . . ."

I smile, my heart beating faster as Kevin slips his hand inside his jacket.

"But I think that it's our time *now*."

I reach for his hand. "*Yes*, it is," I say, beaming, eyes welling up with tears as he pulls out . . . an envelope.

"Coldplay," he says, fanning two concert tickets in the air as my heart sinks. "You know how I wanted to go last year, but you had the flu? Well, they're coming back in May, and I decided to go all-out: VIP entrance, backstage access, front-row seats—hell, we might even meet Chris Martin!"

Coldplay? I don't even really like Coldplay. I mean, "Fix You" is an okay song, but . . . *Coldplay*?

"Kevin," I begin, searching his face as my confusion builds to anger. "What the . . . hell?"

"Wait, what?" he says, a little stunned. "You're not happy? Lena, do you realize how hard it was to lock down these tickets? I thought you'd be . . . a little more excited."

A tear trickles down my cheek and I'm vaguely aware of the violin trio creeping toward our table again. Vivaldi has never sounded so vile.

"Babe," Kevin mutters. "What's wrong?"

"What's *wrong*?" I reply, shaking my head. "Kevin, I thought you were going to . . ." I pause, looking away.

"Oh," he replies after a long beat, my words sinking in as he lowers his head. "Lena, I . . ."

"Please, Kevin," I mutter, embarrassed, eyes downcast. "Just don't."

"You know I care about you," he says, pandering. "And I know we've been talking about . . . *things*, but . . ." He stops again, rubbing his forehead as if this conversation has upgraded his tension headache to a full-fledged migraine. "Listen, I need to be honest with you. I don't know if I'm ready to take such a giant leap. I mean, are you?"

"Giant . . . *leap?*" I reply, wondering if the room is spinning or if it's just the champagne.

He scratches his head. "I know we have fun together, but do you think we're really . . . *compatible?*"

I shake my head. "After two years, you're seriously asking me that?"

"Lena," he continues, shaking his head, "you don't even like hiking."

"Hiking? Are you kidding me?" I grip the edge of the table. "This isn't about hiking! Kevin, we've talked about the future, we—" I take a deep breath. "That day at Tiffany, I showed you the ring I liked. I thought we were on the same page—that you wanted to move forward. I mean, you got the salesgirl's card!"

Kevin looks like a suspect under police interrogation, one who's about to plead the Fifth. He closes his eyes, then opens them again. "Listen," he says, pausing as he runs his hands through his hair. "Lena, you're accomplished, funny, beautiful . . . special."

Why does it feel like he's reading my obituary aloud?

"But just because you've been with someone for two years," he continues, "well . . . it doesn't automatically mean you should be together . . . forever."

"Right," I say, equal parts heartbroken and furious. "Then tell me. What does it mean?"

"I don't know," he says, furrowing his brow. "I look around at our friends and colleagues, and it just feels sort of like a factory, like people, well, are all on this conveyor belt chugging along, and that when they reach that time in life when society expects them to get married, they feel obligated to do it. It's like the next step of the assembly line. It doesn't even matter if it's true love, a soul connection—whatever you want to call it. They just settle for the person next to them on the conveyor belt." He pauses, tugging at the collar of his shirt. "I don't want to do that."

"Wow," I say, dumfounded. "So that's what you think of me? Just a passing human on a . . . conveyor belt?"

"No, Lena," he says, face softening. "Sometimes I worry that's how you see . . . me."

I gape at him. Honestly, I don't know what to say, and all this right before we were supposed to fly to Seattle tomorrow. I'd envisioned the moment we'd announce our engagement to my aunt Rosie, my late mother's older sister who raised me after she passed. I must have turned the scene over in my mind a hundred times, imagining the expression of joy on her face when I showed her the ring, how Kevin would be smiling lovingly in his puffer vest with his arm tucked around my waist.

I feel silly and foolish and nineteen shades of embarrassed when the waiter catches my eye from a nearby table and flashes an expression of pity. *He knows.*

"Kevin," I finally say, tears stinging my eyes. "This isn't a conveyor belt. It's real life. I thought you wanted to move forward. I thought . . . wrong."

"I'm sorry, Lena," he says, reaching his hand across the table, but I don't take it. It feels like the entire restaurant is watching as I sling my purse over my shoulder and rise to my feet, the chair beneath me screeching against the hardwood floor. Wobbling in my heels, I adjust the hem of my dress as I eye the exit. I already know I'll forever despise sequins—and Vivaldi.

"Goodbye, Kevin," I finally say.

I watch his mouth open and close, his lips forming words—a sentence or two, or three—but I can't make any of it out. All I can hear is the pounding in my chest and the nauseating sound of Baroque music. Kevin reaches for my arm, but I lurch forward, extricating myself from his grip as I bolt for the door.

2

I drop my keys into the bowl on my apartment's entryway table, beside the withered houseplant that has long since given up on life, then sink into the sofa and burst into tears—mascara pooling under my eyes like raccoon rings.

SOS, I text to Frankie, our emergency code. She immediately FaceTimes, even though it's after midnight in New York.

"What's going on? You okay?"

Through fits of tears, I download the unfortunate events of the evening.

"Maybe this is just a misunderstanding," she says, in triage mode. "Has he called? Texted?"

"No, not a peep," I say with a sigh. "And it's *not* a misunderstanding." Stomach growling, I walk to the kitchen, wishing I would have at least ordered an appetizer before my life imploded. Instead, I stare into my fridge, surveying my options: a pack of raw chicken breasts, spinach, a container of couscous from the market, yogurt, and a bottle of sauvignon blanc, which I grab from the upper shelf. Nothing sounds good, nor do I have the energy to cook. I want takeout—stat.

"I know how hard this is for you," Frankie says. "You really like Kevin, and I see why: He's successful. He cooks. He likes dogs. His parents are normal. Don't they even drink eggnog on Christmas Eve—*in matching pajamas?*"

I groan. "Please, don't rub it in."

"Honey, listen to me. What happened tonight royally sucks, but . . . it might be for the best. Yes, Kevin may be great," she continues, "maybe just not great for *you*."

I let out another hiccup of tears and pour the sauv blanc into my glass. "Easy for someone who's happily married to her soul mate to say."

"That may be true, but Christian and I don't have a perfect marriage—not by a long shot. I mean, sometimes I don't think he's even *listening* to me—like this morning when he came back from the market with two bags of groceries, none of which were on my list."

I know that Frankie's only trying to help, but her situation pales in comparison to mine. So what if Christian missed the memo on the organic tomatoes! Kevin missed the memo on *everything*! I slump back into the sofa, covering my face with a pillow for a long beat before I resurface, Kevin's words replaying in my mind.

"There's something else," I begin, shaking my head, still trying to make sense of it all. "He had this bizarre . . . conveyor belt theory."

"I'm sorry, what?"

I bite the edge of my lip. "I don't know. It was something about how . . . we're all on this assembly line in life, and that most people just end up partnering with the person that happens to be next to them."

"How romantic," Frankie scoffs.

I nod. "He accused *me* of only wanting to be with him because, well, right place, right time."

Frankie's quiet for a beat, then she lets out a big sigh. "Oh, Lena. I hate to say it, but he might have a point."

"Hold on—you're actually taking *his* side?"

"I love you, but listen. You can't treat a relationship like a career, and I know how you run your career."

I cover my face with the pillow again.

"All I'm saying, Lena, is that Kevin was—is—great on paper, but you're so goal-oriented that maybe you've been in a rush to seal the deal. Like, you might have overlooked some of his less-appealing qualities." Frankie pauses, smirking. "I mean, he's pretty uptight."

All I can think of is hiking. I hate hiking, but I could have tried harder. Should I have tried harder?

"Honey, I know this probably won't be easy for you to hear, but I don't think Kevin was . . . your guy."

"But he was—is," I rebut, as I peer out of my pillow fort. In this moment, I realize that everything I thought to be true, everything I banked on to happen, has all just slipped from my grasp. But how? I did all the right things. "Frankie, how did I get this so wrong?"

"Maybe you were too busy checking the boxes on your list to see that Kevin was just the person next to you on the assembly line."

I groan. "Can we *please* stop talking about assembly lines?"

"Sorry," Frankie replies with a little laugh. "Hey, why don't you fly out for a visit? I'll help you work through this, and maybe we can spruce up your online dating profile."

"Honestly, I'd rather become the person who adopts all the stray cats in the Presidio than dip my toe into the online dating cesspool."

"Oh no," she replies with a laugh. "You're not turning into a cat lady on my watch."

"Fine," I say. "But I'm leaving for Seattle tomorrow, remember? Kevin was supposed to meet Rosie." I sigh. "So much for that."

"His loss," Frankie replies without a second thought. "And I'm glad you're going home—you need that—but, come visit soon."

"I will. I promise."

We hang up, and I quickly place an order for Chinese, then crawl into bed to call Rosie.

"Hi," I say to the only mother figure in my life. "It's me."

"Lena!" Rosie sounds the same—bighearted and wise—but also a little tired, which is when I realize it's after ten, and I've woken her up.

"Sorry, it's late," I begin, "but, Rosie, it's been . . . a *day*."

"Talk to me, dear. What's going on?"

"It's Kevin," I say, wiping away a tear. "We broke up."

"Oh my goodness," she replies. "What happened?"

I feel gut-punched and paralyzed. Unlike corporate drama, this isn't a situation I can fix with a spreadsheet. "I thought he was going to propose," I finally say, "but . . . nope. Literally the opposite."

"Oh, Lena," Rosie says, her voice like a salve. "I'm so sorry. This hurts, I know. But you'll get through it. We'll figure it all out when you get home."

I exhale deeply. *Home*. I can almost taste the salty air. "I'll be on the afternoon flight tomorrow—without Kevin, obviously."

"To hell with Kevin," Rosie replies. I immediately picture her face—strong and steadfast, with a mischievous twinkle in her eye. "We'll have more fun without him."

THE PLANE TOUCHES DOWN IN CLOUDY SEATTLE THE NEXT DAY, JUST AS THE workday is ending. I gather my things and race to baggage claim. If I'm lucky, I'll be able to cab downtown in time to catch the 7 p.m. ferry to Bainbridge Island. How long has it been since I visited? Two years? *Too long.* Yes, work had always been the mitigating factor, but Kevin, too. I feel a pang of regret, recalling the recent holidays I'd spent with his family instead of making the long-overdue trip home.

When my mother died, I was only twelve. Her absence, especially at that delicate age, knocked the wind out of me in one fell swoop, but Rosie was there to pick up the pieces—to lift me from my despair. And she did, brilliantly. In some ways, it was as if she were always meant to be my mother, and I her daughter.

Mom and I had been living with Rosie for almost two years when Mom passed. Before that, I'd never known a consistent home. We'd shuffled through as many grungy apartments as Mom did boyfriends. I lost track of the number of elementary schools I attended, always the new kid. Fortunately, I was nothing like her. She was plagued by highs and lows and would spend days in bed fighting her demons.

While I thrived under Rosie's care, Mom deteriorated. She tried to work on her art, but without consistency. Half-finished canvases littered the floor of her bedroom. New boyfriends came and went, and when they went, she'd disappear, sometimes for days. When she would finally return, her eyes were vacant and her heart somewhere else.

After a particularly bad heartbreak, she'd been missing for two days when a sheriff knocked on the front door, delivering the crushing news no young girl should ever receive. A drunk driver going the wrong direction on a freeway off-ramp had plowed into her.

I remember feeling as if I'd detached from my body—my young soul hovering above, watching the scene play out like a movie: Rosie weeping, the sheriff offering his awkward condolences, me in the fetal position on the living room rug. It didn't feel real. How could it be real? How could she be . . . gone?

MOM WAS UNDENIABLY COMPLICATED, AND IT TOOK ME YEARS OF THERAPY TO realize that although she's sorely missed, her absence quelled the turbulent waters. In fact, after she was gone, the sea was like glass. Maybe her soul feels that way, too.

As the cab veers off the freeway, dipping toward downtown, my heart contracts. *Seattle.* Memories seep in, hitting me at all the angles: Pearl Jam at the Showbox, afternoons puttering through hidden corners of Pike Place Market (in Doc Martens, of course), and all those rainy Saturdays hunkered down in cozy cafés, lingering over foamy vanilla lattes with friends. In some ways, the city is just as I left it, though I can't really say the same thing about myself.

I think about Café Vita, tucked beneath the Market. It was a mainstay for me the summer after college, when I interned for a venture capital firm before moving back to New York. I smile, recalling all the hours I spent at the café before and after work. It felt like my second home, and I can still picture the cast of characters: Spencer, the barista, smiling behind the old La Marzocco; Annelise at the cash register with her cat-eye glasses and that whole Lisa Loeb vibe;

Vaughn, the creepy/not-creepy regular in the dark trench coat with clunky headphones who ordered a *doppio con panna* at seven-thirty every morning. I laugh to myself, remembering the time Spencer asked him what he was listening to. We all assumed it would be heavy metal, but no. "Mozart," he replied, as if there were no other plausible answers. "Always Mozart."

At least it wasn't Vivaldi. I cringe at the memory of last night as I board the ferry. A few minutes later, the captain blares his horn, the familiar sound like a giant hug as I slip into a seat on the main deck. How many times have I ridden the ferries to and from the island in my life? A thousand? More? Memories, like old friends, creep out of the corners of my mind—of Rosie taking me to dentist and doctor appointments in the city and late-night trips home with friends, gliding through the Puget Sound on vessels that looked like gigantic illuminated layer cakes in the night. I breathe in the familiar scent of sea air, engine oil, and burnt coffee in the galley. *I'm almost home.*

Thirty minutes later, when the ferry docks on the island, I wrangle my bags and disembark, flagging down a cab in the terminal parking lot. The road that leads to Rosie's waterfront home on Manzanita Bay appears untouched by time—the local farmstand's sign for fresh eggs, the blue spruce at the bottom of the hill, my old friend Natalie's house with the gazebo in front where Robbie Fenway tried to kiss me the summer I turned fourteen, though I made a quick exit the moment he leaned in with puckered lips. It wasn't that I didn't like him. It was the braces—*both* of our braces. We'd all heard the rumor about the couple in ninth grade whose orthodontic gear got stuck together during a make-out session. The fire department had to be called. Yes, Robbie was sweet, but the risk of humiliation loomed large.

It all feels just like yesterday, but also a million years ago. As the cab veers left, passing a quaint Craftsman with a picket fence, I imagine Robbie, all grown up, but with that same goofy smile and acne scars on his cheeks, married, with a couple of kids—a swing set in the backyard and a wife who bakes blueberry muffins. While my life raced on at the speed of light the past ten years since I've lived in California, it seems as if Bainbridge Island remained fixed in time, just as I left it.

"Is this the place?" The cabdriver grunts, pulling into the gravel driveway and me from my reverie.

Too overcome with emotion to speak, I nod, pay the fare, and heave my bags from the trunk. As the driver motors away, I gaze up at the old house perched on the sparkling inlet of Manzanita Bay. Built in 1922 and buffered by five wooded acres, the sprawling white farmhouse has five bedrooms—six, if you count the attic. From the outside, the house looks like something out of a Bing Crosby Christmas film. The interior is just as charming—with a big open kitchen, expansive windows facing the sea, and a woodburning fireplace in the nearby living room.

I make my way along the brick walkway leading to the front door. Rosie's beloved hydrangeas with their enormous lavender and pink blooms line the path. *Why did I stay away so long?*

I don't knock, just turn the knob and let my bags drop to the floor with a thud as I breathe in the familiar scent of the smoldering fire, Rosie's sandalwood perfume, and . . . memories. *I'm home.*

3

"Rosie!" I call, peering into the living room, where I find her, book in hand, sitting in her chair by the fireplace, the embers glowing orange and crimson in the dim light. Before she can get up, I rush to her side, immediately noticing the wrinkles around her eyes and the pronounced hollows of her cheeks. She turned seventy last month; my time away has aged her—perhaps us both.

"I'm so glad you're here," she whispers, pulling me to her chest. "I've missed you so much." Her eyes are glossy in the firelight.

"I'm sorry I've been gone so long," I say, my heart contracting.

"No apologies," Rosie says, holding her hand to her heart. "For me, you've never left."

I nod, sinking into the overstuffed chair beside her as I watch the flames dance in the fireplace.

"Do you want to talk about it?" she asks.

I sigh. "About Kevin?"

Rosie nods.

"I don't know if there's anything to say," I begin. "Just that I feel shell-shocked and stupid. We were together for two years. I thought this was . . . *it*."

"I know," she replies. "These feelings are real, dear, but they'll pass in time. Someday you might even feel grateful for all of this."

"Grateful?" I shrug, recalling the look on Kevin's face last night, the humiliation seeping from my pores. "I don't know about that." I let out a long sigh, burying my face in my hands. "How did I get this so wrong? I thought we wanted the same things."

Rosie shifts in her chair. "Honey, you can't approach love like a business plan."

"Yeah, that's pretty much what Frankie said." I sigh. "Guilty as charged, I guess."

She smiles, setting her book aside as I eye the spine.

"Rosie!" I exclaim, laughing for the first time in twenty-four hours. *"Fifty Shades of Grey?"*

She shrugs, her chin-length gray hair thinner than I remember. "Well, I'm not getting any younger. I figured I should know what all the fuss was about before it's too late!"

"So?" I crack a sly smile. "Is it . . . good?"

She grins, pausing for a second. "Well, I wouldn't call it great literature, but . . . *interesting*? Yes, indeed."

Rosie and I have always shared a love of reading. While my apartment in San Francisco may be sparsely furnished, books are stacked precariously high on my bedside table, just as they're piled up in stacks in Rosie's living room.

"Tell me, did Kevin like to read?" Rosie asks, eying me curiously.

I pause for a moment, recalling him—headphones on, iPad in hand—binge-watching shows on Netflix while I kept my nose buried in a book. "No, actually."

"Hmm," Rosie replies. "You used to say you could never be with someone who didn't love books."

I look away wistfully.

"Your 'business plan' was flawed."

"More like doomed," I reply, eying the shelf on the far wall. "I see you're still collecting your rocks."

"Crystals, dear," she says, nodding proudly. "They're quite powerful, you know, and healing." While Rosie and I are similar in most ways, I didn't inherit her affinity for all things woo-woo.

"Pull down that pink one, top right?" she continues.

On my tiptoes, I reach for the stone, feeling its coolness against my skin, before handing it to Rosie. "No," she says, quickly. "I want you to hold on to it."

I look down at the square-shaped pale pink stone in my hand. It's almost iridescent in the dim glow of the firelight.

"She's quietly wise, this one," Rosie muses.

I'm not sure if all crystal lovers refer to their rocks as "she," or if it's just a Rosie thing.

"And incredibly powerful. Rose quartz is one of the most beneficial crystals for the heart. It has a way of bringing about harmonious love."

"Harmonious love, huh?" I say, a little sarcastically, setting the rock on the table between us. "I love you, Rosie, but I think it would take a truckload of rose quartz to fix my love life."

"Why not keep it for a while?" She grins. "You'll see."

"Okay," I concede, but only because I know it'll make her happy.

Rosie's wise eyes search my face. She's always been able to read me, sometimes eerily so. "Let me ask you a question," she begins again. "How did Kevin make you *feel*, I mean, when you were in his presence?"

I shrug. "I don't know. I guess I've never really thought about that."

"Well, you should, because it's everything. It's how I knew about Bill. With him, it all just felt . . . *right*. We fit."

"Let me guess," I say with a tinge of sarcasm. "Like two puzzle pieces?"

"Well, yes, actually."

I roll my eyes.

She looks toward the darkness outside the window where the waves crash onto the shore, saying their good nights. Unlike me, Rosie has known love—true love. As I watch her smiling peacefully, I wonder if she's thinking of him.

Though Bill died shortly after I was born, Rosie's vivid descriptions made me feel as if I'd always known him: the fly fishing tackle box in the mudroom, his raspy voice, love for shepherd's pie. They loved to laugh, Rosie told me, but especially to dance. I liked to imagine the two of them in the living room, feet stepping in time to an old jazz record—Rosie squealing with delight when Bill dipped her in his arms. After his death, she never remarried, never even dated. When I once asked her why, she told me that she didn't need to, that her heart was already full.

She pats my arm, sensing my disquiet. "You'll find your way, honey."

I think of my mother and the revolving door of boyfriends and romantic disappointments—her version of the "conveyor belt," I guess—and I can't help but wonder if I'm destined for the same parade of disillusionment.

Rosie smiles again, her eyes big and wise. "Remember, the heart is a muscle you must flex. It takes practice."

"I don't know," I reply, unsure. "Maybe I'm just destined to be alone. It would be a lot easier."

"And a lot lonelier," she counters.

I can't help but wonder if Rosie's happy living alone on this island by the sea, puttering around the house with her crystals and her memories.

"Well, I should be getting to bed," she says with a yawn. "I put fresh sheets on your bed, and there are towels in the bathroom."

I give Rosie a hug. "Thanks for . . . everything."

"Good night, dear," she finally says, her voice cracking a little as she cradles my face in her hands, eyes a little misty. "I'll see you in the morning."

I sit in silence for a long moment, soaking up the comfort of home as the fireplace's final embers crackle and spark, glowing red and orange. When my gaze turns to my mother's bedroom door across the room, memories rush back, hitting me in rapid fire.

I'm thirty-five, but I might as well be ten years old again, hair in braids. Fighting back tears, I walk ahead, across the room, placing my hand on the doorknob, cold to the touch.

Inside, the coverlet is tucked tight over the empty bed. The only remnants of her are a cardboard box filled with tubes of dried-up paint on the floor and two art easels perched against the far wall, one holding a landscape painting, the other an in-progress, but not-quite-finished still life—a ceramic pitcher nestled beside two ripe pears. I walk closer, unable to take my eyes off the canvas, the scene so simple, but somehow majestic. I hear my mother's voice in my mind. "Sometimes the most beautiful things in life are right in front of our eyes. We just need to learn to see them."

I sigh, opening the top drawer of the dresser and lifting a moth-eaten wool sweater. I hold it up to my face, breathing in its scent, though my mother's essence has long since disappeared. Feeling the heaviness of this moment—and of the last twenty-four hours—I turn to the bedside table, where I notice a framed photo beside the lamp. I reach for it, blowing dust from its rim. There I am—only three, maybe four—sitting on my mother's lap, looking up at her with wide eyes. I'm holding my little stuffed bunny, the one I loved but tragically left behind in some apartment. By the time I realized it was gone, it was too late to turn back. *Snowball.* His name was *Snowball.*

For the first time, I realize how expertly I've hidden away the past, compartmentalized all these painful memories into the far corners of my mind, locking the dead bolt and throwing away the key. But now the door is open—wide open—and it's all here, vying for my attention.

I see it, and yet I don't want to see it: how I'm allergic to unchartered territory and bristle at the unknown; the way I buckle when things don't go according to plan, maybe because Mom never had a plan.

I close the door behind me as if to shut it all away again, exhaling deeply as I wander to the kitchen, reaching for a bottle of pinot grigio chilling in the fridge. Looking for a corkscrew, I rifle through a drawer beneath the counter, where I notice an old brass key affixed to a tag that reads GUESTHOUSE.

The little cottage on the edge of the property has long since been locked, especially after I snuck inside with my high school boyfriend, Mike, and it became the site of my first official (braces-free) kiss. Rosie of course had found us, and from then on the guesthouse remained off-limits, and, as I got older, just a distant memory.

Overcome with curiosity, I tuck the key in my pocket, uncork the wine, filling a glass to the brim before finding a coat hanging on a hook beside the back door. Outside, the full moon dangles low on the horizon, piercing through a channel of incoming clouds. It lights up the bay like a superpowered floodlight, casting ambient light on the edge of the property, where the guesthouse sits, perched on the cliffside.

The breeze whistles through the fir trees, jostling the wind chimes on Rosie's back porch as I make my way across the lawn, dodging raindrops with each step. I follow the gravel path to the door and peer through the window into the dark space before finally inserting the key into the lock. The hinges groan, as if releasing decades of pent-up tension. Brushing away a cobweb, I step inside. There's just enough moonlight to make out my surroundings: a desk; a twin bed, neatly made; a painting on the wall of waves crashing onto the shore.

IT FEELS STRANGE TO BE HERE AGAIN IN THIS FORBIDDEN SPACE—STRANGE, BUT also weirdly comforting. I place my wineglass on the desk, then extract the rose quartz from my pocket, blowing away a thick layer of dust from the nightstand. I set it beside Rosie's collection of sparkly crystals and found treasures from the shore.

I've just washed up here, too, and I feel suddenly weary as I sit down on the old bed, the coils beneath me stiff and springy. The wind howls outside the cottage as I rest my head on the pillow. I know I should get back, but the trek across the lawn feels as daunting as traversing the Saharan desert without a camel—or water. Instead, I pull the ancient patchwork quilt over my body. What would be the harm in resting here, just for a little while? Eyelids heavy, I shift to my side, yawning, as I pull the blanket over my tired body. Rain pelts the roof overhead, and it sounds just like a lullaby.

PART TWO

4

Bright light streams through the window—too bright. I groan, burying my face in the pillow. Last night is a blur, and it takes me a long moment to find my bearings, but when I do, it all comes rushing back: Bainbridge Island, wine, the guesthouse. *The guesthouse.* I sit up, rubbing the sleep from my eyes. *What time is it? How long have I been asleep? Rosie must be making breakfast.* I freeze as my surroundings come into focus—the antique pane windows fitted with wispy linen drapes, the crystal chandelier overhead, the . . . black silk negligee I'm wearing, and nothing else. I gasp, reaching for the white duvet to cover my chest. This is not the guesthouse, nor is it Bainbridge Island.

Where the hell am I?

"Hello, *mon amour*," a shirtless man says from the doorway holding a silver tray, which is when I let out a shrill scream.

"What was that for?" he continues, walking closer, setting a breakfast tray with croissants and scrambled eggs beside me. "Did you have a bad dream?"

My eyes dart around the room, pausing briefly when I notice an oversize candle in a thick glass jar on the nightstand. It's gigantic, like weapon-size, and, when I creep a few more inches to the right, fortunately in my grasp. With any luck, I can hit him over the head, stun him long enough to get out of here.

"What was it this time?" he asks, my heart racing as he inches closer. "The plane crash dream, or the other thing—you know, the one when you try to speak and nothing comes out?"

His accent is thick—French, definitely—and also *familiar*, though I can't quite place him, nor do I have the slightest recollection of how I ended up here. I've been kidnapped, obviously—and probably drugged. Rosie's undoubtedly looking for me at this very moment, probably even called the police. My hands tremble as I clench the herculean candle under the sheet, adrenaline coursing through my veins. I feel like I'm in a horror movie, but the terror is real. *If he gets any closer, I'll . . .*

"I know what'll cheer you up," he says with a mischievous grin. He plants his elbow on the bed, the edge of his face resting in his palm. "What *always* cheers you up." He brushes a lock of his wavy brown hair from his eyes, then reaches under the covers, caressing my left thigh.

"Get your hands off me!" I scream, adrenaline taking over as I reach for the candle, leap out of bed, and race to the corner of the room, where I stare at him, shaking like a frightened animal.

The man laughs, walking toward me, as if he thinks this is some sort of game, albeit a sick one. "Feeling feisty this morning, I see."

I hurl the candle toward him, but he ducks, and it shatters against the wall leaving a mess of jagged shards of moss-green glass and chunks of candle wax beside the window.

"Lena? What the hell?" He shakes his head, muttering something in French, which I can't understand. "I get it. You're not in the mood. But there are better ways to convey the message than destroying a Monique Pierre candle." He sighs. "I guess that's what I get for marrying an American woman."

Marrying . . . me?

He's obviously delusional, but I have no business arguing with my kidnapper. I'll have to play nice until I figure out how to get out of here.

"*Merde,*" he grunts as he glances at his gold Rolex, then slips into a tailored white shirt and pulls on a pair of pants. "I made coffee with those beans you love from Seattle—get it while it's hot."

Okay, so he's a *hospitable* kidnapper? Still, I'm hardly in the clear. At any moment he might handcuff me to the bed. Instead, he laces up his shoes and heads to the doorway.

I clear my throat. "So, you're . . . just going to leave me here?" My voice is jittery and high-pitched.

He shakes his head, obviously confused.

"You're not going to . . . tie me up or anything?" I continue, instantly regretting the words that have just flown out of my mouth. Apparently I am the idiot who feeds her captor ideas.

"No, my naughty, naughty wife," he says, shaking his head with a laugh. "But we can do that later, if you'd like."

Wife. I stand still, speechless, as he reaches for his cell and wallet, blowing me a kiss from the doorway. "Oh, be sure you arrive before six, okay? Just to make sure everything's perfect. You know how important this night is for me."

"Before six," I mutter despondently, as his shoes clack against the hardwood floors.

When the door clicks shut, I fall to my knees, exhaling deeply. I'm relieved to be alone, though I imagine he's probably locked the door from the outside. Why wouldn't he? I tell myself not to panic, though goose bumps erupt down my arms. Maybe I have a head injury? I check my scalp for lumps—nothing—which is when I determine that I must have been drugged. I've seen those *48 Hours* specials, where the innocent woman's drink gets spiked, and she ends up in a strange hotel room—or worse.

No. I'll find my way out of here. But first I need to get dressed.

I glance around the room, but the jeans and sweater I was wearing last night appear to have vanished—he destroyed the evidence, no doubt—so I tiptoe to a nearby closet, where I'm shocked to find a smorgasbord of female wardrobe selections. He probably stocks the shelves for his victims, I think, though I don't waste any time dwelling on any of the nuances of a criminal's mind. This is my chance to escape, and I need to move *fast*.

I pull on a pair of black leggings and a light gray hoodie, both of which fit like a glove, then slide my feet into an expensive-looking pair of nude sandals that I find on the shoe rack—exactly my size—which is when I hear a thud coming from the adjoining room. Fresh adrenaline surges through my veins as I tiptoe out of the closet, grateful to find a steel poker resting against the bedroom fireplace. I grab it.

The parquet floorboards creak beneath my feet as I make my way to the doorway. I cautiously survey the apartment's grand living room and well-appointed chef's kitchen, admiring the Lacanche stove and impressive collection of red Le Creuset enamelware. *Apparently it's possible for psychopaths to have impeccable taste.*

Confirming that I'm alone, I drop the poker, just as a mass of black fur descends upon me like a whirling dervish. I lose my footing, and moments later I'm lying in the kitchen, flat on my back, pinned by four paws and one overly exuberant wet tongue.

"Down," I say, struggling to sit up. "I mean, no! Stop! No! Halt?" The enormous canine obeys, retreating to the living room where he lies down on the rug with a defeated sigh that echoes my own befuddled exhale. Well over 150 pounds, he looks like a Saint Bernard, with a white chest and front legs and a brown patch on his midsection—cute, if you're into beasts that slobber.

Where the hell am I?

I eye the balcony outside the windows—in a city, obviously. But where? Seattle is the only logical explanation, and yet . . . this is *definitely not Seattle*. I study the scene outside the paned glass, following the rows of gabled roofs and quaint centuries-old-looking stone buildings, as far as the eye can see. On the street, below, an older man ambles along the sidewalk—a cane in one hand, a baguette in the other. When I look out into the distance, the hair on my arms stands on end. It's impossible, of course, but there it is: unmistakably the Eiffel Tower, sticking out of the low clouds like it was painted against the horizon.

I gasp, clutching the edge of the windowsill. *Paris?* No. Absolutely *no way*. I really must have been drugged and the effects are still wearing off. *Water. I need water.* I find a glass in the kitchen and fill it, then guzzle every last drop.

After a quick twist of the front doorknob, I'm relieved to discover that it's unlocked. (Climbing out the window wasn't exactly a welcome Plan B.) But, before making my exit, I pause, noticing a cell phone plugged into the wall on the kitchen counter. I tuck it into my hoodie pocket, then open the counter drawer, which, good news, appears to be the junk drawer. There's a handful of bills and some loose change, which I also stuff into my pocket. As I make one final glance around the apartment for anything useful, a framed photo on the coffee table catches my eye. I pick it up to get a better look. My eyes nearly pop out of their sockets. There I am, in a fluffy white *wedding* dress, hair swept into a loose bun and arms wrapped around . . . the French kidnapper.

No. This isn't happening. This is not *real. I'm just dreaming, or under the influence of some sort of psychedelic substance. I went to sleep in the guesthouse on Bainbridge Island. How could I have woken up here? With him? Married?* My stomach churns and my mouth waters. I stumble to a potted plant beside a nearby window and vomit into the well of a bespoke urn.

On my knees, I wipe my face and take a breath, glancing down at the vintage-looking diamond ring hugging my left ring finger. The oval-shaped yellow diamond is staggering, and I let out a little gasp as the picture frame slips from my hand. Its collision with the parquet hardwood floors leaves a jagged, spiderweb-like pattern on the glass, blurring the smiles in the photo—only their gazes remain visible— four piercing eyes. That's when it hits me.

Sebastian. His name is Sebastian. I shake my head, struggling to process the memories as they rise to the surface, one after the next, like waves depositing lost relics onto the shore. Was it six years ago? Seven? We met at a mutual friend's wedding and, being the only two singles at the reception, the two of us spent most of the night talking . . . well, mostly questioning the institution of marriage.

"Want to make a guess at how long they'll last?" Sebastian whispered to me as the newlyweds took to the dance floor with Elvis's voice crooning through the speakers: "I . . . can't . . . help . . . falling in love with you."

"What are you talking about?" I fired back, a little indignantly. When he didn't respond, I studied his face with curiosity. "Aren't you happy for them?"

"Sure, sure," he replied. "I'm just saying that they probably have no idea that this is as good as it gets. It's all downhill from here."

Initially, I balked at his sentiments, which struck me as indifferent, but his words lingered—frankly, they hit me to my core. After all, I'd witnessed the very same thing in my mother's life before she passed. The endless stream of relationships that began with fireworks and ended in loathing, the constant search for *the one*, only to find him . . . and lose him—on repeat.

"Perhaps you're just jaded," I said, sizing him up—at least ten years my senior and handsome. *Too handsome.*

"And perhaps you're just naive," he rattled off with a facetious smile.

I dismissed his words with a wave of my hand as I took another sip of champagne. Still, maybe there was some truth to his cynicism? What did I know about love, anyway? Only that it ended. But then I thought of the happy couples in my life, Christian and Frankie, for example.

"Well," I concluded dismissively, "I think they're going to be just fine."

"Sure, maybe," he replied with a knowing wink as we watched the happy couple on the dance floor.

"So, you're anti-marriage, then?"

He shook his head. "You're missing the point."

"Please enlighten me, then, oh, wise one."

Sebastian leaned in closer. "I'm neither anti-marriage, nor do I think they're doomed. I'm just a realist. One person can't be your *everything*. I just think people should remain open to the other people and experience that life brings, you know?"

I raised my eyebrows. "Sounds like something a Frenchman would say."

"*Touché*," he replied with a laugh. "But tell me, why must everyone be so hellbent on putting love in a box? Not everything is destined for . . . forever. Some relationships burn hot in the beginning—so hot there's little fuel left to sustain them. Others simmer at a medium heat, and maybe even get better with time. All I'm saying is that nobody knows for sure. But when we find ourselves in beautiful moments"—he paused—"like this one . . . we should enjoy them to their fullest." He paused, brushing his hand against mine, letting it linger a little too long.

I shifted my chair back, his words equally obnoxious and provocative.

"Care to dance?" Sebastian asked.

I took a sip of my wine and smiled my reply. *Why not?* I thought as he led me out to the dance floor, where we both smiled and waved at the bride and groom and their adorable flower girl twirling around in her white tulle dress.

As he whisked me around the dance floor, thoughts of my mother crept in. Big-hearted and sensitive, she lived her life on a hamster wheel of sorts, chasing love but never catching it. And for what? To end up exhausted and disillusioned? Alone? For her, love only disappointed. It remained within view, but always out of reach. Why? Were her problems a function of her own flaws, or because of the men she fell for—men who could never love her completely?

When the song ended, I told Sebastian I had a headache and needed to sit down. Honestly, though, he rubbed me the wrong way.

I couldn't decide what bothered me more: his flippant hypothesis on love and commitment, or my deep-rooted fear that he was right.

After returning from her Caribbean honeymoon, the bride called me to confess that she'd purposefully seated Sebastian and me at the same table in the hope that we'd make a connection. "Did you two hit it off?" she asked. "It sure looked like it!"

"Yeah," I said. "He was . . . fun." I didn't have the heart to tell her that Sebastian had scrawled his number on the back of a napkin at dinner, and that I'd tossed it in the garbage can later that night.

SEBASTIAN'S ENORMOUS CANINE PRESSES HIS NOSE AGAINST MY LEG, LEASH in his mouth. I clutch my head, reeling. Nothing makes sense. Nothing at all. All I know is that *I have to get out of here—and soon.*

"Hey, buddy," I say, scratching the dog's neck as I eye the gold tag on his collar. "You're name's Claude, huh? Very distinguished." I smile, fastening his leash as his tail wags faster—and precariously close to the lamp on the end table. "C'mon, boy. Let's go for a walk."

I haven't been to Paris since 2012, not that the five-day trip with Frankie left me with any real aptitude for navigating this city. I'm *lost*—in the most disturbing sense of the word.

"Claude, slow down!" I scream, clutching the leash with all my might as he barrels out of the building and down the street. "Heel!" I continue, which I immediately decide is pointless, because I don't know the word in French—or any French for that matter—which I assume he understands. Obviously—he's a French dog. In any case, I have no idea why I decided to escape with a Saint Bernard who outweighs me, but I'm now regretting it—especially when he makes a beeline for the park ahead, where an older, chic-looking woman with black-rimmed glasses seems to be waving—at me?

"Mademoiselle Gateau!" she says, approaching. Claude leaps up and plants a slobbery kiss on her left cheek; obviously he knows her. *"Bonjour!"* she says, wiping the slobber from her cheek, unannoyed. *"Ce soir c'est le grand soir! Êtes-vous prêts, toi et Sebastian?"*

I shake my head, utterly confused.

"Ah, not in the mood for French today, I see?" she says in English, laughing. "No problem. I ran into Sebastian at the café. He said you had a rough morning. Poor thing. Well, *c'est la vie*. You must snap out of it. The big opening is tonight!"

"I'm sorry," I say, tightening my grip on the leash when Claude spots a pigeon and lunges. "Um, how do we know each other, again?"

The woman's smile fades. "Oh, sweet child," she says, holding the back of her hand to my forehead. "You're sick. Shall I call a doctor?"

"No . . . I'm fine," I mutter, fumbling for my phone. "I just . . . need to call my aunt."

She furrows her brow. "Honey, let me help you, I—"

"Thank you, but . . ." I pause as Claude darts ahead, pulling me with him. "I . . . have to goooooo."

We zigzag through park benches, narrowly missing several picnic baskets, before I spot a café a few blocks ahead where a waiter points to an empty table. I tie Claude's leash to a metal railing then sink into a street-facing chair, catching my breath.

The photo in the apartment. The Frenchwoman just now, who seems to know me. The shoes in the closet—just my size. *Am I losing my mind? No. Impossible. I must stay rational. This is only a dream.* I drive the edge of a fingernail into my palm, wincing inwardly. *Wake up, Lena. Wake the hell up!* Sadly, the only result of my self-inflicted pain is a fresh blood blister and bevy of worried glances from people at nearby tables.

I pull the cell phone out of my pocket, noticing the photo on the main screen—another one of me and . . . Sebastian, he in a navy suit, me in a figure-hugging pink minidress—if you could call it a dress, more like a scrap of fabric. The hemline barely reaches my thighs. I study the photo closer. We're clinking champagne glasses as if we're celebrating—as if we're *happy*. My face recognition unlocks the phone and I scroll through the photo album. Claude wearing a Santa hat; snaps of exquisite-looking dinners; trips to sandy beaches;

Sebastian in bed—his chiseled chest starkly contrasted against the crisp white linen sheets. I bury my head in my hands. *Enough.*

I dial Rosie's number as quickly as I can, but something's wrong—an error message chimes, in French—words I don't understand. I try again, with the same result, then try Frankie. Fortunately, the call connects, and she picks up.

"Hi!" she says. "Where are you?"

"Um, in Paris."

"Duh," she says, unfazed. "Are you still home?"

"Frankie!" I begin, my voice shaky. A teenage boy walks by the café holding a baguette over his shoulder like a rifle. *What is it with the French and their baguettes?* "Listen, something *happened.* Something's . . . not right."

"What are you talking about?"

"I don't know," I say, my hands shaking. "I went to sleep last night at Rosie's—on Bainbridge Island—and I woke up here . . ."

"So, you had a bad dream, then?" I can picture her eyes narrowing in problem-solving mode. "I know you've been homesick since you guys moved to Paris. It's only natural to—"

"What do you mean, since we *moved* to Paris?"

"Um," she replies, unamused, "if you're joking, Lene, this isn't funny."

"I'm not joking." I bite the edge of my lip. "Frankie, I'm scared."

There's a long silence on the other end of the line before she speaks again. "Where are you right now?" she asks. "I'm worried."

Tears sting my eyes, but I blink them away. "Like I said, in Paris! With an enormous dog!"

"Good, you're with Claude."

"How do you know Claude?"

She mutters something unintelligible, though definitely in French. *When did Frankie learn to speak French?* My life feels like a snow globe, overly shaken and with jagged cracks on the verge of exploding.

"Lena, did you hit your head or something?"

"No! I mean . . . I don't think so?" I pause. "I think I was . . . kidnapped."

"Okay," she says slowly. "Can you tell me what street you're on?"

I glance up at a nearby street sign. "Um . . . Rue Street?"

"Lene," she replies with a sigh. "*Rue* is the French word for street. *Which one?*"

I take another look at the sign. "Uh . . . Cler?"

"Rue Cler, okay. Stay put. I'll jump in a cab and be over in a few minutes."

"Wait, you're in Paris, too?"

"Wow, you really are in a state." She pauses. "Don't leave, okay? I'll be there soon."

As I tuck the phone back in my pocket, a pretty woman in her mid-twenties, dressed in jeans and a tight-fitting black top, waves at me from a nearby table. Her dirty blonde hair is swept back into a low bun, with wisps effortlessly framing her face and a cigarette in her left hand. Apparently she knows me, though I don't recognize her at all.

"Lena," she calls out, before rattling off something in French.

Here we go again.

I walk toward her, shaking my head, confused.

"English today," she says with a nod. "Right. Sebastian told me you had a rough morning."

I furrow my brow. *Rough* hardly describes what I'm going through, but I don't stop to explain. Instead I triage. "You talked to . . . *Sebastian*?" Maybe all these people—Frankie, the woman in the park, this woman at the café—they're all in on some prank? My best friend *is* the practical joker type—not one of her most redeeming qualities, I'll admit. How can I forget the time she'd lacquered a bar of soap in our shower with clear nail polish? Uh-huh.

And yet, this is far beyond the scope of Frankie being Frankie. In fact, it sort of feels like I'm starring in one of those awful reality shows, where they put a poor soul in some nightmarish situation that brings him to the brink of despair while his friends crack up off-camera.

But there are no cameras. Just me and a very large dog in PARIS, where I have a husband, apparently, and there's a woman with impressively high cheekbones who is staring at me.

She tilts her head quizzically. "Uh, are you okay, Lena?"

The million-dollar question. I shrug, shaking my head. "I don't know."

She shrugs, any trace of concern on her face gone. "Well, whatever you're going through, snap out of it, okay? As I was saying, I talked to Sebastian earlier—well, like fourteen times already this morning, and *merde*. We have a lot to do. If we can somehow pull off this event, it'll be a miracle." She lets out a belabored sigh before the corners of her mouth form a smile again, albeit a forced one. "What are you doing here, anyway?"

"Uh," I say, pausing when a cab motors by—not Frankie. I turn back to my chic interrogator. "I was . . . just taking a walk."

"Hmm. Well, since you're here," she says, extinguishing her cigarette, "we have catching up to do. You heard that the florist fell through for tonight, right?" She sighs. "Something about a sick kid. I mean, who bows out at the eleventh hour like that? Anyway, I've been on the phone all morning, and I think I've just found a suitable replacement. Oh, and I'm picking up your dress in an hour. I'll bring it over to the apartment around three, okay?"

My dress. The florist. Sebastian. Tonight. I clutch Claude's leash tightly with one hand and rub my forehead with the other.

"Lena?" she adds, raising an eyebrow. "You really do seem *off.*"

"Uh," I say with a sigh. "It's what Sebastian said. I'm . . . having a rough morning."

Her phone buzzes on the table, rattling the espresso cup in its saucer beside her right hand. "Ugh, it's this guy I went out with last month," she says, frowning. "He's been ringing me all week. *Men.* They have no idea when to give us space." She rolls her eyes.

"Right," I mutter as a cab pulls up beside me. Frankie—*thank God.* She leans her head out of the open window and waves. "Get in!"

The sight of my best friend's face is just the tonic I need. I run across the cobblestone street to the opposite side of the black Mercedes.

"No way," Frankie says. "There's no room for Claude." She points to the woman at the café. "Leave him with Ella. She can take him home."

"Ella?"

"That's what assistants do, right? Besides, we have a lunch reservation. You can't exactly bring a 150-pound dog into the restaurant."

Ella. My assistant. Right.

"Um, okay," I say, turning back to the table. "Would you mind bringing Claude home for me? Something's come up, and I . . . need you to take him."

Ella nods begrudgingly, then flashes Frankie a saccharine smile as she takes Claude's leash.

"Thanks," I say, dashing back to the cab.

"I'm sorry we couldn't meet up for drinks last night," Frankie says, giving me a hug. "Our flight got in so late. It would have been after eleven before we arrived."

I search her face as my eyes well up with tears.

"Lena," she says, her expression shifting to concern. "Talk to me. *What the hell is going on?*"

5

I let out a long sigh as the cabdriver speeds down a narrow street, barely missing a woman on a bicycle with a bouquet of tulips in her front basket. "Frankie, I don't know what's happening to me."

"Have you eaten?" she asks, giving me a long and very maternal look in the way that only best friends can—best friends who also remind each other when it's time to wax their upper lips.

I shake my head.

"Well, then, no wonder why you're acting like a lunatic." She glances at her watch. "You need food. Christian's down at the d'Orsay." She rolls her eyes. "My museum-obsessed husband. He got us a lunch reservation in the restaurant there."

I laugh, remembering a story Frankie shared a few years ago about one of their first fights as a married couple: His idea of celebrating their anniversary was a trip to the Guggenheim. Hers? Not so much.

"Guggenheim-gate," I say, winking. The familiar phrase momentarily quells my anxiety and for a moment, I feel normal again. I may be in Paris, and apparently married to a perfect stranger, but Frankie is still Frankie . . . at least, I think she is.

She groans, obviously just as perturbed all these years later. "I mean, who *actually* considers the Guggenheim a romantic destination?"

I grin, even though we both know that Christian and I share an affinity for art. In some ways, I'm as close to Christian as I am to Frankie. After all, I was there the day they met. I smile, recalling how I dared her to go talk to the handsome guy sitting at the end of the bar; the rest is history. Yes, Christian has been as much of a friend to me as Frankie has—especially that year when she juggled her full-time job by day and MBA studies by night. Christian and I kept each other company.

"You mean fluorescent lighting doesn't do it for you?"

Frankie laughs as I rest my head against her shoulder, breathing in the scent of her trademark perfume—Chanel No. 5, a gift her grandmother gave her when she was in college. Everything about Frankie is, in fact, the same—her chest-length, curly dark hair, the little scar on her left hand, the way she's always been able to take one look at me and *know*. "I'm so glad you're here," I whisper, basking in the comfort of familiarity.

"All right, so let's debrief," she says, looking deep into my eyes. "Did you have a fight with Sebastian? Is he being rude to you? Do I need to talk to him? Or maybe you're just being too sensitive? Remember how you flipped out on your wedding day?"

"I . . . flipped out on my . . . wedding day?"

"Do I have to remind you that it took me a half hour to get you out of the bathroom?" she scoffs. "Look, Lena. Whatever you're going through, I'm sure it'll blow over. I know you have a somewhat . . . *complicated marriage*, but he adores you, and that's a fact. Didn't he just whisk you away to Nice last month?" She makes a swoony-looking face. "I mean, count your blessings. At least you're not spending your summer vacation at the Smithsonian." She laughs. "But, seriously, let me know if you want me to talk to him. After all, there's nothing like a dress-down from your wife's best friend." She smiles, flexing her right arm. "Did I tell you? I've been doing CrossFit. Look at these guns!"

I don't know if I'd call Frankie's petite biceps "guns," but I can't help but admire her bravado. She has more strength in her little finger than most people have in a clenched fist. Still, the image of

Sebastian's physique in bed this morning is fresh in my mind, and
I know that in Frankie's hypothetical matchup, she would certainly
be the underdog.

"Listen," I say, searching her big hazel eyes. "Something's going
on with me—something bad."

She frowns, the bravado disappearing from her face, and in its
place, deep concern. "Lena, what's happening? Are you hurt? Did
someone . . . do something to you?"

I shake my head. "No. I mean, I don't know. It's just that I . . . woke
up this morning . . . in Paris, with Sebastian, and . . ." I pause, my
heart racing. "I don't know any other way to explain it, but, Frankie,
this is not my life."

She nods. "So, you're having a midlife crisis."

"No, no. Not a midlife crisis. I'm not even old enough for that, am
I?" I sigh. "But a crisis? Yes."

"You sure you didn't hit your head?"

"Honestly, I'm not really sure of anything right now."

"Maybe you got some bad booze last night? Did someone spike
your drink?"

"I *wasn't* roofied. I told you. I fell asleep at my aunt's house—on
Bainbridge Island."

Frankie thinks for a long moment. "Well, I've heard that absinthe
can really mess you up, like, it can send some people into psychosis.
Isn't it banned in the US?" She nods to herself. "That's probably it—
you're coming off of absinthe."

If only it were that easy. I sigh, looking out the window as we
motor down a street lined with opulent old apartment buildings.
It's the type of scene you find on postcards from Paris, complete
with a macaron shop on the next corner. Its pale pink sign sways
in the breeze.

"Listen, Frankie," I say, turning back to her. "I know this all
sounds far-fetched, but you have to believe me." I bite the edge of

my lip. "This life that's supposed to be mine?" I shake my head, eyes stinging with fresh tears. "It's not."

"Okay," Frankie mutters, rubbing her forehead. I wait for her to continue, but she doesn't. Instead, we sit beside each other for a long moment, cloaked in a heavy and cloistering silence.

"You think I'm crazy, don't you?" I finally say. "You think I've lost it."

She looks out the window, deliberating for a beat. "Listen, I don't know what's happening to you, and yeah, it's a little hard to make sense of, but whatever you're going through, we'll get through it together, okay?"

I nod, more than a little forlorn as the cab pulls to a stop in front of the Musée d'Orsay. Frankie pays the fare, then slips her arm in mine as we follow the path to the entrance.

"If I've learned anything in all these years, it's that museums usually have surprisingly good places to dine. And thank God for that. Do you know how many times I've left Christian standing in front of some ancient nude while I slipped off to get a glass of chardonnay?"

"When you've seen one ancient nude, you've seen them all, right?" I say, playing along.

"There's my girl," she says, squeezing my arm.

I smile, admiring Frankie's ability to cheer me up and help me find my way. Even now, when I'm spiraling (or possibly concussed, poisoned, or in a state of psychosis—maybe all three?), the sheer presence of my best friend is like an IV drip of dopamine—with a side of Xanax and a shot of electrolytes.

"Let's hurry!" she says when the rain starts, quickening her pace. As she reaches for my hand, it unlocks a memory—of us sidestepping mud puddles on our first day of college. She'd just finished her first class, but I was lost, and late to mine.

"Didn't you bring your map?" she asked, referencing the bundle of papers we received in our orientation.

I shook my head. "Sorry, I'm hopeless with maps."

Frankie reached into her jacket pocket, the humid air making her curls even curlier. "I've got one, and I can read it. Now, tell me where you're going."

With her help, I found my classroom that day, and I was only two minutes late. She was my compass then, just as she is now.

"Come on," Frankie says, pulling the hood over her head as the rain intensifies. "We're going to get soaked." The sky overhead looks like it was painted by a moody impressionist. When we reach the entrance, she squeezes my hand. "Don't worry. I won't tell Christian about any of this."

"You can if you want," I say with a shrug. "I trust him. Besides, maybe he'll have some insights on what's going on with me?"

Frankie nods. "True. My husband may not be a charming Frenchman with a home in Nice, but he *is* a damn good problem solver." She grins. "Come on. Let's hash it all out over a bottle of Sancerre."

WE TAKE AN ELEVATOR TO THE THIRD FLOOR, FOLLOWING THE MOUTH-WATERING scent of roast chicken to the restaurant, which looks like a page torn from Marie Antoinette's Versailles, with gilded woodwork, crystal chandeliers, and the enormous fresco on the ceiling. Christian waves from the far corner, where he's seated at a window-facing table clad in crisp white linen and set with handblown glassware in a myriad of colors. I'm grateful to see an open bottle of white wine at the ready. *I need a drink.*

"Lena!" Christian says, standing to give me a hug. "We're so excited to celebrate with you two tonight."

I look at Frankie, then back at Christian. "Okay, can someone please tell me what's going on tonight?"

Christian laughs. "You're kidding, right?" He laughs, reaching for Frankie's hand. "We wouldn't have missed it for the world."

"I'm not kidding," I say, straight-faced. "Missed what?"

"The hotel opening, obviously," Christian continues, a little confused.

"Hotel opening," I mutter blankly, the words triggering zero memories, as we take our seats in the crowded, light-filled restaurant.

Christian looks at Frankie, then back at me. "Have there been any issues?" he asks, pouring us each a glass of wine, which I immediately sip, well, gulp. "I mean, with the opening."

"Honey," Frankie says to her husband. "Lena . . . isn't . . . *feeling well.*"

Christian frowns. "Oh no! You're sick?"

"Something like that," I say as Frankie studies my face. I know she's waiting for me to take the lead, and I do, telling Christian what I'd explained to his wife in the cab.

He clears his throat. "So, you have . . . amnesia?"

"Yeah, it's like that, but not accident-induced, at least as far as I know."

He nods, leaning back in his chair thoughtfully. Christian is still as handsome as he was seven years ago when Frankie and I spotted him in that New York bar—tall, with dark hair and a shadow of stubble on his face. I noticed him first, not that it matters. He flashed a smile at us while sipping his martini. I remember the cheese-stuffed olive in his glass, the song playing through the speakers: "Summertime Sadness" by Lana Del Rey. I'd have walked over and introduced myself if it weren't for the fact that I was in a relationship at the time—a bad one, yes, but still a relationship. Instead, I told Frankie—who was single—that I'd get the next round if she accepted my dare: walk over to the mysterious hottie at the end of the bar, introduce herself, and slip him her number. While Frankie was, and is, by no means shy, approaching men at bars wasn't exactly her thing. Shockingly, though, she took a sip of her cosmopolitan, squared her shoulders, and rose to the occasion.

In some ways, I lost my best friend that night. Well, not exactly, though she did spend the rest of the evening talking to Christian—and the next evening, and the next, and many more for weeks. Three months later, she told me they were talking about marriage and that she'd be moving out of our Brooklyn apartment and into his *très* chic loft in Tribeca.

Such is life, I told myself. In fact, after she moved out, I even bought a framed print of the words *c'est la vie*, which I hung in the bathroom we used to share, right above the toilet. I missed her—oh, I did—especially when I found myself single again. I had to remind myself that while some things change, others remain the same. In this case, even though I'd lost Frankie as my roommate and 24-7 sidekick, I didn't lose our friendship; it just looked a little different. We had a new plus-one: Christian. I even crashed some of their date nights. "You're always welcome," my best friend assured me. She never broke that promise.

This is why I feel comfortable opening up to Christian. I trust him, of course, but I also respect him. He does, in business, what emergency room doctors do in triage mode. He's the guy struggling corporations hire to sort out their messes and save them from collapse. Can he save me?

"So you remember nothing?" Christian asks, gesturing to the waiter for another bottle of wine.

"Zero," I say, leaning back in my chair. "Maybe I should see a doctor?"

"No," Frankie says quickly. "You know what they do to people in France who act a little—"

"Crazy?" I say, finishing her sentence.

She nods cautiously, lowering her voice to a whisper. "I watched a YouTube video about it once. They can lock you up here."

Christian chuckles. "I see we have a professor of YouTube University." Frankie rolls her eyes.

"Babe, this isn't funny! I'm just trying to help!"

"Okay, okay," I say quickly. "So Plan B, then."

"Did you call your aunt?" Frankie asks.

"Yeah, I tried her earlier," I reply, pulling out my phone. "But I didn't get through." I dial Rosie's number again, with no luck.

"Let me try." Frankie keys in the digits, then frowns. "That's weird."

I glance down at my phone—which I feel like hurling across the room—when a text notification, in French, pops up on the screen from someone named . . . *Jacques*? I can't make out the message.

Frankie looks over and studies the screen. "It says"—she pauses, exchanging a glance with Christian—"good luck tonight, and, uh . . . congratulations on the hotel opening."

I shrug. "What's with all the heart emojis?"

"You know the French," Frankie explains. "They're very . . . emotive."

"Wait," I say, confused. "How do you know French?"

She sighs, looking at me as if I've just asked her if Santa Claus is real. "Wow, you really are worse for wear. Honey, remember, I got my master's at the Sorbonne?"

I shake my head. "No, you didn't. You went to NYU."

Frankie turns to Christian, then back to me, as the waiter arrives with our food. We eat in silence for a few minutes—each of us contemplating the mismatched pieces of this maddening puzzle.

"Lena, the thing I can't figure out," Frankie finally says, looking up from her arugula salad. "When we visited last summer, you were fluent. What happened?"

"I don't know," I reply, eyes downcast.

She sighs. "Okay, well, I need to find a restroom."

After she's gone, I bury my face in my hands.

"She's just worried about you, that's all," Christian says. "I am, too." When I remove my hands, our eyes lock for a long beat, before I turn away and he pushes his half-eaten steak *frites* aside. "What's the last thing you remember? Maybe we can start there."

That look in his eyes—I've seen it before, a long time ago. I close my eyes tightly, opening them again as I part my lips to speak, but no words come out. The memories streaming through my mind have no business resurfacing. In fact, I've spent many years trying to purge them from my brain: That night in New York, at that little Italian restaurant by Carnegie Hall, when Frankie was pulling an all-nighter with her grad school study partners, and Christian and I met for dinner. She knew, of course. It wasn't some salacious secret. She loved that we kept each other company. We had her blessing, and yet, each of us knows that she would not have blessed what transpired that night.

I could blame it on the bottle of Barolo, though Christian drank far more, or the hilarious off-Broadway show we stumbled into later that night, or maybe the dimly lit subterranean bar we slipped into afterward, Christian's six-foot-four-inch frame barely clearing the doorway. In any case, both of us knew—and know—that a line was crossed that night. The way he looked at me, the way I'd linked my arm in his after the show, the brush of our knees under the bar counter as we sat close—too close. We were dangerously near the edge, that night, and we both knew it.

When the bar announced last call, and it was time to for us to hail our individual cabs, we lingered outside, huddling together to stay warm. True, it was twenty-two degrees, but it wasn't the Arctic air that pulled our bodies close, it was something else—something far more intense. It felt like a force, a magnet, even, and it rendered us both weak.

A part of me wanted to give in that night; to melt into the warmth of his strong arms and surrender, even tell him the truth: that sometimes I wished it were me, not Frankie, who had approached him at the bar all those years ago. I could have said all those things that cold night, but I didn't. I couldn't. Instead, I got into my own cab and told him goodnight, because I love my friend.

I always will.

Our eyes meet again, but I don't let my gaze linger.

"Hey," Frankie says, slipping back into her seat. "French restrooms are something else. I always forget that you're supposed to tip the attendant. I mean, what if I didn't have any euros on me?"

"No soup for you!" Christian says grinning.

Frankie shakes her head, a little annoyed. "Honey, I'm talking about the bathroom, not soup."

Christian and I exchange a knowing look—obviously she hasn't seen that Seinfeld episode.

"*Soooo*," Frankie continues, underwhelmed as she shifts in her seat to face me. "How are we going to get you through this day?"

"I don't know."

"I was just asking her what she remembers," Christian says.

"Good thinking," Frankie continues. "Lena, what *do* you remember?"

I plant my elbow on the table, resting my head against my right palm. "Like I said, I flew from San Francisco to visit my aunt Rosie on . . . Bainbridge Island."

"San Francisco?" Frankie asks, shocked.

"Uh, yeah, where I live—and work."

Frankie looks at Christian, then back at me. "*Oh-kaaaaaay.*"

"Kevin, my boyfriend, well, ex-boyfriend, and I broke up the night before. I thought he was going to propose, but he gave me Coldplay tickets instead."

"Coldplay tickets?" Frankie folds her arms across her chest.

I nod. "It was brutal." They listen skeptically, as I continue. "That night, on the island, there was a full moon, a big rainstorm, and I . . . fell asleep there—in the guesthouse."

"Maybe it was all just a dream," Frankie suggests.

"Okay, but if it was, does that mean I'm still dreaming?"

Christian shakes his head. "No, you're not. You're very much here, and this is very much real." He points to my left hand. "See that scratch on your finger? You're bleeding—that's proof."

Proof of what? That I just got dragged across Paris by an enormous dog? I blot my tiny cut with the edge of my napkin as Frankie fumbles for a Band-Aid in her purse.

"Maybe you're a time traveler," Christian continues, intrigued. "No, wait! An interdimensional being? Or maybe this is some kind of simulation!"

Frankie laughs. "Uh, I think someone's been watching *way* too many sci-fi movies."

"Hmm," I say, doubtful. "What day is it?"

Frankie glances at her phone. "April eighth, 2023."

"I was on Bainbridge Island yesterday, April seventh."

Frankie nods. "The time travel theory is officially debunked." She looks around. "Christian, let's get the check and take our lost girl home."

He gives the waiter his card, then signs the bill, before we make our way to the exit.

"Absinthe," Frankie says conclusively as we walk out to the street. "That's the explanation. It'll pass soon, but we need to get your head on straight so you can crush it tonight."

I groan, thinking of this illusive "event." "Can you, maybe, fill me in a bit more?" I ask. "Talk to me like I'm a five-year-old."

Frankie nods. "Okay, so, Sebastian is a hotelier—you know, the owner of a *hotel chain*?"

"Come on, I'm not a complete moron."

"Okay, okay, but you did say five-year-old." She grins. "He owns the La Maison Rouge Hotel Group. They have properties in the ritziest locations in France—you know, Nice, Saint-Tropez, Avignon, places like that. Anyway, his company just completed the build-out of their latest location, La Maison Rouge Paris. The opening party's tonight. It's why we're here—to celebrate with you guys."

"Right," I say, nearly tripping on a cobblestone. "And do *I* work for the hotel group?"

Frankie shakes her head. "No, well, yes, in the sense that you're married to Sebastian, but no, not in a direct way. You're an event planner."

"An event planner?"

"Yeah, one of the most successful ones in Paris, in fact. Last month you threw a party for Brigitte Macron."

My eyes widen. "You mean, the first lady of France?"

Frankie grins. "That would be the one. You're a rockstar in the event world, and you're hosting the party tonight."

Suddenly my hands feel clammy. "Why do I have a sinking feeling this is going to be a disaster?"

"Don't be ridiculous," she continues. "When we talked on the phone last night, it sounded like everything was set, but, of course, you don't remember."

"I don't."

"Anyway, you told me that all the heavy lifting was pretty much done. Think of it like this: The musicians have taken their seats. Their instruments are tuned and polished. All you have to do is step out on the stage and . . . conduct."

"An orchestra led by a tone-deaf conductor?" I mutter. "What could go wrong?"

"Maybe hold a clipboard," Christian offers jokingly. "People will think you've got everything under control."

Neither Frankie nor I find this funny, even if he's only trying to lighten the mood. Still, I can't shake my lingering sense of dread. "Guys . . . I just . . . want to go home."

"I get it, honey," Frankie replies, reaching for my hand. "And I know that everything must seem backwards and upside down right now, but I promise, it'll all be fine." She glances at her watch. "It's only two. I bet you'll snap out of this fog in an hour or two. And tonight, I'll be right by your side. SOS is our code under normal circumstances, but tonight just touch your right earring twice, and I'll have your back." She smiles. "You also have that assistant of yours to pick up the slack." Frankie's tone makes it obvious that she's *not* a fan. I nod, thinking back to my exchange with Ella earlier today. She seemed nice enough—definitely a go-getter. "Put her to work, Lena."

Frankie's right, I can do this. If I can handle an egotistical CEO just before earnings, I can pull off a party for a bunch of boozed-up French people. I'll go through the motions, put one foot in front of the other until this bizarre delusion fades. And it will fade. *It has to.*

I glance down at my phone to find an incoming text from Sebastian. Mon amour, I haven't heard from you. Just checking to make sure that you're feeling better and that everything's set for tonight. Meet you there, okay?

I hand my phone to Frankie, groaning. "What am I supposed to text him back?"

"Here," she says, typing with her thumbs. "You'll say, 'Hello, handsome, I—'"

"No," I exclaim. "Do *not* flirt with him."

She laughs. "Okay, how about, 'Hey there, I was just thinking of you. Feeling better. Everything is on track for tonight. XO.'"

"Sure," I finally say, taking in the absurdity of it all. "Send it, I guess."

"Sent," she says, handing back my phone. "Now let's get you back to your apartment. We're staying in an Airbnb a few blocks from you. Why don't we circle back around five to pick you up? Sound good?"

I nod.

"Okay, now go put on a dress. Get glammed up. And don't forget red lipstick, and heels—Frenchwomen always wear heels."

"I hate heels."

She winks, facetiously. "Well, that's a shame, because you happen to have a closet full of them."

"Right," I say nervously. "Okay. I'll do my best."

"That's the spirit," Frankie says.

6

"How much time do we have until guests start arriving?" I ask Frankie as the cab pulls up in front of the hotel.

"Plenty," she replies, glancing at her watch. "At least an hour."

I nod, nervously peering out the window at La Maison Rouge Paris, which is perched on a quaint street in the Montmartre neighborhood. It's beyond charming, with enormous cypress trees that flank the lantern-lined entrance and the warm amber glow of candlelight flickering from the sills of each guest room window. Tightly bunched arrangements of red roses line the steps leading to the gilded double door.

"What do you think?" Ella says, suddenly materializing behind me. She's dressed to the nines in a red-sequined minidress that accentuates her petite frame and ample cleavage. I feel plain in comparison, having selected a high-neck long-sleeved black gown. She points to a gold sign beside the entrance: UN ENDROIT POUR TROUVER L'AMOUR. "A place to fall in love," she translates, grinning. "Sebastian loved your idea!"

A place to fall in love? *More like a place to have a mental breakdown.*

"The flowers look great, don't they?" she continues, smoothing her hair, which is curled and pinned to one side. I feel instantly less glamorous with my tight bun.

"They do," Frankie interjects when I don't reply. "Now, how can I help? Put me to work!"

"Absolutely not," Ella replies. "You're a *guest*. Please, come in, and have some champagne. Sebastian insisted on top-shelf tonight!"

Speaking of Sebastian, I spot him ahead, smiling confidently in the hotel's foyer beside an ice sculpture of a man and woman—nude, in the David style—embracing as their lips meet. Christian gazes up at it curiously. Everything about the hotel is grand—from the lush velvet drapes to the crystal chandeliers overhead.

Ella shifts in her heels as Sebastian approaches, beaming when he kisses her hand. "The place to fall in love," he says, slipping his arm around my waist. "My brilliant wife."

"Um, hi," I say awkwardly.

"Hello, *mon amour*," he whispers, pressing his lips against mine. Miraculously, I don't flinch—or whack him over the head with my Chanel handbag. I remain frozen, haunted by Frankie's warning about the fate of psychiatric patients in France. Whether it's true or not, I make a mental note not to raise any eyebrows.

"It's all perfect, isn't it?"

I nod obediently.

"I have you—and Ella—to thank."

"*Merci*," Ella says as she slips her arm into Sebastian's in an easy, familiar way.

I don't care, of course (and *why should I?*). Besides, it's just the French being, well, *French*, but I can't help but wonder: Does this assistant of mine have a *thing* for him? When I catch Frankie's eye, I can tell she concurs. What's with my assistants these days, both in reality and this alternate one?

"Your vision is nothing short of genius," Ella says, batting her eyelashes at Sebastian.

"A beautiful party, surrounded by beautiful women," he replies. "I am the luckiest man in Paris."

When I feel my heels wobbling beneath me, I'm grateful for Frankie's steadying grip on by arm, especially when Sebastian reaches for my hand. "Darling, come with me. I want to show you the most magnificent suite."

I search Frankie's eyes. *Don't worry!* she telepaths to me. *Go!*

"Suite?" I ask nervously as he leads me to the elevator.

"Yes," he says, tucking his arm around my waist. "On the top floor."

When the elevator door shuts, Sebastian inches closer in the dim light, his breath on my skin. "I've missed you," he says, running his hand along the length of my arm, leaving a trail of goose bumps in its wake.

I'm surprised by the surge of electricity coursing through my veins, but also relieved when the elevator doors open again. Sebastian leads me to the end of a dim hallway, swiping a key card beside a door to our right. "*Voilà*," he says, weaving his hand in mine as we cross the threshold.

The suite *is* truly magnificent, in fact, it rivals any of those loved-up couple posts you see on Instagram, depicting the Parisian life of pied-à-terres, exquisite pastries, and indulgent bubble baths.

I eye the elaborate bed, where Sebastian seems to be luring me. My heart beats faster with each step, especially so when he takes me into his arms and delicately presses my body against the wall, running his hand along the edge of my thigh. When he kisses me, I feel light and fluttery—like the only thing that exists is the few square feet we occupy.

"Wait," I say, coming to my senses. I take a step back and smooth my dress. "Shouldn't we go back downstairs and greet our guests?"

He shakes his head and pulls me back into his arms. "Let's be fashionably late," he whispers in my ear, his breath like a feather on my neck. "I want you."

When he kisses me again, I'm powerless to resist. Maybe this is it? Maybe this is love—*the* love I've always wondered about, but never found, and all because I tossed a scrap of paper in the garbage can after a wedding reception? Could this be my chance to get it right?

As if they have a mind of their own, my fingers find the buttons on Sebastian's shirt and unfasten them one by one. I stifle the cautious part of my brain, the one that tells me I'm being foolish, that I've lost my mind, as he begins to unzip my dress, kissing the top of my spine, just as his . . . pants vibrate. "*Merde*," he says, running his hand through his hair before reaching into his pocket and eyeing his phone. "I should probably take this."

"Right," I say, standing up as he makes a beeline to the bathroom, speaking in a hushed voice—in French.

"Everything okay?" I ask when he reappears.

"*Oui, oui,*" he says buttoning up his shirt. "It was nothing, my love." He kisses my cheek before helping me with my zipper. "But you're probably right. We should be good hosts and head downstairs."

"Yeah," I say quickly. "Totally. I'll just . . . get my heels."

He smiles at me warmly in the elevator, but I can't help but feel a shift. Whoever called, whatever their conversation, it sucked the passion right out of him.

"THERE YOU ARE!" FRANKIE SAYS AS I ENTER THE FOYER, WHERE A DOZEN PEOPLE are milling around. "Where've you been?" she whispers. "I was beginning to worry." She pauses, then frowns. "Oh dear, your lipstick is smudged. Wait, were you . . . ?"

"Up in the penthouse suite with Sebastian," I say nervously.

Frankie laughs. "Well, I'm glad that you two are . . . staying the course . . . despite, you know, your state of mind. What was it . . . like?" She gazes off into the room nostalgically. "I mean, when you've been married as long as Christian and I have, things can get a little, well, *routine*, you know? I can't even imagine the thrill of experiencing that 'first time' again."

"No, no, we didn't . . ." I pause, eyeing the entrance where a couple in their sixties have just walked in. They're both regal-looking, like they belong in a chateau adorned with Louis XV furniture. The woman holds herself like a countess, exuding a certain zest that somehow makes her more alluring than any other woman in the room. Even the younger men in attendance seem to fall under her spell, including one talking to Ella who can't keep his eyes off her.

"Who's that?" I ask Frankie, who pulls a folded page from her purse.

"Ella asked me to give you this," she says. "The guest list—with notes on each attendee—food preferences, quirks, et cetera."

"So, my cheat sheet?" I look over the page with little luck. "Great—it's in French." I sigh, handing it back to Frankie. "Can you make any sense of this?"

She scours the document in her hands, then nods. "Bingo. That woman is Claudine Trousseau, or Madame Trousseau, as she's known—one of the most famous lingerie designers in France. She and her husband have just returned from their seventeenth-century chateau in the south, and according to these notes, Sebastian's been entertaining her interest in investing in the La Maison Rouge Hotel Group."

I furrow my brow. "Great, so I have to kiss her butt."

"Bingo," Frankie says as Sebastian crosses the room, whispering something in Ella's ear. She straightens his collar before he slips away to greet Madame Trousseau.

"Frankie," I whisper, "was he just *flirting* with Ella?"

"Of course not," she says, though her tone is far from convincing.

I wave and smile at people I don't know, avoiding conversation at all costs. "Where's Christian?"

"Oh, probably off gawking at the hotel's art," Frankie quips, reaching for a glass of champagne. "It's fine. I told him that you're my date tonight, anyway."

"Thanks," I say, "for being here for me. I . . . don't know what I'd do without you."

"Uh, you'd be a disaster. And you're welcome."

An hour passes, and then another. There are a hundred or so people mingling and milling about, enjoying the flowing champagne and piped-in jazz music. The party is a success—at least as far as I can tell—that is, until I pass Madame Trousseau. I feel obligated to stop and say a brief hello, but I immediately regret the decision when she turns to the woman beside her and mutters something in French, her expression cold and guarded.

"I'm . . . sorry for . . . interrupting," I say quickly, finding my way back to Frankie, who's just snatched an hors d'ouevre from a passing waiter.

"You have to try these," she says between bites. "They're insane!"

"Frankie, I totally flubbed. I went over to say hi to Madame Trousseau, and, I don't know . . . I must have offended her somehow, because she totally blew me off."

"Are you sure? Maybe you misread the situation?"

I nod. "Maybe."

"Don't worry about Grandma Trousseau," Frankie says, popping another bite into her mouth. "Let Sebastian handle her."

"Right," I say, noticing a man looking at us from the other side of the room. He's a little younger than me, well dressed, with light brown hair that falls just over his left eye. He slicks it back after taking a sip of wine, flashing a smile in our direction. I nudge Frankie's arm. "Do you see that guy looking over at us?"

"You mean every guy at this party?" Frankie laughs, slipping her arm in mind as she whisks me across the room, taking a quick glance over her shoulder as we round the corner. "Come on, let's find the restroom. I'm pretty sure I have an enormous chive wedged between my two front teeth. I also need to borrow your lipstick."

"Sure," I say, digging through my purse, where I find my phone buzzing. It appears to be the same person from earlier today at the museum, with all the emojis. "I can't wait to get out of here," I say, tucking my phone away with a sigh.

"Me, too," she says, puckering at her reflection in the bathroom mirror, then applying a coat of matte-red lipstick. "Want me to round up Christian and have him get us a cab? I'm sure no one will notice if we slip out—make a little *French exit*."

I nod. "Yeah, but I should probably find Sebastian first. What should I tell him?"

"That you have the stomach flu," Frankie suggests. "That always works."

I smile, turning to the bathroom door, when Ella walks in holding a manila envelope. "There you are," she says, her skin flawless and fresh. *Twenty-somethings*. "Great party, right?"

"Yeah," I say, smiling awkwardly.

"All right, before I forget, I wanted to confirm that I've booked the flights to Saint-Tropez. We depart tonight at midnight. It was tough getting a charter, but"—her voice shifts into a singsongy tone—"guess who pulled some strings?" She smiles, clearly proud of herself.

"Uh, thank you?" I say, a little confused. "I'm sorry, I guess I somehow missed the memo that we were leaving tonight. Seems a little weird to get on a plane so late, and after this big event. I haven't even packed."

Ella shakes her head. "No, no. *You're* not going." She laughs. "Just Sebastian and me." She opens the manila envelope, sorting through papers. "Oh, and I booked that suite he loves—the one with the balcony that overlooks the terrace with the citrus trees."

I take a step back, my gaze alternating between her and Frankie. "The two of you are going to Saint-Tropez? Why?"

"For his . . . business meeting," she says, pausing to clear her throat. "You know, Madame Trousseau."

"Then why are you going?"

"He . . . asked me to come along to . . . smooth out the edges."

"To . . . smooth out *what* edges?"

"Well . . . all of them," she continues, a little surprised. "Lena, that's what I do."

"I bet that's what you do," I say, shaking my head. "It was you, wasn't it? The one who called Sebastian when we were up in the suite before the party started?"

She shakes her head. "I don't know what you're talking about."

"But you do," I continue, my jaw tensing. "You're having an affair with my husband, aren't you?"

Frankie looks like she's on the verge of a heart attack as Ella gasps, placing her hand on her chest. "Absolutely not."

Her response is believable enough, though I reach for the envelope in her hands for proof, pulling out the hotel reservation details.

"This says there are two rooms booked," I say, after reading the reservation details. "One is a single; the other for *two*." I hand the page to Frankie; she nods, confirming my quick detective work.

Once confident and poised, Ella suddenly looks like a frightened field mouse shivering in front of a broom. She rubs her forehead. "Lena, I'm so sorry. I . . . thought you knew. I . . . thought you and Sebastian had an . . . *understanding*."

"An understanding?"

Frankie tugs at my arm. "Lena, let's go, okay? Don't worry, we can sort this all out later."

"No," I say. "I want to sort this out right now."

Ella looks terrified, though I can't tell if her expression is born of empathy or regret. She merely nods, steadying herself. "Lena, after all these years, surely you know that Madame Trousseau is . . . Sebastian's lover."

I'm so stunned, my mouth falls open. I don't deserve to feel betrayed, and I have no grounds to feel the anger that's rising up in my chest, but it's there nonetheless.

"Really I . . ." Ella continues, a bit forlorn. "I had no idea that you weren't aware, I mean, especially because—"

"Thanks, Ella," Frankie interjects. "It's been a long night. I think we should find ourselves a cab." She hustles me out of the restroom into the lobby and tells me to wait while she looks for Christian.

I nod despondently, staring ahead where Sebastian stands in the far corner, locked in conversation with *The Madame*. Her husband is gone, off with his own lover, I assume. And yet, I can't help but imagine the lingerie she's packed for their romantic weekend. Will he hold her the way he held me tonight? Does he love her? Does he love me?

I don't have any answers, but I do know one thing: Sebastian certainly showed his true colors all those years ago. In fact, he predicted this. I'm so trapped in my mind that I hardly notice the figure beside me—just another insignificant person in this bizarre charade—that is, until he whispers, "*Hello, mon chéri*," in my ear.

I take a step back, eyes wide. It's the guy from earlier—the one who was smiling from across the room. He seems normal enough—in other words, I don't get the feeling that he's the type who'd drag me into a dark alley—and yet, something about his presence feels off, and why is he standing so close?

"Excuse me, who are you?"

"Oh, I see we're role-playing tonight," he says, extending his hand. "Hi, I'm Jacques." When he inches closer and places his hand on the small of my back, slowly letting it creep lower, I take another giant step back. My heel catches on my dress, and I stumble sideways, flailing my arms as I desperately try to reclaim my balance. But gravity has her way with me, cruel as she is, hurling my body sideways and directly against the edge of the ice sculpture.

As I wobble in my heels, I clutch its cold edge for balance, which turns out to be an ill-fated idea when a chunk cracks off and the whole thing begins leaning to the left, taking me down like a felled tree. *Timber!*

The next thing I know, I'm on my back, sprawled out on the floor. I barely feel the pain—just a throbbing sensation along my right leg, and I suspect I'll have a nasty bruise in a few hours. Oh, but I do feel the gazes of the other party guests boring into me like lasers. The room is abuzz in a chorus of whispers, and here I am, lying on the floor beside a slightly pornographic ice sculpture, part of which is presently dripping onto my forehead—French water torture.

My vision blurs as the room begins to spin. Is this the end? If I close my eyes tightly, will I wake up from this nightmare and find myself back in the guesthouse on Bainbridge Island? For a moment, I think yes. This is the close of my wild delusion, the final scene of a chilling dream. Any second now, I'll sit up in bed, in a cold sweat, relieved to be home. I'll call Frankie, and we'll have a good laugh.

Oh, but no. When I open my eyes, I'm still here, in Paris, lying next to the disgraced ice sculpture. The only bright spots are Christian's and Frankie's faces hovering over me—dual lighthouses calling out to me on a stormy sea. Jacques? Gone.

Frankie kneels beside me, placing her hand on my cheek. "Lena, can you move your legs? Is anything broken?"

"Yes, and no—at least, I don't think so."

"Good," she says, nodding, before looking up at Christian. "I'll get us a cab, can you—"

"I've got her," he says, effortlessly lifting me into his strong arms.

The partygoers hover, gawking and whispering. There's no empathy in their eyes; this is sheer entertainment, though I'm relieved not to see Sebastian or Madame What's-Her-Name in the peanut gallery. He probably took her up to the penthouse to pick up where *we* left off, but I don't care. I just want out of here.

When the crowd doesn't budge, Frankie rattles off something in French, then follows up with, "What's wrong with you people? Step aside. We need to get her out!" She sounds pissed, and I love her for it.

A miniature cab is waiting outside, and Christian helps me into the backseat. "I don't think there's room in here for me," he says to Frankie. "You two go ahead. Stay with her tonight. She shouldn't be alone. I'll find a ride back to our place, okay?"

"Okay," Frankie says, her eyes beaming with love as she leans out of the window to give him a parting kiss.

At first we don't speak, maybe because neither of us knows where to begin or what to say. But when my phone buzzes in my purse, I glance at the text message, then hand it to Frankie. "Tell me," I say, my stomach in knots. "This person who's been texting me, that man who came on to me tonight. Frankie, tell me what's happening. Make it make sense."

She looks out the window for a long moment, then back at me. "Okay," she finally says, taking a deep breath. "Lena, it's true, Sebastian is having an affair. But . . ."

"But?"

"So are you."

I nod, quietly processing the bomb she's just dropped. "How do you know?"

"Because you told me, on the phone two months ago."

I can't immediately pinpoint what I'm feeling, but it's a mix of shame and sadness, with a pinch of disgust. Here I am, a supposedly happily married woman, who's just found out that her husband has a lover, and—news flash—so does she! I shake my head, feeling the weight of Frankie's revelation.

I lean my head against the side of the car. "It's all so sad."

"Yeah," Frankie replies. "But I'm not judging you, honey."

I sigh. "You should. I'm judging *myself*."

"I mean, at least he's cute."

I grimace. "Jacques?"

She nods.

"Of course his name would be Jacques."

We both laugh—for no reason and every reason—before slipping into silence again.

"Frankie," I say after a long moment. "I'm . . . not in love with him—Jacques—am I?"

"No way. You were very clear that this was just a . . . thing."

"A thing." I bite the edge of my lip. "Okay . . . and what about Sebastian? Do I . . . love him? Do I truly love him?"

She smiles, her eyes curious and wise. "You profess to, yes, but, honey, you're the only one who knows the answer to that question."

I nod, letting her words sink in as the driver pulls up in front of the apartment building. When we step out of the cab, I clutch my back. "Oh man, I think I pulled something."

"Advil and ice," she says, helping me into the building.

Inside the apartment, Claude gives us an exuberant welcome before we peel out of our dresses and heels, shedding the trappings of this very bizarre evening. I lost an earring somewhere, which strikes me as oddly hilarious. I imagine my stray bauble lying on the floor of the hotel lobby, right beside the ice sculpture, which, by now, is probably becoming a puddle.

"What are you laughing about?" Frankie asks.

"Everything," I say as she tosses me a pair of pajamas from a dresser drawer.

She smiles, changing into her own pair, before bringing me a bottle of Advil, an ice pack, and a mug of herbal tea.

While Frankie takes Claude out to relieve himself, I think about today's shocking chain of events. I'm no closer to understanding what's happening, just that it's happening . . . only to me. I just hope that tomorrow this big hot mess of a nightmare will all fade away. It has to.

A few minutes later, Frankie climbs into bed next to me, and we lie together in silence for a long while, cloaked in the protective blanket of our seventeen-year friendship. There are no words—not now, at least none that need to be spoken. The fact that she's here with me is enough. Two tired souls sharing space. We'll figure out the rest later.

I think back to meeting Sebastian all those years ago, how I'd bristled at his theories on love. At the time, I wondered, worried, even, that there might be a grain of truth to it all. After today, however, Sebastian somehow makes Mr. Conveyor Belt more appealing. At least he wasn't living a double life.

I exhale deeply, my head sinking into the pillow, where I first opened my eyes this morning. "I love you," I whisper to Frankie, her dark ringlets cascading over the white sheets. "Love you, too," she replies, yawning.

With moonlight streaming through the windows, I look over at Frankie—mascara smeared under her eyelids, mouth gaped open. I wipe away a little drool from her cheek with the edge of my sleeve when she begins to snore. She sounds like a baby elephant with a head cold. I smile to myself. Two best friends, sharing a king-size bed in Paris under the most ridiculously unbelievable circumstances. Yes, *this, too,* is love.

PART
THREE

7

A rooster crows from somewhere nearby—as in, right outside the window. I sit up, panicked, looking down at my unmanicured hands, with a thick accumulation of dirt under the nails, before noticing the ring on my left hand. I eye the modest diamond nestled in an art deco setting. It has the look of a family heirloom—something passed down from a great-grandmother who baked gingerbread cookies. Obviously, no one Sebastian's related to.

Sebastian. I gasp, looking around the room. *Frankie!* I turn to my left, scouring the strange, empty bed—wondering, worrying. I'm not in Paris, nor am I home.

No! Not again! Apparently yesterday's "bad dream" has morphed into a real-life *nightmare*—and a recurring one. I catch my breath, scratching the back of my neck, immediately noticing raised red welts along the backs of my arms. An allergic reaction or stress? I'm not sure, but *I'm breaking out in hives.*

Cautiously, I climb out of bed and tiptoe to the partially open doorway, peering out to find a staircase leading to the lower floor. "Hello?" I say, my voice high-pitched and a little mousy. "Is anyone . . . there?"

I step back when I hear the thud of heavy boots clacking against creaky hardwood floors. My heart lurches as a tall, bearded man appears in the doorway. "Morning, sleepyhead," he says with a smile. "I can't remember the last time you stayed in bed past eight. Must have needed the rest, I guess."

"Uh, yeah," I say, tugging at the edge of my sweatshirt, which is when I realize that I'm *not wearing pants*.

"I made a frittata," he continues, clearly unfazed by the state of my half-clothed body. "Come grab a slice before it gets cold. The weather's supposed to turn this afternoon—might even hail. We've got our work cut out for us today."

I nod, quickly closing the door behind me, before I run to the bathroom, where I peel off my sweatshirt and have a look at myself in the mirror. This hive situation is *real*, but, surprisingly, yesterday's bruise on my upper thigh is gone. Still, the memories of Paris continue to linger—the ice sculpture, Jacques whispering in my ear, Madame What's-Her-Name. I shudder.

Yes, I'm out of that nightmare, but now in another one? I look out the bathroom window, which only ignites more confusion. There's a flower garden just below, a red barn in the distance, row after row of trees brimming with white blossoms, and cows grazing in a nearby pasture dotted with wildflowers. The scene is as charming as it is foreign. In fact, I feel like I've just woken up in a freaking Norman Rockwell painting. Cue the pumpkin pie.

So I'm on a farm? I don't know any farmers. Wait, I do! I mean, I *did*. Tall dude with a beard—who are you? He looked vaguely familiar, but my memory isn't cooperating. *Think, Lena, think.*

Farmer John. Yes, Farmer John! I mean, his name wasn't really John, but after a few dates, six or seven years ago, Frankie anointed him with the moniker, and it stuck. I guess we did, too, somehow?

Nathan! His name is Nathan. We met at a farmers' market in the city shortly after college, when Frankie and I lived in that fifth-floor walkup in Brooklyn with those awful neighbors who were always slamming their doors. I approached his stand to buy a bag of . . . apples, I think? Or were they potatoes? No—definitely apples. Anyway, he was sweet, earnest, and, oh, yes, ruggedly handsome. Though not my usual type, after a streak of bad dates with Wall Street men (don't even get me started on Harry the hedge fund executive, whom Frankie nicknamed "Hedgehog," though he wasn't nearly as cute as the mammal of the same name) I decided to do a complete one-eighty. Yes, John, er, Nathan was a breath of fresh air—honest, uncomplicated, hardworking. He'd just taken over his family's farm in the outskirts of Lancaster, Pennsylvania, if I'm not mistaken—on acreage his ancestors had farmed for generations. I liked him—I really did. But when he texted at the eleventh hour to reschedule what would have been our third date, I was miffed and went dark. That was the end of us—or was it?

"Honey?" he calls from downstairs, just as the insufferable rooster crows again. "You coming down?"

"Um, yeah," I reply a little nervously, as I scramble to find a pair of pants. "I'm . . . just getting dressed."

I survey the closet with a disappointed sigh, sorting through stacks of practical, drab-looking wool sweaters and neatly folded, heavily worn jeans. My uniform, I take it. I catch a glimpse of myself in the bathroom mirror. My cheeks are rosy, my hair long, shockingly so (hello, Laura Ingalls Wilder), which is when I notice a jagged scar on my stomach, beneath my belly button. It doesn't have the fleshy pinkness of a fresh wound—probably years old. Appendicitis, maybe? Rosie had hers taken out in her thirties; she'd warned me that I'd probably lose that game of genetic roulette. Fun.

Rosie. I want to call her, desperately, to hear her voice, to have her tell me that everything's going to be okay, that I'll snap out of this, but there's no trace of a cell phone on the nightstand—not even a charger. Life off the grid, I guess.

I throw my hair into a messy bun, before cautiously opening the bedroom door. Following the mouthwatering scent of breakfast, I head downstairs and turn right, which leads to the living room. It looks like something clipped from the pages of *Country Living*, with its river-rock fireplace, overstuffed sofa, and the serene landscape painting hanging on the wall. Just ahead is the kitchen—and, oh, the kitchen! Sunny and bright, with a wall of windows facing out to the garden, polished copper pots hanging over an enormous vintage range. In the center of the room, a large rustic wood dining table holds court, where Nathan sits, sipping coffee.

"There you are," he says, looking up from the array of kraft paper packets laid out in front of him. "Just getting the seeds organized."

"Um, cool," I say, clutching the edge of a chair to steady myself.

He eyes one of the seed packs, then sets it aside. "I say we ditch the San Marzanos this year. Remember how long they took to germinate last spring?"

"Yeah," I say numbly. "Totally."

He pauses. "And the spider mites didn't help matters, either."

I feel a chill running down my spine. A few days ago, I was in San Francisco, running point on earnings for a major Fortunate 500 company, and now I'm a . . . farmer, dealing with . . . spider mites?

"Definitely," I say, doing my best to play along.

Nathan nods decidedly. "All right, then. We'll ditch the San Marzanos and go with"—he pauses, reaching for another seed pack—"a mix of Brandywine and Queen of the Night." He gestures to the stove. "Grab some breakfast, honey."

I nod, luckily locating a cabinet containing plates on the first try. The cutlery drawer is a bit more of a goose chase; fortunately, Nathan doesn't seem to notice.

"You like?" he asks, after I slide into a chair and take a bite.

"Delicious," I say quickly, eying a shelf stacked with dozens of mason jars on the far wall—an impressive collection of pickled carrots, cucumbers, and tomatoes. Apparently we're pickle people.

He seems pleased, and his face relaxes. "We're a little late on squash. I mean, we do have some starts in the greenhouse, but I want to get the acorn and sugar pies in the ground today—before it heats up this weekend."

I nod, completely lost.

"Hate to put this on you, but can you do the cows this morning?"

"Do the . . . cows?"

"Yeah."

My eyes widen. "You mean, milk them?"

Nathan laughs. "Yep, that would be the thing."

"Right, right," I say with a nervous laugh.

"And the chickens," he continues.

I nearly choke on my last bite. "Milk the . . . *chickens*?"

He chuckles. "Quite the *comedienne* this morning, aren't you?" *Ha ha.*

"Well," Nathan continues, sighing as he rises to his feet, "these seeds aren't going to plant themselves." He pauses, reaching into the pocket of his Carhartt pants. "Oh, I almost forgot. Can you give these to Barb and Babbs?" He hands me a seed pack with the words "Big Max" written in black ink. "What our kale farmer neighbors want with giant pumpkins is beyond me, but you know how Babbs is when she gets an idea in her head."

"Right," I say, eyeing the coffeepot on the counter. *Good old Babbs.*

Nathan places both of his strong hands on my shoulders, then kisses the back of my neck, which sends a tingling sensation down my arms. I can hear Frankie's teasing voice in my head: "Farmer John is a hottie!" He was and *he is.*

"Hey, what time will Frankie and Christian be here tonight?"

My eyes light up.

"Uh, I'm not sure."

"Okay, let me know," he continues, heading to the back door. "I want to time the carnitas."

A man who cooks breakfast—and dinner? *Why did I ghost this guy, again?*

"Good luck milking the chickens," Nathan says with a grin before slipping out the door.

I down a cup of coffee, then slide my feet into a pair of green boots. "All right, cows, I'm coming for you," I whisper under my breath.

Zigzagging through the garden, I pause to admire rows of flower beds, munching a sprig of mint from a terra-cotta pot—at least, I think it's mint. A butterfly lands on a rosebud as I breathe in the fresh morning air and gaze out at the orchard in the distance with dense rows of apple trees clustered with pale pink blossoms that look like cotton candy. What a contrast from yesterday, in Paris, with my thousand shades of self-loathing. I may be far from home, out of my element, and more lost than I've ever been in my life, but there's something comforting about this place. The light-green shoots bursting from the ground! The fresh air! The chickens roaming around. I pause, watching one particularly plump hen feast on an enormous . . . earthworm. I cover my mouth, squelching the shriek that nearly erupts from my mouth. *It's nature*, I tell myself. *It's just nature.*

I find the cows in the barn, happily chomping on bales of hay in their individual stalls. *All right, this isn't rocket science*, I tell myself. *Find a pail, grab a nipple, milk the cow!* Easy peasy, right?

I square up beside Maybell, at least that's what her tag says, rolling up my sleeves. "Hi," I begin, lowering myself onto the stool in her stall. "I'm Lena, and I'm going to, um, be doing the milking today."

Maybell lets out a long, dissatisfied moo, as I lean in. "I know this is a little uncomfortable—for us both—but it'll be fine," I continue, feeling a little like a gynecologist before a pelvic exam. "Now I'm going to start *the process*." I raise my hand up slowly, reaching for one of her engorged breasts—nipples? I don't know. I've never done this before. I don't even have a phone to google it! "Okay, okay," I say, as she becomes increasingly agitated. "I'm just going to reach right here, nice and easy, and then we'll—"

Suddenly Maybell flinches, sending me off the stool and swiftly face down on a bed of hay. "Listen," I say, picking bits of straw out of my hair. "I know you don't like this. I'm not loving it, either." I peer into her enormous brown eyes. "But I *need* you to cooperate." Tentatively, I take my seat on the stool once more. "Let's make a deal: You hold still for a few minutes, and I'll get out of your hair. After that, we don't have to see each other again. Cool?" I nod to myself. "Cool."

I place the pail underneath her and cautiously get back to work. Fortunately, she upholds her end of the bargain, but not before I somehow manage to squirt milk directly into my left eye. "Not so bad, right?" I say, laughing as I wipe my face with the edge of my sleeve. She moos as if to say, *You know it.*

"Okay, you can tell I'm nervous, can't you? You know I've never done this before." I nod to myself. What I need is a poker face. Lady Gaga's song pops in my head, and I bolt out a few stanzas, humming along. Maybell's apparently a pop music fan, because by the time I finish the song, the pail is nearly full, which gives me a strange sense of relief and accomplishment. I may be a city girl who works in corporate America, but I can do this.

The next six bovines aren't nearly as cooperative, but somehow I manage to finish the job and funnel my harvest into a nearby refrigerated holding tank before moving on to the chickens, at a complete loss about my impending task. No milking, fortunately, but what?

I peer inside the coop, where a bevy of animated hens startles. Eggs? I don't see any, just piles of fresh excrement. I cover my mouth, nearly losing my breakfast, but fortunately the two women waving across the pasture from the other side of the fence give me the courage I need to hold it together, or, at least, pretend.

"Um, hi," I say, leaning my shovel against the coop before walking over to them.

The pair of fifty-something women in overalls smile as I approach, and I remember the pumpkin seeds Nathan handed me earlier. These must be the kale farmers.

"Hi, sweetie," the taller one says, her graying hair cut short. "Nice day, isn't it? Cooler than usual, but the kale sure loves it, right, Babbs?"

The other woman nods. Wearing a pair of denim overalls and a flannel shirt, she proudly displays a woven basket piled high with greens. "The first of the lacinato! It'll be in the salad we bring by tonight."

I reach into my pocket. "Oh, I have . . . seeds for you—from Nathan."

"Wonderful!" Babbs exclaims, obviously thrilled.

Her partner folds her arms across her chest, less enthused. "Babbs has this cockamamie idea to do a pumpkin patch for local children this year—you know, bales of hay, bobbing for apples, that kind of thing. I keep telling her we should stay in our lane. We're kale farmers, not pumpkin people." She shrugs. "But, happy wife, happy life, right?"

I love them already. "Right," I say, grinning.

"Hey," Barb continues, a little cautiously, "how are you feeling . . . about tonight?"

"Tonight?"

The two women exchange a knowing look. "You know, seeing Frankie's . . . baby for the first time?"

Frankie's . . . baby? I steady myself as I take in her words. My best friend is a . . . mother? The same best friend who'd never once talked about having babies? The same one whose job working for a nonprofit sometimes meant so much to her that she chose service over her own husband's birthday last year? All facts, but even if this is true, why are these women looking at me as if I'm an antique teacup on the verge of cracking? Sure, I'm surprised, but why wouldn't I be anything but happy for Frankie?

"I know it's been hard for you, honey," Babbs adds, "given all you've been through."

"She'll do just fine," Barb interjects. "That baby is going to love her auntie Lena."

Frankie has a baby girl? I force a smile, at a loss for words, but Babbs quells the awkward silence.

"I don't think I've ever told you how difficult things got shortly after we met." She pauses, smiling at Barb for a beat. "The two of us were both passionate about organic farming—and each other." She laughs. "We were toiling away at our jobs in the city, each with our own agricultural dreams. Little did we know that we'd applied for the same highly competitive government grant to pursue farming in Lancaster County. Anyway, when Barb called to tell me she was chosen, it felt like an arrow to the heart. Here was this person I was falling in love with, and I should have been happy for her. But the truth is, her good news only amplified my own disappointment— that is, until I came to my senses and willed myself to see the bigger picture." She smiles at Barb, then looks out to the surrounding property. "Losing that grant hurt—it did. But it was a blessing in disguise, not only because it gave me the dose of humility I obviously needed, but it also opened my eyes to the unexpected joy that can grow out of disappointment. That grant of Barb's was the beginning of this beautiful life we've shared together—I was just too thickheaded to see it in the moment."

Barb nods. "You're probably experiencing your own version of this, sweetie," she adds. "But you'll see, good things can grow out of the weeds. I promise."

I smile politely. These sentiments are sweet, for sure, but they've read me entirely wrong. "I'm okay," I say with a nervous laugh. "Really. I'm thrilled for Frankie and Christian. Honestly, I have zero interest in motherhood."

Babbs and Barb exchange a curious look.

"Seriously, no diapers for me, please."

"Well," Babbs says, eyeing her pack of seeds. "We should probably get back to work before the rain starts." She smiles strangely. "See you tonight, sweetie."

I swallow hard. *Clearly, they know something I don't.*

WHILE NATHAN IS OUT IN THE GARDEN BEDS, I RETREAT INSIDE, WHERE I FIND A phone charging in the kitchen—*yes!*—and immediately call Rosie.

"Hi, dear," she says, her familiar voice calm, natural.

I clutch the phone as if squeezing Rosie's hand, tears stinging my eyes. "I miss you so much."

"My dear girl," she continues, sensing my distress. "What's wrong?"

"Everything," I say, half laughing, half crying.

"Ah," she says knowingly. "Did a coyote storm the chicken coop again?"

I swallow hard, shaking my head. "No, no . . ." I whisper. "Not that. It's just that . . . Rosie, I'm scared."

"Scared of what, dear?"

"This is going to sound crazy," I begin, exhaling deeply. "But . . . hear me out, okay?"

"You're not crazy, and I'm listening."

"Rosie, *I'm stuck*. Something's happening to me, and it all started when I came home to see you and fell asleep in the guesthouse."

She's quiet for a long beat, processing all I've just said. "When did you say you were here—in *the guesthouse*?"

I pause, struggling to recall the passing of time. "A few days ago? I don't know—it's all a blur."

"Okay, honey, listen to me, and listen to me *carefully*—"

The connection suddenly glitches, and Rosie's voice sounds pixelated before I lose her entirely. When I try dialing her again, I can't get through.

Deflated, I sink into the sofa in the living room, scrolling through photos on the phone. "Hey," Nathan says, breaking my reverie as he slides onto the sofa beside me.

I look up nervously, before turning back to a photo of the two of us on our wedding day. I'm dressed in a simple white satin gown, he in a suit. We're standing beneath a tree brimming with white blossoms.

"Best day of my life," he says, looking over my shoulder. "Well, that and the day you said yes. Gosh, I was a nervous wreck, remember?"

I nod, pretending to follow along.

"I wasn't sure what you'd think of my grandmother's ring." He pauses, smiling. "Especially after Christian proposed to Frankie with that enormous rock." He sighs. "I was so worried you'd be disappointed, but then I saw the way your eyes lit up when I slipped it on your finger—it made me love you all the more."

I glance at the ring on my finger, the art deco setting and its prewar diamond, imagining it on Nathan's grandmother's hand as she tended the farm, raised children, kneaded bread dough, and suddenly I'm struck with a strange sense of belonging—to something bigger than myself, to a past and a family I may never know, but still, for now, they're mine. It's both comforting and disconcerting, but also sort of . . . beautiful.

"Hungry?" he asks, changing the subject.

I shake my head.

"Me, either. The frittata was pretty filling, wasn't it?" He glances at his watch. "Besides, Christian texted—they'll be here at five, and I should probably get the pork in the slow cooker."

I nod, continuing to scroll through photos, until one catches my eye—and Nathan's.

"Honey," he begins, his eyes filled with worry. "Are you sure you want to . . . go there right now?" He pauses, sitting beside me. "You've been so happy lately. Why spoil it?"

At first I don't understand what he means, but then I look closer at the photo—of me—standing on the front porch, cradling my noticeably swollen belly. My heart seizes. I know nothing of pregnancy, of course, only that I am—or *was*—pregnant in this photo . . . in this life. I might have been four, maybe five months along. Bright-eyed and rosy-cheeked, I look blissfully happy. *What happened?* Heart racing, I continue to swipe, finding more photos of my pregnant self, which is when it hits me: The scar on my stomach; my apparent unease about seeing Frankie with her baby tonight; the neighbors' concerns. Suddenly it all makes sense. A baby was growing inside of me—our baby—and then it wasn't.

I HAVE NO IDEA WHAT TO WEAR—BOTH BECAUSE I'M OUT OF SORTS AND, WELL, there's little to choose from. *Come on*, I think, staring into the nearly bare closet. *You've got to have a dress in here—somewhere?* I parse through the hangers until I find a simple white linen maxi dress. I slip it over my head, then give myself a long look in the mirror. *Good Lord, I need highlights, and some concealer—stat.*

I'm still reeling from the photos when Nathan smiles at me from the kitchen. I feel the instinctive urge to put on my boots and run, though I realize it's a dumb idea. Where would I go? A neighboring farm? Hail down an Amish man pushing a plow? And then what? Call the police and tell them that I woke up married to a man I didn't marry, and that this has happened *twice*? As real as this is to me, I realize how crazy it sounds. No, the only way out of this is *through*. I must stay the course until I find my way home.

"You look pretty," Nathan says, looking up from the stove, where he's stirring a simmering pot. *Do I?* I wonder. *Plain* would be a better word to describe my appearance, and yet Nathan smiles at me with adoring eyes, which momentarily puts me at ease, until I remember that Frankie and Christian will be arriving any moment. I should be thrilled to see my best friends, so why do I feel a pit in my stomach? Why do I sense that a storm is brewing?

"Do you need any help?" I ask, willing myself to get a grip.

He shakes his head. "No, honey. I've got everything handled." He pauses, smiling tenderly as I walk to his side. "Maybe pour the wine?"

"Sure," I say, catching a whiff of his freshly washed skin—musky and masculine. I feel a flutter in my stomach as he points to the bottle of white on the counter. After locating a corkscrew in a nearby drawer, I get to work, pouring us each a glass.

"Cheers," Nathan says, clinking his glass against mine before we each take a sip. Our eyes linger for a long moment as we stand together in the kitchen, emotions coursing through my veins. This man might have been the father of my child. It's bizarre and heartbreaking and beautiful—all at the same time. He feels it, too, I can tell: the weight of it all, this wound that will always be ours, and ours alone. But is it love that binds us together, or only pain? I take a step closer, longing to know if this is—or was—the great love of my life. Lost in the moment, I touch Nathan's face, but he immediately steps back and rubs his forehead. "I . . . I'm sorry, Lena . . ." He turns back to the pot on the stove. "I . . . need to finish dinner. We don't have much time until our guests arrive."

"Right," I say awkwardly, leaning against the kitchen counter. *What just happened? Why did he pull away?*

Nathan sighs. "Sorry. I . . . just want this dinner to be perfect."

As his voice trails off, I eye the elaborate spread on the counter-top: homemade tortillas and various delicious-looking accompaniments for the carnitas. I want to say, *Uh, you're amazing. You know that, right?* But then I see his face, awash with anguish and pain, but also something else: distance. After we lost the baby, did he simply shut down? Or did he shut me out?

"Nathan," I say, searching his face.

"Oh," he says, the pained expression on his face shifting to practical. "Do you mind picking some flowers for the table? I meant to do that, but it slipped my mind."

"Sure," I say, reaching for a pair of scissors on the kitchen table. Outside in the flower garden, I snip some early-blooming roses and a bit of rosemary for greenery. I think about how Nathan had bristled at my touch a moment ago. Maybe we're both just out of practice after experiencing such an enormous loss? Or is it something else—something bigger? I've read about couples struggling through their shared grief, marriages swallowed up by pain, but it's an entirely different thing to live it.

Nathan nods approvingly when I hand him the flowers just as the doorbell rings.

I head to the entryway—my heart beating faster with each step.

On any other day, I'd be excited to see my best friend, but today I'm a bundle of nerves, though immediately relieved to find Barb and Babbs on the front porch.

"Hi, sweetie," Barb says, handing me a chilled bottle of white wine.

Babbs kisses my cheek, before setting the aforementioned kale salad on the dining table. "It smells amazing in here. Nathan working his magic, I see."

I grin, pouring them each a glass. When the doorbell rings again, my smile disappears.

"You've got this," Babbs whispers, squeezing my hand.

I take a deep breath as I open the door, smiling hesitantly at Frankie, Christian, and the adorable baby girl in his arms.

Frankie, baby on her right hip, practically tackles me with a side hug. "I can't believe it's been this long," she says, her eyes welling up with tears. "How are you . . . doing?"

"Uh, well," I begin, feeling the urge to bring my best friend up to speed on what's been happening to me, but I hesitate when the baby coos.

"Emma, meet your godmother, Auntie Lena."

Emma is, in a word, perfect. She looks just like Frankie, and Christian, too, in the weirdest way.

"Can you believe she's already six months old?" Frankie exclaims, eyeing me cautiously. "Do you want to hold her?"

I shake my head. "I . . . don't know anything about babies."

Frankie laughs. "Well, they eat, and they poop—repeat. That's about all you need to know."

I smile, catching Christian's eyes for the first time. He looks exhausted—and thin.

"And they also have a knack for robbing their parents of sleep," he adds, grinning.

Frankie lifts Emma from her husband's arms. "Christian's been amazing with her," she says. "He's the only one who can get her down at night. He sings her songs and reads her books and does all the voices."

Christian smiles proudly. "She's Daddy's girl."

Frankie turns to me, lowering her voice. "He freaking loves her."

I smile, watching the two of them with their daughter as Nathan appears and greets our guests.

"You okay, sweetie?" Frankie asks, sidling up beside me while rhythmically bouncing up and down and side to side, baby Emma strapped to her chest in a complicated-looking contraption.

"Yeah, totally," I say quickly.

"Emma had colic for the first three months," Frankie continues. "She's out of the woods—*thank God*—but I guess I got used to the bouncing. It was the only way we could get her to sleep. Christian used to have to sit on one of those exercise balls and bounce her until she dozed off." She laughs, turning to her husband. "Remember that, honey?"

He grimaces. "All too well."

"Wow," I say, taking it all in. "Sounds . . . challenging."

"To say the least. But she's so much better now—only wakes up two times for feedings."

I practically choke on my wine. "I'm sorry, did you say she wakes up *two* times in the night?"

"Yeah," Frankie replies. "But it sure beats five!"

"Right," I say, a little stunned as she takes my hand and leads me to the living room sofa.

"Is this weird for you?" she asks, continuing the bouncing while I sit. "I mean, I know it must be, and I hate it. Lena, I'm so sorry that . . ." Frankie shakes her head. "I don't even know what to say."

I don't know what to say, either. I want to tell her about my situation—about everything—but she's too busy with Emma, who's just tossed her pacifier on the floor and is beginning to fuss. I pick it up and hand it back to Frankie.

"Have you two been . . . *trying*?" she asks.

"Trying?" My eyes get big. "Oh. As in, like, trying to *make a baby?*"

"Yeah." Frankie bounces more vigorously when Emma starts to fuss again.

I shrug. "I don't know. I . . . guess."

"Well," she continues, "maybe it's time to consider some *alternatives.*"

I lean back, sighing.

Frankie moves closer. "I mean . . . there's always IVF," she says, lowering her voice, "or maybe, even . . . adoption?"

"Adoption?" I shake my head, as Frankie lifts Emma out of the contraption and nestles in beside me on the sofa.

She tugs the edge of her shirt to pull down her bra, revealing her enormous left breast. "You don't mind, do you?" She smiles as she wedges Emma's mouth against her nipple. "I think she's just hungry. Poor thing—that long drive from the city was a lot for her."

"No, no," I say quickly, as my pulse races. "I . . . I . . ." Tears sting my eyes. "I mean, it's totally cool." Suddenly my hands are clammy, and my heart feels like it might spontaneously combust. "I'm just going to . . . run to the bathroom."

I close the door behind me and gasp, looking at myself in the mirror as I fight back waves of emotion. I don't deserve to cry. There's no reason for me to feel grief about something I didn't even experience— that I didn't live. So why does it hurt . . . so much?

"THIS KALE SALAD IS AMAZING," FRANKIE SAYS, BOUNCING EMMA ON HER LAP between bites. "I'm definitely going to need the recipe."

Barb and Babbs smile, pleased, then Christian launches into a story about Emma's first few months, with Frankie interjecting every few sentences. Parenthood sounds brutal, but also surprisingly beautiful. The two of them are like soldiers who went through war together and came out on the other side with battle wounds but also medals of bravery and a deep bond.

"I'm sorry," Frankie whispers, when Nathan abruptly changes the subject. "I didn't mean to—"

"It's fine," I reply, forcing a smile. "Really."

"Really?"

Well, it's not really fine, I want to say, especially when I catch Nathan's pained expression. True, I don't exactly know Nathan at all, but it somehow feels as if I do. We've also been through war together, but our battle wounds cut deep. Without thinking, I reach my hand under the table to find Nathan's, but whatever tenderness I feel in the moment disappears when he pulls his hand away and reaches for the wine bottle to refill Barb's glass.

AFTER EVERYONE'S GONE, NATHAN INCHES TOWARD ME IN THE DARKNESS, where I'm curled up in bed. "I know tonight wasn't easy for you," he says. "But you handled it all with so much grace."

"Thanks," I say, shifting my head on my pillow.

He rests his hand on my stomach, lovingly tracing the scar beneath my belly button. I don't flinch or pull away, mostly because I can barely feel his touch. The skin around my incision is numb—maybe I am, too. Maybe both of us.

"It's been such a long road," he whispers. I can hear the pain in his voice. "But I wonder if we're finally reaching the light at the end of the tunnel."

I reach for his hand under the covers. There probably won't be a tomorrow, at least not for the two of us. If today is anything like yesterday, I'll drift off to sleep and wake up beside someone new, in another strange life filled with its own land mines and complexities. But right now I can't stop thinking about this one: the cows in the barn, the quirky kale farmers on the other side of the fence, my handsome farmer with his delicate heart—the life we built with our hands and the baby we made . . . and lost.

There are so many things I should say to Nathan in what will likely be our final moments. I want to tell him that, despite our gigantic loss and the latent grief that might linger for years to come—forever, maybe—we can rise above it. Like Babbs said earlier today, there's joy in the weeds—we just need to find it.

I stroke Nathan's hair as his breathing becomes shallow and rhythmic. He's a *good* man, and this would be a *good* life—cozy, comfortable, happier than most, though far from anything I'd expected or envisioned for myself. Yes, unexpectedly beautiful, even in its rawness and grit. And yet, here we are, not only crippled by our grief, but also unequipped to face it.

I yawn, listening to the rhythmic pounding on the roof overhead—hail, just like Nathan predicted. But there's no barometer for what's next. If I stayed—if this was my forever—how long could I endure? Would we find a way to push through the pain and come out on the other end? Would time heal us, make us whole? I don't know. I don't know anything. But maybe tomorrow it'll all make more sense.

PART
FOUR

8

I wake with a heavy feeling on my chest. Yes—*Frankie, the baby, the bouncing, my miscarriage . . . Nathan.* All heavy things, but this is an altogether different sensation, like pressure on my sternum. Something is *on* me.

I pat the air until my fingers hit a tuft of fur . . . *animal* fur, which elicits a shrill cry. Less *meow* and more *reeeeeaaaaaaaar*, it's definitely a cat—an *angry* cat. I fumble to turn on the lamp beside me, before locking eyes with a very large feline inches from my face, back arched and ready to pounce.

"Yikes," I mutter, pressing my back against the headboard. "Hey, now! Let's be nice, okay?" The cat makes a guttural sound, jumping off the bed and hissing at me from a corner of the room. *She knows.* I cringe, thinking of yesterday's experience with Maybell the cow, and before that, the French dog, who, though nice enough, dragged me halfway across Paris. *Animals always know.*

It's been three days since I found myself in this mess, but it also seems like three years, maybe even a lifetime—or rather, lots of mini-lifetimes. I feel like I'm stuck on one of those nauseating carnival rides I used to be able to stomach as a teenager. I want off. I want my life back, but I have no idea how to make it stop.

I swallow a lump in my throat, willing myself not to cry, then notice the skinny silver band on my ring finger.

Silver? Really? I'm a gold person.

I rub my eyes, which feel itchier and more swollen by the minute. Fortunately, I spot two prescription pill bottles on the bedside table: Prozac and desloratadine. The label on the second reads: "Take daily for cat allergy." I ignore the Prozac and pop the second without wasting another second. Now to figure out . . . *where* I am, and, more importantly, *who* I'm with. The nondescript bedroom provides few clues—just the basics: a king-size bed with a drab gray duvet that bears evidence of multiple claw marks, dingy white sheets (if you could still call them white), and a dresser that looks like it was purchased at IKEA and begrudgingly assembled. I peer out the window and everything comes into focus—the dark sky overhead releasing a slow and steady drizzle, the cobblestone streets below, the PUBLIC MARKET CENTER sign in giant red letters. My heart practically leaps out of my chest. I'm in *Seattle*—in an apartment overlooking Pike Place Market, just a stone's throw—well, a ferry ride—away from Rosie. I'm home! Sort of.

I walk to the adjoining bathroom to pee, immediately wincing when my rear hits the toilet's cold rim. *He left the seat up. Great.*

After taking a look at myself in the mirror, frowning at my dry skin and mid-length hair, with dark roots, I slip out of a ratty, oversize Nirvana T-shirt, then look down at my stomach. I run my hand along my skin, where the scar beneath my belly button was yesterday, but now it's . . . gone. My miscarriage, Nathan, life on the farm in Pennsylvania—it's all just a memory, and today? The beginning of another one.

I throw on a sweater and jeans before slipping my feet into a pair of black-and-white-checkered Vans, steadying myself as I place my hand on the doorknob. *Here goes nothing.*

"Um, hi?" I say, stepping cautiously into a very messy living room, where boxes are stacked along the far wall. I peer inside one, which is filled with . . . toys—no . . . fidget spinners? I bought Kevin's nephew one as a stocking stuffer last Christmas, but I'm at a loss for words, eying the various models—pandas, frogs, ducks—especially when I turn to the kitchen, where dishes are piled high and a huge stack of unopened mail teeters on the kitchen counter.

Like in a game of Jenga, I pry out an envelope with my name on it and a return address from a legal office on Bainbridge Island, quickly tucking it into my back pocket before going on another dumpster dive, this one leading me to a credit card bill. My eyes get big when I see the staggering balance and history of minimum payments, but when I notice the name beside mine at the top of the page, I gasp.

Mike Hanson? No way. I would never marry Mike. How could I?

"Hey," he says, looking up at me in his boxer briefs and yawning as his belly bulges from the hem of his T-shirt like a deflated pool floatie.

"Um . . . hey," I reply, more than a little shocked. Let's just say, the last time I saw him he was a little more *Magic Mike* and a lot less . . . *Pool Floatie Mike.*

"Lena, it's *after nine,*" he says, confused. "Why are you still here?"

I shake my head, confused. "Still here?"

He lets out a disappointed sigh. "Babe, you're late again. I know you hate that call center, but it pays the bills."

Call center? I imagine myself stuffed into a windowless cubicle wearing a headset, fluorescent lights glaring overhead. *So, I'm a telemarketer. No wonder I have a prescription for Prozac.* Mike lifts one of the fidget spinners from a nearby box—this one a duck, which he spins between his fingers, grinning like an eleven-year-old boy. "You won't have to do this for long. My business is going to hit it big—especially with the NFTs I'm working on."

I stare ahead blankly.

"Remember? When someone buys a PetSpinner, they get a matching NFT," he explains. "It's freaking genius. Each one is unique, with a specific name. Like this little dude." He holds up the toy in his hand. "His NFT name will be 'Dr. Reginald Duckworth.'"

I rub my forehead, thoroughly disturbed. "*Sooooo* . . . how much did all that cost?"

"Well, it wasn't exactly cheap," Mike replies, scratching his left butt cheek as he walks to the kitchen. "But, trust me, it'll pay off. People *love* personalization." He rummages through the fridge, pulling out a slice of cold pizza. "I mean, Tickle Me Elmo was a sensation back in the day, but just think: What if Tyco had been able to pair each Elmo doll with an NFT?" He nods confidently.

I'm speechless, recalling the Mike I dated when we were teenagers. In high school, he was student body president and budding entrepreneur. By our senior year, he already had a successful pressure-washing business under his belt and was voted Most Likely to Succeed by our classmates, who, as it turns out, couldn't have been more wrong.

We remained in a long-distance relationship through our first year of college, which was when things began to sputter. True, Mike had his setbacks—some of which were beyond his control, like the death of his father and a bike accident that left him with two casted legs. But messing around with drugs, dropping out of school, and the kicker—cheating on me—was *all him*. By our sophomore year, I pulled the plug, and for good.

"Hurry," he says, wiping a smattering of pizza sauce from his chin as he cracks open a beer can. "If you leave soon, you can at least clock in for a partial day."

I clench my fists. "I'm sorry," I say, shaking my head. "Are you actually standing here in your *underwear*, telling *me* to get to work?"

He shrugs. "Well, yeah, babe. You have a job."

"And what about you? What about *your* job?"

"That's not fair," he says, folding his arms across his chest like a petulant child. "I'm working my ass off to get PetSpinners off the ground." He sighs. "Come on, you know when you get like this it kills my mojo."

"Gotcha," I say, flipping on the kitchen light switch, but the bulb overhead only makes a pathetic buzzing sound. "Well," I continue, handing him the credit card statement. "Sorry to . . . 'kill your *mojo*,' but it seems you've racked up quite the debt."

He tosses the statement on the counter with an eye roll. "You wouldn't understand. You're not an entrepreneur."

Mike's obviously frustrated, but I press on. "You really expect *me* to dig us out of this hole?" I shake my head. "What happened to you, Mike?"

I think back to a few years ago, when Frankie and I decided to google our exes over a bottle of wine. At the time, Mike's LinkedIn page had painted a more appealing picture of his decade-plus without me than the present scenario. Apparently he owned a successful construction company outside of Seattle. Still, our messy breakup left me with little closure, and I'd always wondered if I was partly to blame for the way things ended—the cheating, the drugs, all of it. I mean, I knew he made those choices, but what if I'd been there for him, especially after the accident?

Clearly, this is the outcome: a long and expensive downward spiral, reminiscent of the movie *Singles*, when Bridget Fonda's character laments her disappointing boyfriend: "Somewhere around twenty-four, bizarre becomes immature." Mike is, ahem, *thirty-five*.

"Give me a break, Lena," he says with a huff. "Why all the hate?"

"Hate? Mike, it's almost ten a.m. You're unemployed and cracking your first *beer*."

He frowns. "Baby."

"*No*. Don't *baby* me. That might have worked when we were nineteen, but not now." I feel disgusted for my younger self—for my present self. How could I put up with this? "I'm leaving, Mike—leaving you."

"Lena, wait," he pleads as I reach for what must be my purse on the counter. "Lena Bena!"

I cringe. Once a term of endearment, the nickname only elicits repulsion and regret. I walk through the door—without looking back.

OUTSIDE ON THE STREET, I'M BORDERLINE-HYPERVENTILATING—AS IN, I COULD use a brown paper bag *right this second*. Sure, like anyone, I'd wondered what my life might look like if I'd stayed together with my first love. But this? It's a disaster. *I'm* a disaster, and I'm spiraling. *Get it together, Lena.* I look through my purse. No phone—disappointing, but I'm not going back up there. Fortunately, I do find a few small bills, a pack of gum, and a credit card. First order of business. Caffeine. Second? Catch a ferry to Bainbridge Island. *Rosie will help me sort all of this out*, I tell myself. *She'll know what to do.*

While Mike was a disappointment, Pike Place Market is not—in fact, it's just as I remember. This little corner of Seattle has always held a special place in my heart, born out of that year after college when I worked for a venture capital firm on Pike Street. They packed so many desks into that loft it probably violated every fire code. I laugh to myself, remembering the aroma that wafted from the market's fishmongers on warm days. My coworkers complained about it, but I didn't mind. To me, it smelled like home—the sea, salty air, ferry engine oil—as was the little café downstairs, tucked inside the heart of the Market. Café Vita was, to me, what Central Perk was to the characters on *Friends*. Filled with regulars—mostly recent grads like myself, and exhausted interns precariously balancing cardboard drink trays to lug back to their bosses—the place exuded warmth and belonging.

I walk to the edge of the Market, then down the stairs, where I'm happy to spot the old sign hanging from its awning. My heart surges as I walk inside, breathing in the familiar scent of freshly ground coffee beans, scones baking in the back kitchen, and—I pause, doing a double-take at the man standing behind the counter—Spencer? We met the summer after I graduated from college, when I began my first job. I'd stop in at least twice a day—it was a very overcaffeinated time in my life—and Spencer and I became fast friends.

He waves from the cash register as I walk ahead, a little taken aback. "Lena?"

"Hi," I say, grinning. "Wow, it's been . . . a long time."

Spencer looks a little confused. "If you don't count the times I see you passing through the Market every other week."

"Oh," I say, my cheeks burning. *That's right. I supposedly live here.*

"But . . . I'm glad you finally stopped in," he continues. "Best coffee in the neighborhood . . . well, the world." He grins. "I was beginning to worry you'd gone Starbucks on us."

"Me?" I laugh, rubbing my neck—no more hives, thank God. "No way."

"Want to sit down?" he asks, pointing to an empty table as he peels off his apron.

I nod, overcome with the feeling of déjà vu. "This place is just as I remember." I smile. "You, too."

He eyes me curiously. "Should I take that as a compliment?"

"Yeah, I mean, it's like nothing's changed. It's been at least ten years, and . . . you're still a barista."

"Still a barista," he says, extending his hand. "Pleased to meet you."

My cheeks flush. "Sorry," I say, regretting my choice of words. "I didn't mean it like that. I guess I just didn't expect to see you still here. Weren't you planning to head to grad school—in Chicago, right?"

"You know what they say about best-laid plans."

"Believe me, I'm the living proof of that right now."

"What do you mean?"

I sigh. "Well, for starters, I just . . . kind of . . . left my husband."

"Oh," Spencer replies, his eyes filled with concern. "I'm sorry to hear that."

"Don't be—really. Let's just say that Mike and I were . . . never meant to be."

"What can I do to help?"

I shrug. "Maybe make me something to drink, like the old days?"

He smiles. "Still like chai lattes?"

"Yeah," I say, impressed by his recall, "though I haven't had one in ages."

After Spencer finishes making my latte, he pours a coffee for himself and joins me at the table I've claimed. As we sip our drinks, we catch up on the past twelve years. Spencer tells me that a few years ago, Café Vita's elderly owner asked him to run the place after he got sick, with the understanding that someday Spencer would be able to purchase the business and make it his own. For now, however, he still dons an apron. "I guess it seems like a small life, when you think about it," he muses. "I've spent my entire career in this little café, but I've come to love it—the regulars, the way you can turn someone's day around with the perfect amount of foam, or just a smile. Maybe it's not the most important work, but it's mine."

"Of course it's important work," I counter, thinking of my own career. It's true, I'm at the top of my game. I've climbed the corporate ladder, even made VP, but these past days have made me wonder if something's missing.

"When this place is finally my own," Spencer continues, "I'm going to make some changes—like, new lighting, marble countertops on the bar, mobile ordering."

"Just tell me you won't get rid of these old chairs." I pat the edge of the threadbare wing chair, its green velvet fabric worn and tattered in the best of ways.

"Oh no, I couldn't. All of you old-timers would riot."

I laugh. "We would."

Spencer points to the wall behind me. "And you know what else? I'd rent the adjoining space and make it our roasting headquarters. I've always felt that we could do more with our beans, though the owner has never been that motivated. I could make it happen, and I'd give a chunk of our profits to South American farmworkers."

"That's beautiful," I tell him. "Here's to manifesting all of it."

He searches my face. "You believe in that stuff?"

"What, manifestation?" I chuckle. "Not really. Besides, all I seem to be able to manifest these days are dysfunctional relationships." I shrug. "How about you?"

"I guess you could say I'm open to it," he continues. "We have this word puzzle here at the café, and one day last week the answer to the daily riddle was 'tilapia.'"

I furrow my brow. "Like the fish?"

Spencer nods. "So that morning I said the word *tilapia* out loud."

"Let me guess: You went home that night and found a bunch of fish on your doorstep?"

"Not quite. My neighbor invited me over for a tilapia dinner. It was so random, I had to believe something bigger was at play. Oh, and the mango salsa was amazing." He pauses, flashing a smile. "Hey, maybe I manifested *you* back in my life?"

"Oh? Do tell how you managed that."

"Can't say." He grins. "That would break the rules of manifestation."

"Okay, fine," I reply, laughing again. "If you *did* manifest me, can you, maybe, manifest me a better life?"

"Hold on," Spencer says, closing his eyes, then pressing his fingertips together rhythmically. "Done."

It feels good to laugh with him, just like the old days. When we met, all those years ago, he invited me to dinner at his family's home on Queen Anne Hill. I was in my early twenties then, but the memories are still fresh in my mind: His mom pulling baked ziti from the oven and his dad teaching me how to play the game Rummikub, which soon became a staple for Spencer and me. It was a lively household, filled with love. Though his younger sister was off at college, his twelve-year-old, adorably rowdy twin brothers hiked a football back and forth in the living room, big brother Spencer the self-appointed referee. "Happy chaos," was how his mom described their family life. Truth. But it was also, somehow, perfect.

"So, what's next for you?" Spencer asks, extracting me from my memories.

"I need to go home, to my aunt Rosie on Bainbridge Island," I tell him.

His eyes get big. "Oh, I guess you didn't hear the news?"

"What news?"

"The ferry workers are on strike. The whole fleet is shut down."

I lean back in my chair, defeated, before I remember my (nearly maxed-out) credit card. "I guess I could take a cab."

Spencer shakes his head. "A *two-hour* cab ride? No way. I'll drive you."

"No," I say. "I couldn't ask you to do that."

"A little road trip with an old friend?" He smiles. "I'm game. Really, it's no problem at all. Just give me a moment to get things sorted with the staff, and we can be on our way."

"THIS IS FUN," HE SAYS, HANDING ME A WRAPPED SANDWICH. I CAN'T HELP BUT notice the tattoo on the inside of his right arm, which appears to be a series of dates. "Checking out my ink, huh?"

"Oh yeah, I guess I just . . . didn't peg you as the tattoo type," I say with a little laugh.

"Well, I don't believe in types." Spencer grins. "But I'll admit, it took my mom a minute to warm up to it last year. Didn't last long, though." He extends his arm to me. "See, these are my parents' and siblings' birth dates."

"Wow," I say, running my finger along the edge of his arm. "That's actually pretty cool."

He nods. "They're with me, wherever I go."

I smile. Family is so important to him. I've always admired his closeness to his siblings and parents—a family dynamic I always wanted but never got to experience.

His 1990s-era Volvo station wagon shudders a little as we gain speed on I-5. With any luck, I'll be home this afternoon, and Rosie will help me snap out of this.

"Do you mind if I borrow your phone? I guess I left mine at the apartment."

"Sure," he says, handing his iPhone to me.

I dial Rosie's number, but there's no answer, just the familiar cheery greeting on her answering machine. "Hi, it's Rose-eeeee! Sorry to miss you. Leave a message, pretty please, and I'll call you back!" I try three more times before handing the phone back to Spencer with a sigh, willing myself to stay positive as I unwrap my sandwich—grilled cheese and sweet pepper—and take a bite. "Um, *this* sandwich is *divine*."

Spencer smiles. "You like?"

"Um, *love!*"

"That's good feedback," he says. "I almost put it on the menu six months ago, but my girlfriend said it was awful, which kind of knocked the wind out of my sails."

"Your girlfriend, huh?"

"I mean, *ex*-girlfriend." He smiles. "Funny how it always comes down to the little things. Like, could you really be with someone who doesn't appreciate the epicness of a cheese-and-pepper sandwich?"

"I'm with you there," I say, laughing as I take another bite.

"How about you?" Spencer continues. "What's your hard stop?"

I think of the toilet seat left up in the apartment this morning, the mounting pile of debt, before my mind turns to Kevin, with fresh perspective. "People who don't read books."

"I couldn't agree more." He nods. "So books were the reason your marriage failed?" he asks. "Or, rather, the lack of books."

I shake my head, my mind jumping from Sebastian to Mike and then Nathan. "Maybe I bring out the worst in people."

"No way," he fires back, his expressive blue eyes flashing before turning back to the road. "You're Lena! Lena the Great!"

I smile at the memory of his nickname for me, which grew out of our frequent Rummikub benders at Café Vita. After I finished work and his shift was over, we used to recruit randoms to battle us. Either he or I would always win, of course—usually me.

He clutches the wheel nervously. "Listen, I don't know how to say this, but, back in the day, every guy at Vita had a crush on you." He pauses. "Including me."

I gasp, letting out a nervous laugh. "No! You *did not!*"

"I did."

"But . . . you had a girlfriend, didn't you?"

"Carrie? Yeah. When we weren't broken up. I used to fantasize about asking you out on a date, actually, but I could never get the courage up. Besides, I always knew you were out of my league."

"Out of your league?" I scoff. "I never once thought that."

It's the truth. I didn't. But I also never looked at Spencer through a romantic lens. On top of that, back then I was leaving Seattle for New York to take a job that I thought would look good on my LinkedIn profile.

We sit in silence for a long moment, staring out the windshield and listening to Mazzy Star's "Fade into You," each of us replaying scenes from our pasts—the wrong turns and the right ones, and maybe even the doors we never tried to open.

9

By late afternoon, Bainbridge Island is in sight. I feel a million shades of nostalgic as we reach the Agate Pass Bridge, exiting 305 to the turnoff that leads to Manzanita Beach and the old gravel drive that brings me home. I look out the window, heart bursting. Every Douglas fir and cedar tree seems to be swaying in the breeze as if they're all waving hello. For the first time in these past days, I feel a shred of hope. I'm home, and I know Rosie will help me snap out of this.

"Wow, this place hasn't changed a bit," Spencer says, pulling the car to a stop in Rosie's driveway. "Remember, that summer we met, you invited me over for a clam bake on the beach?"

"Oh, that's right!" I say, memories rushing back. "We swung on that old rope swing . . ."

"And your bikini top almost fell off," Spencer adds.

I cover my face. "No! Tell me it *didn't*."

"You were in the clear," he assures me. "But it was close to being the most epic wardrobe malfunction this island's ever seen."

I laugh, reaching for my purse. "Well, thank you for coming all this way just to get me home."

Spencer smiles. "My pleasure."

I feel bad not to invite him inside, but Rosie and I have private things to discuss, and yet, there's time. He could at least come in for a little while. "Hey," I finally say. "Why don't you pop in for a bit? I know Rosie would love to see you."

"You sure?" he asks, fingering his seat belt.

"Sure," I tell him.

Gravel crunches under our feet as we walk the path to the front door, which is uncharacteristically locked. I find the spare key under the rock beside the doormat that I painted the summer I turned thirteen. LENA, it says, surrounded by butterflies and hearts.

"Rosie?" I call, peering inside as I bat away a cobweb that runs the length of the doorframe. "It's me! I'm home!" I adjust the painting on the entryway wall, its frame leaning unsteadily to the right. "Rosie?"

Spencer follows me to the kitchen, where I stop in my tracks. Dirty plates and cups litter the countertop; a moldy baguette on the cutting board looks practically petrified.

"Something's wrong," I say, panicked, running to my aunt's beloved reading chair in the living room, which is eerily empty. A layer of dust blankets the cover of *Fifty Shades of Grey* on the adjacent side table.

"Rosie!" I cry, panicked. "Where are you?"

I don't stop when Spencer's hand grazes my shoulder, as if to say, *Whatever's happening, it'll be okay.* Instead, I run down the hallway, past my childhood bedroom to Rosie's, where I find an empty hospital bed with disconnected wires and cords beside a medical monitoring machine. "No, Rosie. No. No, no, no, no, no." I press my hands against the rumpled linens, before falling to my knees.

"I don't believe this," I whisper. "What happened? Why didn't she . . ." I hang my head, lost in grief, the only consolation being the fact that maybe—just maybe—I'll wake up tomorrow and this will all be undone. And yet, I'm devastated.

"So she was sick?" Spencer asks, kneeling beside me, his face mirroring my state of shock.

I shake my head. "No. I mean, not that I knew."

"Come here," Spencer says, pulling me close as I weep. Frankie would call this "ugly crying," which is exactly how I'd describe my present state: blotchy, swollen, hysterical. He holds me for a long moment, and when I finally sit up and wipe away my tears, I feel something crinkle in the back pocket of my pants—the letter from the attorney that I'd tucked in there this morning. I pull it out, tearing the edge of the envelope.

Dear Ms. Westbrook,

As you may know, your aunt, Rosie McAllister, passed away last week, tragically, from an infection she contracted in India. I, and everyone at Branson, Fairchild & Fleming, offer our condolences. Ms. McAllister appointed our firm to handle the distribution of her estate, which, I'm happy to report, she's left to you. Please call our office at your earliest convenience so we may assist in the transfer of assets.

Kind regards,

Mitchell Branson, Esq.

Branson, Fairchild & Fleming

"Wow," I say, taking it all in. In what world would I learn about Rosie's death through an attorney? I shudder. This one, obviously. Did we drift apart? Did she disapprove of my marriage to Mike? I can't ask her to fill me in on the details. I can't reintroduce her to Spencer. I can't tell her about my plight or give her one last hug. She's gone, but hopefully not for real, just in this alternate universe, or whatever it is. I can only hope . . . and long for tomorrow, when my world will no doubt shift again. I may be somewhere else, *with* someone else, but Rosie might still be here, still breathing, still sitting in her chair by the fireplace reading *Fifty Shades of Grey*. Lord, let that be the case. And yet, when I look into Spencer's kind eyes, feel the warmth of his tender smile, I can't help but feel a little guilty for wanting to stay here—just a little longer.

"What can I do for you?" he asks, reaching for my hand. His

touch feels natural, as if we've shared a thousand moments just like this.

I exhale deeply and release his hand. "Maybe pour me a drink?" Although what I really need is to tell him an insane truth: that I'm stuck in some sort of alternate universe and I need to find a way out.

"Done," he says, as we walk to the kitchen. He pulls a bottle of pinot grigio from Rosie's fridge—her favorite—before reaching for two glasses and a corkscrew.

"It's so weird," I say, as he fills my glass. "This place—it's not the same. Her spirit—it's gone."

Spencer hands me a glass, nodding empathetically. "I get it. But that spirit, it's still with you. *She's* still with you."

I search his eyes. "How do you know?"

"Because, when you love someone, they never leave you." He points to his heart. "They stay right here."

I wipe away fresh tears, thinking about the different versions of my life, in Paris and that little farm in Pennsylvania, but especially this one—how a single choice, a certain relationship, can affect everything. I can't help but feel that in this version of my life, I played a role in Rosie's fate—indirectly, of course, but circumstances matter. Maybe if she didn't take that trip, maybe if I'd gone with her . . . All I know is that I messed up, somehow. I need to make it right.

"I want to tell you something," I say, taking a sip of my wine. "And it's going to make me sound, well, clinically insane."

Spencer raises his glass defiantly. "I dare you."

"No, I'm serious. What I'm about to say is . . . nuts—like, certifiably crazy."

He shrugs. "Try me."

"Okay," I say, looking out the kitchen windows. "How about we continue the conversation down by the beach?"

"I'll bring the bottle," he replies as we walk out to the bulkhead.

It's low tide and the beach teems with life—glistening rocks of varying colors, swaths of emerald-green seaweed drying in the sun, a seagull pecking at something in the sand, and legions of baby crabs peering out from barnacle-covered stones. As a girl, I used to love those little crabs and would spend hours peeking underneath rocks to spy on their colonies. Rosie taught me how to determine whether they were male or female. Mama crabs and daddy crabs—my eyes well up with tears again.

Spencer and I sink into two chairs by the shore, in the little area that Rosie referred to as her "outdoor living room." I can still hear her voice in my head, coaxing me to come out and join her for a glass of wine. "Come sit with me, dear! Let's have a party!" I'm here now, but this is no party.

"So," Spencer begins, clearing his throat. "What you said back there. Tell me what you mean."

I take a deep breath, nodding. "So . . . I'm kind of . . . stuck."

"Yeah," he replies. "You alluded to that."

I shake my head. "No, I'm not talking about my marriage, or Mike. It's bigger than that. I'm stuck in . . . life." Spencer nods politely, but I can tell he's struggling to understand. "Listen," I continue, "I warned you this would sound crazy, but I need to talk to someone, to make sense of what's happening to me."

"You've been through a lot," he says, his kind eyes searching mine. "Your marriage, and now this? You're swimming through grief right now."

I nod slowly. "I am—for sure. But it's more than that." I bite the edge of my lip. "Listen, four days ago, I fell asleep in Rosie's guesthouse, and then . . ."

His eyes get big. "And then what?"

I take a deep breath. "And then . . . I woke up in Paris."

"In Paris." Spencer nods, his expression a mix of confusion and doubt.

I lean my head back with a groan. "See, I knew that would be your reaction."

"No, no . . . I mean, keep going."

"Okay," I continue, steadying myself. "So, yeah, I woke in Paris, with this crazy Frenchman. Well, he wasn't crazy." I pause, thinking back to that first morning. "He was actually . . . kind of hot."

Spencer scratches his head. "I see."

"I mean, yeah, but no. He was awful, actually—and *so* not my type."

I can't tell if Spencer's making his exit plan or considering having me institutionalized—maybe both.

"Still with me?"

He nods.

"Okay, so the morning after Paris, I woke up on this little, adorable farm in Pennsylvania. That day, I was married to . . . Nathan." I laugh nervously. "You can call him Farmer John."

"Wait, what?"

"Farmer, er, John, was sweet. The farmhouse, the garden—I even milked cows." I chuckle to myself. "Everything about it was idyllic, really, except a skeleton in our closet." I notice the concern on Spencer's face, so I quickly redirect. "No, we didn't kill anyone . . . but anyway." I pause, collecting myself. "It was all just a memory, a memory replaced with a new set of circumstances: Seattle, Mike, this . . . *you*."

Spencer sets his wineglass down on the old stump that Rosie had fashioned into a coffee table and folds his arms across his chest.

"I know what you're thinking," I continue, swallowing hard. "If someone were telling me this same story, I wouldn't believe them, either. It makes no sense."

Spencer gazes out to the water, then reaches for his wineglass again. "Okay, I think I understand."

"You do?" I reply eagerly, shifting onto my knees. It hasn't been that long—only a few days, really—but my loneliness is palpable. The fact that he understands—or, at least, is trying to understand— makes my heart swell. "Really?"

"Well," he says. "I'm trying to."

I smile, tears stinging my eyes—for Rosie, for the heaviness of these last few days.

Spencer looks thoughtful. "So, these guys you mentioned—they were people from your past, no?"

I nod. "Mike was my high school boyfriend. I met Sebastian, the French guy, ages ago, at a wedding, and Nathan at a farmers' market the year I moved to New York."

He grins conspiratorially. "And you were married to all of them, I mean, in the past few days."

I bury my head in my hands. "I know how this must sound, and I promise, I—"

"I'm not judging," Spencer interjects, "just trying to wrap my mind around it all."

I nod.

"Okay, so this experience you're having, it's . . . giving you a glimpse of what your life might look like had you taken one path or another, yes?"

I shrug. "I don't know, maybe?"

Spencer folds his hands in his lap. "And these men you . . . wake up with each day—let's call them your *insignificant others*—have any of them been more significant than the rest?"

I pause for a long beat. "No. I mean, if you're asking me if I can actually see myself married to any of them in real life." I pause, shaking my head. "But . . ."

"But what?"

"But I guess there have been *significant* moments that have come out of it all."

He leans in. "Romantic moments?"

"No, no," I continue. "More like lessons, realizations, you know? Like, I could never tolerate infidelity, or any shade of that. I don't really like dirt under my nails or milking cows, either, nor could I survive in a relationship with unresolved grief." I pause, laughing. "And I could never be with a fidget spinner entrepreneur."

"I don't know," Spencer says. "Are you sure about this fidget spinner entrepreneur? Maybe he's on to something big?" He chuckles, lightening the mood.

I roll my eyes. "Don't make me relive it."

He laughs. "So how does it end? You finally beam back to real life when you find your perfect match?"

I shake my head, my mind—and heart—completely toast. "I don't know. Maybe? Or maybe I'm stuck on this hamster wheel for the rest of my life." I pause, watching the old barnacle-covered buoy I remember from my childhood bob up and down in the salt water. How I long to be anchored in one place again. "That's why I wanted to come here, to talk to my aunt about it all."

"You thought she would know how to get you out of this?"

"Well, that's what I hoped," I say with a defeated sigh. "That night I arrived at her house . . . I keep turning our conversation over in my mind. I'd just gone through a breakup in San Francisco."

"Wait, so there's *another* guy?"

"Yeah, but this one was in *real life*." I bite the edge of my lip, realizing how weird this all sounds.

"Right, real life, as opposed to this, right now."

"I know, it's . . . all very confusing." I top off each of our wineglasses. "I just keep thinking back to that night I arrived home. Did I miss something?"

Spencer shifts, leaning in. "Now, I'm no physicist, just a humble barista, but I do know one thing to be true." He pauses, reaching for my hand. "*This* is real—you, me, the beach out there." He grins. "It's all real—even if you do turn into a pumpkin at midnight."

"You're right," I say. "I'll remember this, that's for certain. But what if you don't?"

"Of course I will," he retorts, taken aback. "Why wouldn't I?"

"I don't know." I sigh. "Honestly, this all makes my brain hurt."

He rubs his forehead as if his brain is hurting, too—out of solidarity. "So, let me understand what you're saying. When you fall asleep, this all goes . . . poof?"

"Yeah, something like that," I say, before my eyes widen. "Wait! *The guesthouse!*"

He shakes his head, confused.

"The place where I fell asleep that first night, where it all began." Heart racing, I reach for his hand. "Spencer! This could be my way out of this!"

WE WALK AHEAD, PAST THE OLD ROPE SWING HANGING FROM THE ANCIENT CEdar on the edge of the shore—the scene of the crime (or, rather, my near-wardrobe-malfunction) all those years ago.

Spencer follows me across the lawn, but I stop abruptly.

"What is it?" he asks, his expression both worried and confused.

"The guesthouse . . . it was . . . right there. At least, it used to be."

Where the little cottage once stood is now a pile of rubble—splintered wood, chunks of foundation, and fragments of glass. I have no idea what happened, or why, but if I felt stuck this morning, I feel a thousand times more now. This is where I began this journey, and now it's *gone*. My knees feel weak, my heart in stitches. How will I ever make sense of this? How will I ever . . . get home?

We walk across the lawn back to the house, sinking into the sofa in Rosie's living room, where I lean my head against Spencer's chest. We sit together in silence as the sun begins its descent beneath the horizon.

"Did you ever read that book by Maria Semple?" he asks, breaking the quiet. "*Today Will Be Different*?"

I shake my head.

"It's great. So is Maria. She's a local—a regular at the café." He smiles. "Anyway, there's this bit in her novel where she describes a phenomenon that happens when two people are traveling: the 'Competent Traveler' and the 'Helpless Traveler.' The idea is that in any given moment in a relationship, one person can be a mess, so the other has to step up. Let me give you an example. Say we're on vacation together—"

"In Istanbul," I interject. "I've always wanted to go to Istanbul."

"Okay, Istanbul, then." He laughs, playing along. "We've just gotten off the plane, but I have a stomach bug and the airline has lost my luggage."

"So, I . . . make a mad dash to get you some Pepto-Bismol, then chew out the customer-service agent?"

"Exactly. In this scenario, I'm helpless, so you become the Competent Traveler."

"I like it."

He nods. "And since *you're* going through a lot right now—"

"Yeah, I'm definitely helpless."

He grins, reaching for my hand. "Let me be your—"

"Competent Traveler," we say in unison.

"Wait," I add. "Does that mean you'd carry my bags—even if I'm prone to overpacking?"

Spencer nods confidently. "Even if we have to pay the airline's annoying oversize fee."

I have no idea how long we've been talking, but I'm acutely aware of the passing of time as the sun continues its descent.

"I hope I'll see you again," I whisper.

"Don't be such a fatalist," he says. "We *will* see each other again."

I smile. "I need some of your confidence right now."

"You mean my Competent Traveler Energy?"

"Yeah, that," I say, laughing. "Your CTE."

We sit in silence again, the light fading as day gives in to night.

Spencer reaches for my hand, and I let him take it. "What should we do with our remaining time together . . . I mean, before you slip through my fingers at the stroke of midnight?"

I grimace. "Don't remind me."

"Maybe a little Rummikub, for old times' sake?"

"Yeah," I say, my smile returning. "Or just . . . this." I pause when our eyes meet—equally lost and found in his gaze. He takes my face in his hands, kissing me softly, tenderly, but with a force that pulses through my body—from my scalp to the tips of my toes.

Until today, I'd only seen Spencer through that familiar old lens, the friendly barista behind the coffee counter. A good guy. A friend. I'm ashamed that I didn't allow myself to peel back the layers, to see his depth, his heart. How many others had I written off because they didn't fit the mold of what I thought an ideal partner looked like? After all, I had an ironclad checklist: must be financially successful (VP- or director-level minimum; no lawyers unless partner-track), MBA (preferably Ivy League), fit, tall (no less than six-foot-one), no cats, no Ultimate Frisbee, no mustache, good hair, good teeth, no Tevas or Crocs, have a passport, own a tux (bonus points for Tom Ford), iPhone not Android, impeccable taste in furniture (no IKEA!), no Hacky Sacks or vegan diets, no tattoos.

I glance at Spencer's arm, where his family's birth dates are lovingly inked. While my dossier for the perfect partner used to seem normal, it now feels . . . kind of ridiculous. How did I become so closed-minded?

I sigh, resting my head against Spencer's shoulder. In the morning, I'll probably be somewhere else, with someone else—maybe with a tattoo, or a mustache and Tevas, Lord help me. Spencer may or may not remember any of this, but I will. I'll treasure the memory of my sweet barista and how he so *competently* carried my heavy bags, for a little while.

PART
FIVE

10

I open my eyes as an alarm clock blares a few inches from my right ear. It's one of those vintage models with bells on top that you see in old-school cartoons. Antique or not, I have a sudden urge to hurl the abhorrent thing across the room.

After a few failed attempts, I finally manage to silence the contraption. I sit up in bed and notice someone under the covers beside me. *Not again.* Each new day rattles me to my core, and yet I've come to accept my predicament—the mysterious force that beams me from one reality to the next. I don't understand it. I can't control it. All I can do is hold on for dear life.

The figure beside me stirs beneath the sheets; I brace myself, as I've become accustomed to, waiting for the big reveal—today's "insignificant other," the term Spencer so aptly coined.

Spencer. Memories of our time together come rushing back—his kindness, Rosie's passing. I've hardly had time to process it all, and now I'm thrust into some new reality.

I peer across the bed, filled with loathing and anticipation. Which would-be love from my past is he? Someone I met in a bar? My first crush from elementary school? That guy from college, what's-his-name, who spilled beer on me at a Dave Matthews concert? I stare at the human form beside me, cloaked in rumpled sheets. I'll figure out *where* I am later; first I need to identify the male du jour.

"Hey," I whisper, cautiously tapping the edge of his shoulder. When *she* stirs, my left ventricle nearly bursts.

"Wait . . . *what?*" I stammer, inching toward the edge of the bed as the woman beside me sits up and arches her back, stretching her petite arms up to the ceiling with a yawn.

"Morning to you, too, eejit," she says running her fingers through her pixie-length, platinum blond hair. She's about my age, maybe a little younger—pretty, with sharp features, deep-set blue eyes, and a thick Irish accent. Whoever she is, we've never met—at least I don't think so.

"Um . . . what are *you* doing here?" I ask nervously.

She rolls her eyes. "Stop the lights, Lena. After last night, I just can't deal."

Last night? I take a deep breath.

"Listen," I say, covering my bare legs with the edge of the sheet. "I don't mean to sound weird or anything, but are we . . . um, did we . . . ?" I swallow hard. "What's going on?"

She laughs. "Last night's pints are talking, I see. You're obviously in bits."

"In bits?"

"Are ya fecking kidding me? Two years in Ireland, and you're still struggling with the slang?" She shakes her head mockingly, before her expression softens. "I'm just slagging. You know I love ya—but, bloody hell, not in *that* sort of way."

My head spins, trying to make sense of this latest scenario.

"Besides," she continues, stretching her small arms in the air again, "Colm would come after me with a pitchfork."

Colm. Oooooh, this one I remember. The summer after my sophomore year of college, I backpacked through Europe with girlfriends—all of whom, I might add, got mono and had to fly home early, leaving me to finish the last leg of our trip solo. I met Colm Dalton on a train from Paris to Zurich. He was tall—so tall that his head grazed the ceiling of our passenger car. While he did heave my ridiculously overstuffed pack into the luggage compartment, it was his enormous smile and humor that piqued my interest. I don't know if anyone else has made me laugh that hard since. Maybe it's just an Irish thing, or maybe it was . . . him? In any case, when I reached my stop, Colm scribbled his phone number and email address on a scrap of paper, which I tucked into the pocket of my shorts. That night, after I'd settled into my hostel, I reached into my pocket and it was . . . gone, and Colm no more than a few paragraphs in my travel journal.

I met a lot of interesting people that summer, but he was the only one I really remember. "There's just something about Colm," Frankie used to say whenever I'd reminisce about that train ride. I suppose everyone has their what-if person—the profound chance encounter turned into a . . . missed connection—and I've certainly bumped into a lot of them these past few days. But Colm was special.

"The Dalton boys may be thick-skinned," my bedmate continues, her expression softening, "but their hearts? All teddy bear. Colm would be wrecked if you left him. Same with my Declan. Speaking of, I should probably get back and give that arse a talking to. He was fecking locked last night. He actually said to me, 'Bitsy, you need to mind yer tongue. You have the dirtiest mouth in Kinsale.'" She sighs. "Three whiskeys, and there he goes again, *acting the maggot*. Men."

"Yeah, men," I say, doing my best to follow.

Bitsy turns to me, her eyes flashing. "Maybe it wouldn't be a bad idea to, ya know, swing for the other team? It'd sure teach those fecking Dalton boys a lesson."

As she leans forward, I lean back, and she bursts into laughter, smacking her hand against my arm. "Sorry," she says, chuckling. "I couldn't help it."

I shake my head as she climbs out of bed and slides her lithe body into jeans and a sweater, before eyeing her watch. "Colm's train should be gettin' in soon, yeah?"

"Um, yeah?"

"I bet he'll be fiending to see ya. Wish Dec got some of Colm's romantic genes." She smiles, with a sigh. "Hey, thanks for letting me stay at your gaff last night. Nothing good comes from a pub row." She sighs, reaching for a bag by the window. "If that man of mine would stop being such an arse, maybe we could be sisters someday." Her eyes brighten. "Like, real ones."

Sisters. My head spins as I attempt to piece all this together. Her name is . . . *Bitsy? Gaff* must mean . . . house? Her boyfriend, Declan, is . . . Colm's brother? And Colm is . . . coming home—here—soon?

"Well, I better go check on that man-child of mine," she says, turning to the door with a grin. "See ya at the pub tonight—yeah?" She blows me a kiss and disappears out the door.

I EXHALE DEEPLY. IT'S ONLY 9 A.M., AND I'VE NOT ONLY LEAPED TO ANOTHER CON-tinent, but also woken up beside the spunkiest woman in Ireland. I like Bitsy. I can see us being friends in real life, if that even exists anymore.

I glance down at my hand, to my bare ring finger. Maybe we're one of those couples who don't wear rings, or maybe we never tied the knot? I'm hoping for the latter. The last thing I need is another husband. Funny, a few days leading up to this, that was all I wanted. Careful what you wish for, I guess.

I set out for the bathroom, where I take a long look at myself in the mirror. The first glance is always a shocker, but this one? Not as much. I mean, yeah, my hair is lighter, my freckles a little more prominent, but my cheeks are dewy and rosy, my eyes bright. I have the look of someone who's just returned from a week-long vacation— with room service. *But am I happy?* I wonder.

It's too soon to know, I realize. I mean, I haven't even seen Colm! What if he weighs four hundred pounds? What if he has anger issues or, worse, is one of those guys who spends all day filming himself playing *Minecraft*? How would I even know? I met him *once,* for a *few hours,* on a *train.* He could be anyone or anything. He could be a—

Enough, I tell myself, as I make my way to the closet, picking out a sweater and jeans, before having a quick look around the tidy bedroom with its cream-colored plaster walls and wide-plank hardwood flooring. A painting of a castle hangs above the headboard—a flea-market find, perhaps, lovingly carted home and hung on the wall. I'd buy something like that—in another life.

I walk through the doorway to a charming living room and kitchen area, with its low-slung, beam-studded ceiling that hovers overhead like a protective heirloom quilt. At the helm of the kitchen is a vintage stove, which looks like a relic from another era, with its well-worn brass knobs and heating elements soaked in a thousand layers of patina and probably just as many memories. I pour myself a glass of water, then sink into the sofa by the fireplace, where the charred embers in the hearth bear evidence of last night's warmth.

A framed photo on the coffee table catches my eye, and I lean in to have a look. There I am, standing in front of a Christmas tree beside Colm—and a little boy, about six or seven, grinning from ear to ear. I'm immediately confused, and shocked. Could this be . . . our son? It feels like a million years ago, but I think back to Nathan in Pennsylvania, when I learned of my miscarriage. For as long as I can remember, motherhood was a big no-thanks for me, which is why I didn't expect the revelation to hit me so hard, especially seeing Frankie with her baby, knowing I may not be capable of carrying a child of my own. It's like the possibility of motherhood was ripped from my arms at the precise moment I began opening myself up to it.

I try to imagine myself here, cuddled up under a blanket with Colm—and our son?—laughing like we did that day on the train all those years ago. Would he still be funny? Or has time embellished the memories of that day? What if, all these years later, he's actually . . . kind of dull? Maybe the fantasy of the Irishman I met on a train in Europe was just that—a fantasy—and in real life he's just—

My thoughts come to a screeching halt when I hear footsteps

outside. I freeze, watching as the door opens—hinges creaking—and a very tall, and very handsome Irishman walks in with a bouquet of pale pink roses in his hands.

"There's my girl," Colm says, coming toward me, beaming.

"Hi," I say, more than a little stunned. He's just as I remember—and more—with his wild green eyes, chiseled jaw and dirty-blond hair with a kiss of gray at the temples. The years have been good to Colm. More than good.

"My flight arrived early, so I caught the morning train," he continues, sinking into the sofa beside me. *The train.* It's what brought us together all those years ago. "London was grand, of course, but I couldn't wait to get home."

I smile, taking it all in—taking *him* in. I'm both confused and pleasantly lost in his eyes.

Colm runs his hand through his hair. "I had to go, to see it for myself—to see what a big opportunity like that could look like." He sighs. "My bleedin' pride, I guess." He nestles closer beside me. "When Mum asked me to take over the pub, at first it felt like a life sentence. Never getting out of Kinsale, never having the chance to run my own distillery." He sighs, eyebrows raised. "But a funny thing happened. When I got to London and saw the place I'd be managing, I felt this pang in my heart, ya know? I couldn't stop thinking about Kinsale. I guess I love this bloody old town." He laughs. "Besides, the owner of that distillery was a first-class arse."

I grin, doing my best to track what he's saying.

He nods to himself. "I couldn't get your words out of my head, either. You helped me see that family matters more than ego or ambition. The bottom line is that I'm the firstborn, and Mum shouldn't be tending the pub any longer. It's time I take the reins."

"So," I say. "You're . . . staying?"

"*We're* staying," Colm replies, reaching for my hands triumphantly.

I can't help but feel triumphant, too, but also confused. Yesterday I was hurtling through shock and grief—and new feelings. *Spencer.*

And today? Colm's baring his heart and looking at me with adoring eyes as if I'm the only thing that matters in the entire world. I can't help but wonder about the path that led me here—in this life, anyway—the kaleidoscope of roads taken, and not, that make up the story of us.

"You okay, Lena?" Colm asks, searching my face. "Is there something bothering you?"

"No, no," I reply. "I'm just . . . taking it all in. I mean, look at us, two people who met randomly on a train, and we found each other again. What if I'd gotten off at an earlier stop, or . . ."

"Or didn't send me that message on Facebook." He beams. "I never thought I'd see you again, and then there you were, in my inbox." Colm nods to himself. "You've made me so happy, Lena. I just want to make you proud."

I think of Mike, standing in his underwear surrounded by boxes of fidget spinners and cracking his first beer at 9 a.m. Colm couldn't be any more different. "How could I not be proud of you?"

He nods. "I wanted to do big things . . . for you—for us. Are ya sure you can love a man in an apron, filling pints at Dalton's Pub?"

I smile, his big heart on a platter before me to take, and I can't help but feel immediately enamored as I connect the dots. Colm went to London to pursue a big-paying job, but his heart is anchored here, in . . . Kinsale. He's not staying because it's the glamorous choice, but rather the right one.

"I had a look around, and a good think, and I realized that all I need—all I've ever wanted—is right here . . . in that bleedin' old pub." He pauses, smiling. "And in this creaky old cottage with you." He hands me the bouquet of flowers. "Do you like them?"

"I love them," I say, my heart beating faster when our eyes meet again. I recall the same intense feeling the day we met, not that I could tell the difference between run-of-the-mill attraction and, well, *something more*. All I know is that I felt *something* then, and I'm feeling it again—right now.

"Well," I say, breaking our silence as he leans closer. "I . . . better get these into a vase."

Colm nods, reaching into his coat pocket a few times as if he might have lost something. For a moment, his eyes are distant—elsewhere.

"There," I say, placing the flowers on the table.

"I see you've been painting," he says, pointing to an easel and canvas near the far wall of the living room beside the window. A beam of light shoots through the paned glass, illuminating the swath of green grass in the little scene. I walk closer, studying the landscape, much like the one hanging on the bedroom wall. It's stunning, actually. The waves practically jump off the canvas. I can almost taste the sea spray. *I* painted *this*?

Behind my back, Colm presses his chin on my shoulder. "I know I always say it, but I think this one might be your masterpiece."

Me? An artist? Sure, I sketched a bit in high school, but I gave that up a long time ago. Art was my mother's thing, not mine. She tried to teach me to paint, but it always ended with tears streaming down my face. Even though she promised the muddied colors on my canvases were beautiful, I knew they weren't. I would never be as talented as she was. But now? Standing beside this easel, I can't help but wonder if there's more of my mother in me than I ever knew. The thought both comforts and frightens me, especially now. If I can paint like this, does that also mean I'm susceptible to the demons that plagued her? Are they lurking, beckoning me down a similar path? No, I tell myself as I feel Colm's breath on my neck.

He pulls me closer, and my body yields, melting into his embrace like butter; when he kisses me, his mouth feels like home. He tugs at the edge of my sweater, his fingers traveling up the small of my back. I don't ask him to stop, though the moment ends abruptly when the door swings open and a boy, about eight or nine, gallops in.

"Daddy, Lena! I'm home!"

Lena. Not Mom, then who?

11

"Liam!" Colm cries, grinning. "I thought you were spending the day at Grandma's house."

He nods. "I was, but she said you were coming home early." He pauses, pulling a box from his backpack—from what I can tell, a Lego set. "Look, Grammy got me the Millennium Falcon! Can we build it together?"

"Wow," Colm says, ruffling his son's hair. "Sure, big guy. Let's do it."

"Do you want to help, Lena?" Liam asks, smiling up at me.

"Sure," I say, instantly smitten. *My God, I'm a stepmom? Or a bonus mom?* I don't know how to define it, just that this beautiful green-eyed boy has wrapped his arms around my waist, and I already love him.

"I missed you guys," he continues, unloading the contents of the box onto the kitchen table. "I mean, Grammy is fun, but she doesn't make pancakes like you do, Lena."

Rosie's pancakes. Of course, I make him Rosie's pancakes—smothered in honey and with a dollop of whipped cream on top. I can almost taste them.

"I hope you were respectful, son," Colm adds, fusing two Lego pieces together. "Said your please-and-thank-yous, did ya?"

Liam nods. "I even helped carry in the firewood."

"Good boy."

TWO HOURS AND THREE GRILLED CHEESE SANDWICHES LATER, THE MILLENNIUM Falcon is complete. Liam skips off to his room to read a new comic book, and Colm and I head outside, where we sit in two chairs perched on the edge of a grassy bluff overlooking the sea. Seabirds fly in and out of crevices along the hillside, dropping clams against the rocks.

"It's beautiful here," I say, the words slipping out of my mouth without my permission as waves crash against the shore.

Colm grins, eyeing me curiously. "You sound as if you're seeing it all for the first time."

"Maybe I am," I reply, looking back at the little cottage, with its weathered, whitewashed stone façade, cheery, bright red door, and a little chimney poking out of the ailing shingled roof. It isn't fancy—just a couple of bedrooms by the sea—but somehow, it's enough. "I loved what you said earlier," I continue, "about staying here, taking over your mom's pub. You're a good man, Colm."

"Or a stupid one," he says with a chuckle. "How am I ever going to buy you those red-bottom shoes?"

I shake my head. "Red-bottom shoes?"

"You know, the high heels with the red soles."

"Wait, are you talking about Louboutins?" I laugh, shaking my head. "I can assure you, that's the last thing I need." I point to the gravel path leading from the doorway. "Besides, one step out that front door, and they'd be ruined."

"Yer right," he says with a grin. "But I'd actually fancy seeing you in a pair of red-bottom shoes. If you want them, say the word, and I'll do whatever it takes. I'll tap-dance on hot coals."

I laugh again, pressing a finger to his lips, stunned by how easy, how natural it is to be with him. "No more talk of shiny things—or dancing on hot coals, okay?"

Colm nods, his grin fading and his expression far-off. I can't help but wonder if he's regretting his decision, or if it's . . . something else. We sit in silence for a beat, each of us carrying the weight of our thoughts. I feel the urge to tell him about mine, but when I open my mouth to speak, no words come out. While I'd shared my plight with Spencer yesterday, I'm too tired and too lost to find the words again. Besides, Colm is already carrying enough baggage; it doesn't feel right to burden him with anything more. I smile to myself, remembering Spencer's words. I'll be Colm's Competent Traveler, I decide.

"Mum's birthday thing is tonight," he says, eyeing his watch. "We should be at the pub by five. Lord knows she'll have my hide if we're late. Katherine Dalton isn't one to feck with."

"No fecking," I say, grinning. "Let's get ready, shall we?"

"The way you smiled just now," Colm says, taking my hand as we walk back to the house, "reminds me of Jenny." He nods to himself. "Liam's mum would have loved you as much as he does."

Jenny. Past tense. And just like that, the burden Colm is carrying becomes a little clearer.

IT'S A TEN-MINUTE DRIVE INTO TOWN, ALONG A WINDING ROAD THAT'S AS PICTUR-esque as it is nail-biting. At one point I feel as if the car might topple off the side of a cliff. Fortunately, we stay the course, and when we arrive in Kinsale proper, I'm immediately taken by the quaint storefronts that look as if they've been frozen in time. Molly's Sweets, O'Reilly's Hardware—a walk through downtown feels like stepping into the pages of an old fairy tale.

"Damn," Colm says, as we step out of the car with Liam, raindrops hitting our cheeks. He eyes his watch nervously. "We're five minutes late." It's clear that he knows better than to disappoint his mum.

Dalton's Pub is on the next corner—the letters stenciled in gold against black paint. I can already tell I'm going to like this place, with its shutter-flanked windows on the lower level and two ample dormers nestled against the roof. As we approach, music wafts through the air—violin, but not the classical variety, the type that makes you want to tap your feet.

"Grammy!" Liam exclaims, darting through the doorway toward a woman with silver hair swept into a bun, her arms extended out. Her smile is warm, but her eyes? Fierce. I now understand Colm's anxiety.

"Finally! My favorite son has arrived!" she says, kissing Colm's cheek, then frowning. "You weren't thinkin' of standing me up on my birthday, were ya?"

Colm shakes his head, obviously terrified. "No, Mum, sorry—just running a little late, that's all."

"Well, glad you finally made it," she says, hands firmly planted on her hips, as Liam runs across the room to the other children. "A woman doesn't turn sixty-five every day! Come, now, let's get you two a proper round."

At the bar, Colm orders us each a pint. As we clink glasses, Bitsy walks through the door with a tall man—Colm's brother, Declan, obviously. He's handsome just like Colm, though he has their mother's intense eyes—and maybe her temper? In any case, as far as he and Bitsy are concerned, last night's squabble seems long forgotten. They're all smiles as they greet family and friends.

"Bits!" Colm says, barreling her over with a hug. "I see you're still hanging around with this dope. Yer a saint for loving him the way you do. He doesn't deserve ya."

Declan smirks. "Nice to see you, too, big brother."

Colm takes a sip, laughing good-naturedly. "Just slagging, Dec."

"Look," their mother cries when she sees Declan. "It's my favorite son!"

Colm gives his brother a firm elbow to the rib cage. "She just said that about me."

"Liar," Declan replies. "I'm her favorite—everyone knows that."

Colm folds his arms across his chest, but Katherine will have none of it. She takes both her sons by the arm, leading them across the room. They both tower over her petite frame, but it's obvious who's boss, and she looks to be barely five-foot-two.

"Feeling better?" I ask Bitsy as she squeezes into the barstool beside mine.

She shrugs. "Yeah, I guess. Dec and I patched things up . . . I mean, for the most part."

We watch as our partners throw back their heads, laughing with exaggerated hand gestures as Katherine begins to dance.

"Lene," Bitsy begins again, eyeing the revelry. "Do ya ever wonder if this family is, well . . . a bit much?"

"I'll admit, I've never seen a grandma kick up her legs, cancan-style," I say, laughing. "But it *is* her birthday."

Bitsy rolls her eyes playfully. "One day these Daltons could be the death of me."

I smile. "Or maybe the best thing that ever happened to you?"

"Cheers to optimism," Bitsy says, clinking her glass against mine.

"Need anything?" Colm whispers in my ear, his breath sending goose bumps down my neck.

I shake my head, smiling.

"Okay, then, I should probably get up there and make a toast for Mum."

"Yeah, ya better," Bitsy says in agreement, "if you don't want her comin' for ya later."

When the musicians finish their song, Colm kisses my cheek, then makes his way to the little stage ahead, where he taps a fork against his glass, waving for the crowd's attention. "Hello, everyone," he says, taking the mic. "Welcome to our beloved mum's birthday celebration." He clears his throat. "Given that I'm her eldest and *favorite* son, I thought I'd say a few words tonight." He pauses, grinning at Declan. "People speak of the luck of the Irish, but it hasn't always been rainbows and shamrocks for me. I've gone through some tough times, and in the darkest moments, I'll admit, I've wondered if I'm bleedin' cursed. It's only when I pan back and look at the big picture that I see how truly lucky I am, and it all begins with Mum. In fact, I'm the luckiest bastard of them all, because I was blessed with the best mother on the Emerald Isle. Just don't sneeze at her dinner table, or bother her chickens, or side with Mrs. Higgins about the Scrabble contest of 1974. Mum won—enough said." The room erupts in laughter. "And I won, getting to be her son." There's more cheering and applause, but Colm isn't finished. "If you'll allow me a few moments more, I have two announcements to make—both of which I think Mum will enjoy. The first? I turned down a job offer in London to stay here, in Kinsale, and take over this beautiful old fecking pub." Katherine clutches her chest tearfully. The chorus of gasps and cheers is almost melodic. "It's about time Mum retired that apron, got off her feet, and maybe found herself a boyfriend."

Katherine shakes her head, blushing, but it's obvious she's pleased—and deeply touched.

"And while Mum becomes a lady of leisure, I'll be tending to this little hole-in-the-wall that so many of you have loved for generations." Colm steps away from the microphone for a moment, searching the crowd for my face until his eyes meet mine. "But I can't do that without a partner by my side—the ying to my yang, my heart's true home." He swallows hard. "Lena, will you please humor me and join me onstage?"

I smile nervously. "Me? Right now?"

Colm nods. "Please?"

"Go on, girl," Bitsy whispers to me, grinning.

"Okay," I mutter, winding through the crowd to the stage.

"Lena, when we met on that train in Europe thirteen years ago, I felt a spark that was undeniable." He pauses, turning to the crowd. "Unfortunately, she lost my number."

There's more laughter in the room—and a sprinkling of heckling.

"But then, eight years later, Lena sent me a Facebook message. Besides the birth of my son, that was the best day of my life, because . . . we found each other again." He gestures to Declan, who taps Liam on the shoulder. Wide-eyed and smiling, he runs up to the stage, where he stands beside Colm. Both drop down on one knee, and the display of love sends a wave of emotion through the room. Katherine blots her eyes with a handkerchief; Bitsy sobs at the bar, happy tears streaming down her face.

Colm pulls a little box from his coat pocket, and hands it to Liam.

"Lena," he begins, clearing his throat. "We have two questions for you." He pauses, looking up at his dad.

"Lena," Colm begins. "I would be the luckiest man alive if you would be my wife."

Liam nods, then turns to me. "And I would be the luckiest boy alive if you would be my mum."

The two exchange glances, before turning back to me with expectant faces.

"Lena, will you marry me?" Colm continues.

"Lena, will you be my mum?" Liam adds.

I place a hand on each of their shoulders, overcome with emotion as the tears spill from my eyes, rushing down my cheeks like a river in search of the sea. Never in my life have I seen a more beautiful and heartfelt outpouring of love, and I feel it—I feel it deeply. I also can't help but love them back.

"Yes," I say as Colm slips a gold ring on my finger. Studded with tiny diamonds, with three small emeralds at the center, it's modest, but perfect.

The band starts again with an uptempo jig that brings everyone to their feet. Colm lifts Liam over his shoulders, steadying him with one arm and wrapping the other around me.

"Fair play," Bitsy says, clinking her glass against mine and giving Declan a swift elbow to the gut. "You got the *better* brother."

"Welcome to the family, dear," Katherine adds with a wide smile. "You got yerself a grand lad."

I smile, my eyes meeting Colm's—a grand lad indeed.

THE PARTY CONTINUES INTO THE EVENING, BUT BY ELEVEN LIAM IS DOZING, HIS head on his grandmother's shoulder, and Colm and I decide to head home. Given the amount of whiskey consumption, we flag down a cab on the street outside. Colm lifts a very sleepy Liam into the car, where he rests his head on my lap.

On the drive home, we hold hands, both in a quiet, happy daze. I want to bottle this feeling before it passes, and I'm acutely aware that it will—soon.

What will become of them—of this—when I close my eyes tonight? Will we find each other again? Could we ever re-create what we have right now? Where love once bloomed, it can bloom again, I tell myself. But will he feel the same? Will I? Could anything ever be this perfect? I'm not sure.

Colm pays the driver and carries Liam inside, gently tucking him into bed in the little room beside ours. "Poor guy," he says, yawning. "Big night for him." He squeezes my hand, yawning. "We've been practicing for weeks. You made him so happy. You made us both so happy."

"Daddy? Lena?" Liam says, stirring. I planned to call Rosie, but I pause, kneeling to untie his shoes instead.

I smile at Colm. "Why don't you go lie down? I'll tuck him in tonight."

"You sure?" he asks, yawning again.

"Sure," I say, blinking back fresh tears as I remove Liam's shoes, smoothing his hair as he nestles his head against the pillow.

"Sing me a song?" he asks as I pull the blanket snug.

"Sure, honey." I pause, thinking of the lullaby my mom used to sing to me. It's been ages since I thought of it, and yet it's still imprinted on my memory; so is her voice, which I hear right now.

"Hush-a-bye, don't you cry, go to sleep my little baby," I begin. "When you wake, you shall have . . . all the pretty little horses."

My voice falters as I continue, memories rushing back like a burst dam. Her voice. The sweet smell of her perfume. She sang "All the Pretty Little Horses" to me every night, just like her mother did. Mom wasn't perfect—far from it. I watched her fall into the arms of one man after the next, hoping that one of them would stick around, make everything okay. I wish she would have known that she didn't need a man for that. She was enough. And so am I—with or without a fiancé.

I sigh, singing another few verses, until Liam opens his eyes once more. "Is it okay if I call you 'Mum' now?"

I bite the edge of my lip, fighting back tears. "Oh, sweetie, I'd love that."

Liam smiles, satisfied, and rolls over to his side, drifting off to sleep in mere seconds.

I kiss the edge of his forehead, breathing in the scent of his hair—shampoo and pine trees. It's true, I may never be a mother—at least, not a biological one—but if I were, I think I'd be a damn good one. Liam showed me that.

It's nearly midnight, and I don't want to go, but time is ticking. I think of Rosie again, and my heart contracts at the thought of yesterday. I need to hear her voice, to make sure she's actually okay.

I reach for Colm's phone on the kitchen counter—Lord knows where mine is—and dial her number.

"Lena?" she says with a yawn.

Tears sting my eyes as I clutch the phone. She's alive, thank God. "Sorry," I begin. "I have no idea what time it is there, but I just miss you so much and I wanted to call. I hope I'm not waking you up."

"Only from my nap," she replies. "It's three forty-five in the afternoon."

"I'm sorry," I say. "But I have some news that might cheer you up."

"Do tell."

"Colm proposed tonight—with Liam." I pause, assuming that she's up to speed on my life—this version of it, anyway.

"I know, dear."

"You do? How?"

"Because he called me last week asking my permission for your hand."

"He did?" My heart bursts at the thought of this adorably

old-fashioned, yet decidedly modern gesture. I don't have a father or
a mother, so Colm asked my aunt.

"Yes, and he was very sweet."

"So, you . . . approve?"

"Only *you* can approve, honey. And it sounds like you do?"

"I said yes."

"And you're happy?"

"I am, but . . .'"

"No buts."

I sink into the living room sofa. "It just all happened so fast."

"Fast? You've been with him for four years, and in Ireland for
nearly half as long."

"Right."

"Trust your heart, love," she says.

"I think I did tonight."

"Good, then. I shall celebrate. My doctor told me to lay off the
pinot grigio, but what the hell. My girl just got engaged. And, wait! I
just became a grandmother!"

"You did," I say, laughing. "And I can't wait for you to meet Liam.
He's an angel."

"Come home soon," she says, her voice cracking on the last word.
"I miss you so."

"I promise," I say, blowing Rosie an air kiss.

We don't say *goodbye*. We never do. The word used to frighten me
as a child, because when I said it to my mom, it came with underpin-
nings of fear. I never knew when she'd come home, and deep down
I worried that one of our goodbyes might be forever. After she died,
Rosie and I put the word into retirement.

I set Colm's phone on the coffee table, then walk to the bedroom,
where I strip off my clothes, letting them fall into a heap on the floor.
I crawl into bed beside him, pressing my body against the warmth
of his back. "Hi," I whisper, my hand traveling down his arm, to his
hand, where our fingers meet.

"Hi," he whispers back, turning to kiss me. "Did you have fun tonight?"

"The most fun," I say, nestling my head against his bare chest. "Liam's asleep—absolutely conked. I just called Rosie. She was over the moon about our news." I tell him how much it meant to me that he called her before proposing, and that we should book a trip to Seattle soon. When he doesn't respond, I look at his peaceful face. His eyes are closed, and with a sigh, I quietly watch the rise and fall of his chest.

Is this *it*? Is Colm the man I've always been meant for? My handsome Irishman with a heart as big as Kinsale? And if so, how am I supposed to wake up tomorrow somewhere new, with someone else? I dread the thought of it, but most of all, I dread this goodbye. As much as I want to go home, I don't want to leave *this*. I shift, nestling into the pillow. For the first time in all these days, I feel the urge to fight sleep, to stay awake through the night—anything for a little more time. My weary eyelids feel as if they're strapped with bricks, but I will them to stay open just a few more minutes. I don't have any idea what's happening to me or where I'll be in the morning, but I do know one thing, and it fills me with an unexpected sense of comfort: today, I felt love—*real love*.

PART
SIX

12

Taxi horns blare—one after the next—when I open my eyes, peering into the unfamiliar darkness. I don't know where I am, just that I'm not in Ireland, nor with Colm and Liam. Memories of yesterday hit my heart like arrows, and I wince. I've woken up from a beautiful, warm dream, and whatever force that controls my destiny has, once again, dropped me into the abyss.

I sit up in another strange bed, which I'm grateful to find empty. In a blue silk nightie, I shiver as I get up and walk to the window. Pulling back the curtains, I see the sun hasn't yet peeked over the horizon, but even under the cloak of night, I know where I am.

Manhattan.

I spot the High Line in the distance, as well as the Chelsea Hotel's iconic neon sign. I feel like this must be the corner of Twenty-Third and Seventh, where I used to wander in for late-night hot dogs at Chelsea Papaya. To this day, I have no idea how a one-dollar wiener could taste *that* good.

The city lights twinkle through the rain-splattered window, as if to say, *Welcome home, kid.* But I feel neither welcome, nor at home. I just want to be back in my real life, not in this never-ending alternate reality. Also, who is this *man* walking into the bedroom in his underwear?

"Hey," he says, shutting the bathroom door. I recognize his voice, of course. I *know* his voice, even if I'm too shocked to confirm it. He pauses beside the bed, back turned to me.

Adrenaline courses through my body, even before the beam of light hits his face.

"It's going to be a hell of a day," he says, pausing to take a sip of last night's lukewarm nightcap on the bedside table. "Might as well take the edge off." Whiskey on the rocks. I know, because *I know him.*

Every muscle of my body freezes. The man climbing back into bed with me is Christian: *my best friend's husband.*

"No," I say, inching away from him. I turn on the lamp on my bedside table just to make sure I'm not hallucinating. I'm not. "No, no, no, no, no, no, no. This is not happening. You should be with Frankie!"

"Frankie?" he says, thoroughly confused. "We said good night to her at the concert." He smiles. "I got her into a cab, remember? Don't worry. She's fine."

I shake my head. "No, it's not fine, *Christian!*"

"Whoa, Lena. What's wrong?"

I feel dizzy, but not from last night's libations. "Christian, I need you to do something for me."

"What is it?"

I sit up, breathlessly leaning against the headboard. "Describe how we met."

"Wait, what?"

"Christian, please," I say, closing my eyes tightly, then opening them again. "I just . . . need to hear you say it."

"Okay, okay," he finally says.

I wait for him to explain—to make this make sense, if that's even possible. For all I know, Frankie's coming home soon. What have we done? What have *I* done?

"All right," Christian says, propping another pillow behind his back. "Let's take a trip down memory lane. There you were, a *goddess,* sitting on that barstool at the Nomad Hotel bar. I noticed you first, even though you always say it was the other way around. No, *I* watched you walk in. I thought to myself, *I could die a happy man tonight if I could just have one drink with her.*" He smiles, turning onto his side to face me. "And then the miraculous happened—*you* walked over."

No, I didn't. Frankie did.

"I gripped the edge of the bar; I could barely hold on tight enough in your presence." He pauses, shaking his head. "You were a force then, just as you are now."

I look down at the sizable emerald ring on my left hand—cushion cut. Somehow it sparkles in the dim light as Christian inches closer, his hand sliding familiarly across my stomach. *This isn't good. In fact, it's terrible. Terrible, terrible, terrible.*

"What's going on with us, Lena?" he asks, sensing my unease as he pulls away.

Us? Instinctively, I recoil. *There is no us!*

"We were happy, and then . . ." He pauses, looking away.

"Christian," I begin cautiously, "I don't quite know how to say this, but—"

Without warning, his lips meet mine, and I am, at once, powerless to resist. For a moment—a long one—I linger, or, rather, freeze, letting him pull me close, so close that I can feel the beat of his heart against mine. But it's just a moment, I tell myself, a moment that shouldn't be happening. And maybe it isn't happening at all? Yesterday, I was in Ireland under entirely different circumstances. My heart swells, thinking of Colm, Liam. But now I'm here, in the arms of someone I trust—someone I . . . love: my friend, but also . . . Frankie's husband.

"I can't," I say, pulling away, a little breathless and deeply disturbed. *This can't be happening. I would never . . .*

"Right," Christian says, frustrated as he creeps back to his side of the bed, turning onto his side, back to me. I shove a spare pillow in the space between us—the border, I tell myself, which must not be crossed.

This is insane! The last time I saw Christian was with Frankie and their *baby* on the farm in Pennsylvania, and now I'm in Manhattan wearing his ring?

Minutes pass, maybe an hour. I watch the digits on the clock beside me—slow and steady torture—until the sun finally rises, flooding the bedroom with light, which is when Christian lets out a yawn and climbs out of bed.

"Well, guess I better rip the Band-Aid off and get this day started," he says with a groan as he peels off his T-shirt, revealing his six-pack abs. I avert my eyes. "Back-to-back meetings with the LA team." He threads his legs through a pair of trousers, then pauses, turning to me. "Maybe I should bag it? Call in sick. We could"—he sits on the edge of the bed beside me—"do a little more reminiscing?" When his hand dips beneath the covers, I'm instantly transported back to that night in the city, the fire we both felt. It was as real as it was wrong—just as it is now.

"No," I say, stiffening. "I mean, you should go in. It's an important day, right?" I tuck my knees against my chest like a fortress.

"Yeah," he finally says, standing up and walking to the closet. "You're probably right, and I know you have writing to get done."

"Totally," I say, relieved that he took the bait. "I have *so* much . . . *writing*."

"All right," he says, a little crestfallen. "See you tonight, then." He scrolls through his phone, then shakes his head. "Oh, wait, we have that birthday dinner for Frankie, don't we?"

His words sound impossible, foreign even. It's bad enough that I'm here, but how am I supposed to face my best friend under these circumstances, much less look her in the eyes?

"Who's she bringing this time?" Christian asks, straightening his tie. "That woman goes through men like she does hair colors. Remember the last dude?"

I stare ahead blankly.

"You know, what's-his-name with the beard and all those tattoos? I swear, that one had to be fresh out of Rikers."

"Yikes," I say, worried.

"Anyway, my final meeting wraps up at six, so I'll see you at the restaurant, okay? If I'm late, please don't crucify me. You know how the LA team is."

"Right," I say, eyeing his gray suit, which hugs his body in all the right places. "No crucifying."

"Good luck today," he says, before giving me a quick peck. "You're on the home stretch with this one. I'm getting bestselling novelist vibes."

I nod, playing along.

"Well, I can't wait to read it." He smiles, his expression tentative. "You've kept this one pretty close to the vest."

I've written more than one?

"All right, see you tonight," he says, flashing me a final smile from the bedroom doorway.

"Yeah," I mutter. "Tonight . . ."

When the door closes, I lean my head against the pillow, letting out a long sigh.

Okay. I'm an *author*—married to *Christian. What is this, some kind of Freudian nightmare?* I mean, I can write—at least, in the corporate world. But a full-length novel? No. And let's be clear: If Frankie saw me in bed with her husband just now, she'd have my head on a plate. How did the stars align—or misalign—to deposit me here? Maybe that quirky physics professor in college was right. I remember nothing from the course other than his tweed suits and obsession with the so-called "butterfly effect" theory—the idea being that a butterfly can flap its wings in China, for example, setting off a chain of events that could trigger a tornado in Houston, or, in this case, my life.

I should probably get up, get dressed, and figure out my next steps. In the closet, I survey my options, all black and beige. No prints. No florals. No . . . color. Okay, I guess we're into monochromatic? *Am I . . . depressed, or do I just live in New York?* I grab a pair of jeans and a nondescript black sweater, then slip into some sneakers. In the kitchenette, I drop a pod into the Nespresso machine on the counter and down a shot of espresso before making another. The apartment is nice enough, and clean, though very helter-skelter—Amazon boxes stacked by the doorway and a mountain of unfolded laundry on the sofa. I sort through the pile of mail lying on the counter—unopened bills, clothing catalogs, and a postcard from Rosie!

> Hello, darling girl,
> How are you? And Christian? I'm in Bali at a yoga retreat in the jungle! It's gorgeous here! Maybe when I return, you'll have baby news! Oh, do I hope so. I know how difficult this fertility journey has been for you. I wish I could just snap my fingers and make it so.
> How's your novel coming along? Last we spoke, you said that it was more personal than anything you've ever written. Facing our inner selves is a task like no other, which is why I'm sure it'll be your best!
> Well, I must go to sleep, the airport shuttle departs at 6 a.m. Come visit when I'm back! Sometimes I miss you so much it hurts.
>
> Hugs and kisses, and all my love,
> always,
> Rosie

Rosie in Bali? Christian and I . . . trying for a *baby*? The hair on my arms stands on end as I walk back to the living room, to the little desk by the far window, where I sit down and open the laptop. *Who am I?* I open a browser and type my name into Google. I click on a

Goodreads link and see a photo of myself, turned to the side, half smiling. *What's with my smile—and my hair?* I look rigid, pent-up—like I take myself *way* too seriously.

I close the browser and begin clicking through the folders in my iCloud like a private investigator. I scroll through images from my life, well, this one, anyway: Christian and I, sailing on the Hudson, date-night selfies, me in front of the Mona Lisa, Christian in front of Van Gogh's self-portrait. Why me and not Frankie?

I want to pick up the phone again, and dial my best friend, but I hesitate. Instead, I open a folder titled "Third Novel/First Draft." Maybe I'll find a little truth somewhere in my fiction. I click on a document titled "Proposal."

And Then There Was You
A Novel Proposal by Lena Lancaster

Vera Canfield has a loving husband, a fulfilling career as a novelist and a cheeky cat named Elf. From the outside looking in, yes, Vera seems to have it all. But there's something dark brewing in her beautifully curated world—a long-held secret that haunts her by day and keeps her up at night.

I sit up straighter in my chair and shiver, just as my phone rings, and I wince when I see the name on the screen: *Frankie*.

"Uh, hello?" I say, cautiously.

"Dude, where are you?"

"Where am I?" I wonder if she can hear the guilt and self-loathing in my voice.

"Yeah," she continues. "You were supposed to be here a half hour ago!"

"Oh, sorry," I say. "Where again?"

"The park!"

"Okay, as in Central Park?"

"Um, yep, the one and only." I imagine her rolling her eyes. "P.S. Your coffee is going to be cold."

"Okay," I say, a little breathlessly. "But, Frankie, *where* in the park?"

"Alice in Wonderland," she says, obviously annoyed. "Duh."

I immediately recall the bronze statue we used to pass on our jogs through Central Park a decade ago. "Right. I'll . . . be there soon."

THE CAB DROPS ME OFF IN COLUMBUS CIRCLE, AND AS I LOOK OUT AT THE PARK ahead, I realize I have quite a sprint ahead of me. Fortunately, I slipped on running shoes, and I *run*—past a group of tourists taking selfies, past a posh-looking mom pushing a double stroller, past the ghosts of my old life in the city. Twenty minutes later, I'm out of breath and staring up at a bronze statue of Alice in Wonderland—an apt metaphor for me right now. She went down the rabbit hole; I went . . . somewhere.

"You're forty-five minutes late," Frankie says, clearly irritated. Her bleached-blond hair, with an inch of dark roots, is parted down the middle and cut into a blunt bob that lands just beneath her chin. I want to tell her what's happening to me, but I'm too busy wondering, *What happened to my best friend, and who is this rocker chick?*

"Sorry," I mutter, a little stunned. She's wearing an edgy black babydoll dress styled with a choker necklace, and what's that tattoo on her wrist? "Frankie? What happened?"

"What are you talking about?" She takes a sip of her coffee, handing me mine. It's cold, but I don't complain. That's my reward for being late.

"Your hair, your—"

"Oh, do you like it?" She smiles, smoothing the side pieces that frame her face. "I'm loving my new salon on Sixth. Their straightening treatment has changed my life."

I nod, more than a little shocked. "But . . . your curls were so . . . you."

"Meh," she replies with a shrug. "I got my color touched up, like usual, but kept the roots this time, see? It's a thing. Dark roots, light hair. You know, the rocker girl vibe."

"But, Frankie, you're not a . . . rocker girl."

"I know, I know. It's just an . . . aesthetic I'm trying out." She adjusts the choker on her neck, twisting it around as if she has no clue how to wear it. She doesn't. "Also, Townes is into that sort of thing."

"Townes?"

She grins. "Yeah, the new guy I'm dating!"

Not only is Frankie's appearance drastically different, so is her attitude. She's tougher, more jaded. Even her voice—it has an edge to it. I want to know everything, what of life's twists and turns had such a searing effect on her. But before I can open my mouth, she hands me her phone.

"*This* is Townes," she says proudly. "Hot, right?"

I stare at the photo of a man on a subway immersed in a book. "Wait, is that *Infinite Jest* by David Foster Wallace?"

Frankie nods proudly.

"Isn't that, like . . . a thousand pages?"

"He's really smart," she continues. "I saw him on that Instagram page—you know, @hotdudesreading?" She smiles conspiratorially. "Anyway, I may or may not have slipped into his DMs."

Impossible. Frankie would never do something like this!

She shakes her head, as if reading my mind. "Really? You're judging me?"

"No," I say quickly. "It's just that, well, what if he's—"

"A freak?" Frankie shrugs. "It wouldn't be my first encounter. Listen, Lena, while you've been happily married for the last seven years, I've been stuck on the dating roller coaster from hell. I just want to meet someone nice and get off this ride, you know? I'm tired. And . . . I don't know, maybe I want to be a *mom* someday."

You'll be a great mom someday.

My heart aches for Frankie. It hurts to see her like this—so different, so lost. I want to clutch her shoulders, look her in the eyes, and tell her the truth. But I can't, because I'm the reason her life is in a tailspin. I also realize that this isn't the version of Frankie I can confide in. No, this Frankie? She needs *my* help. I need to be her Competent Traveler.

"Everything is going to be okay," I say reassuringly.

"What if you're wrong?"

"I'm not." I pause, thinking back to the day she married Christian, all those years ago, in another life. They'd danced to Nat King Cole, then halfway through busted out a preplanned choreographed dance to "Disco Inferno." It was magical, and they were so in love. And now? Somehow, I've inserted myself into the life that Frankie was supposed to have. I'm the reason she's spinning her wheels, the cause of her unhappiness. I can't turn back time, but I *can* make choices—right now—that might help.

"We'll see," Frankie says with a sigh. "Anyway, Townes is coming to my birthday dinner tonight. I think you'll like him, Lena. I really hope you will."

I nod, though I'm not so sure. I'm also curious about this novel of mine, especially considering what Rosie hinted at—about my fiction bordering reality. "I sent you the pages of my new work-in-progress, didn't I?" *I mean, I assume I share my work with my best friend.*

"Um, *yeah*," she says, obviously annoyed.

I take another sip of my coffee. "And what did you think?"

"I emailed you my comments last week, space cadet."

"Oh, sorry, I . . . I must have missed it."

Frankie smiles. "I really liked it. I did. But, Lena, I have to ask?" She crosses her legs, then recrosses them again. "Is this novel loosely based on . . . *your marriage?*"

"What makes you think that?" I reply, playing coy.

"I don't know," she continues. "I guess I just got that vibe. I mean, Christian is totally on the baby wagon, right? And you've been a little hesitant, like your character, who's on the fence, but going through the motions for her husband."

My God, I'm unhappy, aren't I? All this time, I'd watched Frankie and Christian's beautiful life unfold in real time—happy for them, yes, but also, honestly, a little envious. There was always a part of me, deep down, that wondered if it should have been me, not Frankie, who approached him all those years ago. I think of this morning in bed, the electricity I felt when his lips met mine. We have chemistry, yes, but it's just one part of the complicated recipe for happiness. That's never been clearer to me than right now.

"What else struck you as . . . similar to my life?" I ask Frankie, bracing myself.

"Well," she continues, pausing for a long beat. "Vera and her husband—what's his name—?"

"Preston," I say. The detail is still fresh in my mind from reading my pages this morning—snooping on myself, as weird as that sounds.

"Right, Preston. I mean, the guy's a catch—obviously—and they seem happy enough, at least that's the image they project to the world. And maybe Vera *should* be happy and probably nix all that inner whining." Frankie nods to herself. "Seriously—Preston is practically Husband of the Year." She sighs. "But maybe that's the commentary you're making—the idea that even the most beautiful-seeming lives can still be riddled with uncertainty?"

"Well," I say, taking in her words. "Brava. That's quite the literary analysis."

"Thanks," she says, as a bicyclist hurtles by, spraying droplets from a nearby puddle that splatter onto my pants. "Oh, there was something else." She pauses, lost in thought for a long moment. "Connection. Vera and Preston are compatible, yes; great together in the bedroom, yada, yada; they share a love of art; but something is off with them, you know? Like, he didn't seem all that curious about her work, but went on and on about his. And he thinks *South Park* is funny, but she hates it."

I laugh to myself.

"And then there was the tiniest little thing," Frankie continues. "The slightest detail that I might have missed, and I'm so glad I didn't, because it was so subtle, but so relatable. That part where Vera is at a girlfriend's house and her husband comes home with flowers, kisses her cheek, and asks her how her day was." She pauses. "It wasn't the flowers or the kiss that caught Vera's attention while observing the interaction, it was the '*How was your day?*' I loved how she told her friend that Preston never asks her about *her* day. She's, like, 'Does he even actually care?'" She grins. "Good stuff."

"Thanks," I say, smiling.

"Anyway, go easy on Townes tonight, okay?" Frankie says as we walk to the sidewalk ahead. "Please, no Mama Bear."

I shake my head. "What are you talking about?"

"Oh, I guess you've forgotten about our most recent double date—with Evan?"

"The one with the beard?" I ask, remembering Christian's commentary earlier this morning about the Rikers Island guy.

"Yeah, well, he did kind of have it coming. But not Townes." She grins, hailing a cab. "You'll see."

BACK AT THE APARTMENT, I'M EXHAUSTED, BUT I DON'T DARE CLOSE MY EYES. AS weird and shocking as this reality is, at least I'm here with friends. Besides, who knows where I'll wake up next? For that reason, I want to stay—and stay awake—and for as long as possible. I have things to figure out and a version of my life that needs sorting. But before I can analyze further, my phone buzzes.

The screen reads: *Lucy Sherman: HarperCollins Editor.*

"Hello," I say, picking up.

"Lena! Thank God you answered! We need to talk."

I can only assume this is *my editor*. My *overly caffeinated* editor.

"Okay," I say, letting out a big yawn. "Is everything okay?"

"Yes, yes!" she exclaims. "I read your draft, and I fell in love, Lena. Love, love, love. The way you examine the nuances of marriage. I mean, I laughed. I cried. I felt all the feels, especially that bit when she accidentally breaks his favorite mug while washing dishes and he loses it on her. I mean, it wasn't about the mug. It's never about the mug. But the accumulation of hairline cracks that finally gave in—oh, Lena. It was such a brilliant metaphor."

"Wow, uh . . . thank you," I say, a little stunned.

"Of course, I have some comments. You'll need to fix a few things, but nothing major. It's all *there*. In fact, some sales reps read it over the weekend, and Ernie thinks Target will place a major order, maybe even make it a book club pick. Think of all those women out there in miserable marriages, pushing their red carts around—a captive audience, you know?"

"Yeah," I say, trying to keep up.

"There's just one thing I need to run by you after my meeting with publicity today. Just standard stuff, but I want to make sure you're still on board."

"Still on board? With what?"

"You know, with what we talked about last week. Yes, this is a work of fiction, but the publicity team thinks we could get a lot more leverage if you shared some of your personal life, like pages from your own marriage's ups and downs. Make sense? I mean, we're not asking you to air your dirty laundry or anything, but given what you're going through with Christian, I'm sure you have plenty of material for an *Oprah* magazine essay, maybe, or a *Good Morning America* segment—something like that."

"Wait, what you just said, about the stuff I'm going through with Christian, I—"

"The elephant in the room, right? Honey, how long have I known you? And how long have you been unhappy? Listen, I'm not asking you to do anything that makes you feel uncomfortable." She pauses, laughing nervously. "But hypothetically, if you *were* to, you know, separate, before publication, we could use your personal story to get mega-coverage. With a combo like that, well, I'd be shocked if you didn't make the List your first week."

"As in, the *New York Times Bestseller List*?"

She laughs. "The only one!"

"Listen, Lucy, I'm going to need a little time," I say. "To think this over."

"Right, right," she says with a sigh. "Do hurry, though. I need to get back to publicity. But, Lena, congratulations, again. This is going to be your big book. I can *feel* it."

Lucy—whoever she is—has no idea that I'll be gone tomorrow—at least, if this messed-up situation continues to repeat itself. With four hours until Frankie's birthday dinner, I decide to make another shot of espresso and have a look at the first draft of the novel that my editor has just raved about. Who knows, maybe it's all there, as she says, everything I need to understand—mysteriously veiled in the pages.

13

By the time I reach the final page, I'm practically breathless and gripping the laptop tightly. Before I can process what I've just read—the truth about my life, this one, anyway, spelled out in black-and-white—the door creaks open. I look up to see Christian, as a kaleidoscope of butterflies rises and falls in my stomach.

"Hi," I say, my tone tentative.

He doesn't reply, just opens the fridge and stares inside for what seems like an eternity before pulling out a Heineken and prying off the cap, which he hurls across the kitchen. It misses the trash can, falling to the floor instead. He doesn't pick it up.

"You're back early," I say cheerfully. "I thought you had that meeting with the . . . LA team?"

Christian just stands there, leaning against the black granite countertop, staring off into the distance. He takes a swig of his beer, his shoulders slumped, before his eyes finally meet mine. "When were you going to tell me?"

I shake my head. "Tell you what?"

"Don't pretend, Lena," he says. "I read the email you sent Dr. Miller."

At first I'm confused, but then I remember what Frankie said in the park today—my apparent wariness about fertility treatment. "Oh," I say, closing the laptop.

Christian sits beside me on the couch, rubbing his forehead.

"I can't believe you'd pull the plug on this without talking to me about it."

I reach for his hand, but he pulls away.

"Lena," he continues, eyes filled with pain. "From day one, you've known that being a dad is all I've ever wanted." He pauses, his eyes welling up with tears. "How could you take that away from me?"

"I'm sorry," I mutter, connecting the dots. Christian wants a baby. I don't.

"All these months, all those appointments. Lena, I was excited. So hopeful. I honestly thought you were, too." He shakes his head, deeply wounded. "You should have told me how you felt. You should have . . ."

"Christian," I whisper. "I'm . . . so sorry. I don't know what to say. I—"

"Just tell me one thing: Is it that you don't want to have a baby, or that you don't want to have one . . . with me?"

I bury my head in my hands, my heart on the verge of exploding.

"Yeah, that's about what I expected," he says, rising to his feet. "More stonewalling." He reaches for his keys on the counter, then pauses by the door, wiping a tear from his cheek before reaching for the doorknob. He pauses, back still turned to me. "Lena, I love you, but you're breaking my heart."

I'M LOST IN THOUGHT FOR THE REMAINDER OF THE AFTERNOON, TURNING Christian's words over in my mind, picturing the pain in his eyes. I want to make sense of it all, but mostly I want to fix this disastrous mess that I've seemingly created. Hurricane Lena—the destroyer of her best friends' lives.

I sigh, walking to the closet, where I slip into a black sweater dress and a pair of tall suede boots. As I'm fastening my hair into a bun, it hits me: I know what I need to do to set things straight.

In the living room, I reach for a couple of note cards and envelopes on the desk.

FRANKIE TEXTED ME THE RESTAURANT ADDRESS EARLIER—SOME NEW CHEFFY place on the Upper East Side called Graham's—and when the cab drops me off, I spot her at a window table, locked in conversation with a man whose back is turned to me—Townes, no doubt.

"Hi," I say, sinking into a chair on the opposite side of the table. "Sorry I'm late. Traffic was brutal."

"It's okay, honey," Frankie says, beaming. "I'm just glad you're here." She turns to her date. "Lena, meet Townes."

"Great to meet you," he says, smiling. He seems nice enough—dare I say, normal—and definitely handsome, more so even in real life. Though, when he extends his hand, I can't help but notice that it's quite clammy—no, borderline sticky. I have an impulse to run to the restroom and suds up, but I've just arrived, and I want to do my best for Frankie.

"Tell me," Townes says, eyeing me curiously, "why not take the subway? Might have saved you a solid fifteen minutes."

I laugh a little nervously, wiping my hand on my dress. *Is this guy actually critiquing me right now?* "Oh yeah, your preferred mode of transportation," I say, sparring back. "Frankie showed me the photo."

"Oh, that," he continues with a dismissive laugh. "I'll be honest, one of my friends runs that Instagram account. She put me up to it, staged the whole thing."

Of course she did. I knew he didn't read that book!

"I mean, I was doing her a favor, actually." He shrugs. "Or maybe she did *me* a favor. Seriously, if you could see my DMs right now, well . . ." Frankie and I exchange glances as he drapes his arm, rather awkwardly, around her shoulder.

Charming.

Christian hasn't arrived yet, but when the waiter appears, Townes takes it upon himself to order every appetizer on the menu.

"Um, do you think that might be *too* much food?" Frankie asks, her tone more polite than critical.

"Nah," he replies, perusing the wine list before rattling off his selection to the waiter, which I can't help but notice is a *very expensive* bottle of Barolo.

We've already finished our first glass when Christian finally arrives, his hair speckled with raindrops. "Sorry I'm late," he says, avoiding eye contact with me as he hands Frankie a bouquet of tulips and kisses her cheek. "Happy birthday."

"Ah, Christian! Thank you!" She smiles at me, then back at Townes, who seems unusually stiff. I am, too.

"So," Christian says, sliding into the empty chair beside me as Frankie fills his wineglass. "What have I missed?"

"Not much," I say, feigning cheerfulness. "Just getting to know . . . *Townes*."

"Hey, man," Christian says, extending his hand as the two men lock eyes. "Nice to meet you."

"Likewise," Townes replies, reaching for the wine bottle and helping himself to another large pour, then staring across the table as if he's sizing up a competitor. "So, what kind of work do you do?"

"I'm in finance," Christian says, loosening his tie.

"He's being humble, like always," Frankie interjects, smiling proudly at Christian. "He's a genius, actually. He brings failing companies back from the brink of bankruptcy."

"So, kind of like a corporate fairy godmother, then?" Townes quips.

Christian chuckles. "I guess you could say that, though I much prefer *godfather*." He clears his throat, obviously annoyed but showing miraculous restraint. "How about you? What's your line of work?"

"Townes is a musician," Frankie interjects, swoony-eyed. "He writes his own songs."

"Wow," Christian replies, his expression teeming with skepticism. "That's great. So, you're signed to a record label, then?"

"Well," Townes begins, faltering, "I've had a lot of offers, but I'm not in any rush to sign a contract."

"So you're doing charity work, then," Christian spars back. "I mean, until your career finally takes off."

Townes smirks, but before he can retaliate, Frankie takes the reins.

"Guys," she interrupts, laughing nervously. "It's Friday night. How about we ditch the work talk?"

Townes orders another bottle of wine—the same—and a round of cocktails with the second course. By the time mains appear, he's slurring his words and recounting something funny one of his ex-girlfriends did last summer. Frankie is clearly underwhelmed, and so am I. When he suggests we skip dessert and head to the bar for a round of shots, I decide to have a word with him. That's right—Mama Bear has entered the chat.

"Townes," I say, standing up, "meet me at the bar."

He grins, following behind. "Let's get this party started."

"Not that kind of party," I say, pointing to a stool. "Sit down." I give him a long look. "What the hell do you think you're doing?"

He's obviously a little dazed—and hiccupping. "Hey," he begins, waving to the bartender. "I thought we were all having a good time."

"That's not my definition of a good time, and I can tell you for sure, it's not Frankie's, either."

"Come on," Townes continues. "You all need to loosen up a little."

I roll my eyes, beyond annoyed. "Listen, this is my best friend's birthday dinner, and you're on the verge of ruining it. Either you get your act together, or you head for your beloved subway. Are we clear?"

"You know," he says suddenly with an arrogant sniff, "I don't need this negative energy."

"Neither do we," I fire back. "I think it's time to say goodbyes."

"She's not my type, anyway," he mutters as he stumbles back to the table.

"I see you've got a live one on your hands," the bartender says sympathetically. "Here," he adds, pouring me a shot of whiskey. "On the house."

"Thanks," I say, throwing it back as I watch Townes fumble his goodbyes to Frankie, then stagger for the door. "I could use a little extra liquid courage tonight."

A few moments later, Frankie makes a beeline to me, her expression furious. "Lena, what the hell did you say to Townes?"

"What do you mean?" I ask, feigning ignorance. "He clearly had too much to drink. I just suggested that he call it a night."

She folds her arms across her chest.

"Come on," I say, leading her back to the table. "Let's not let that guy ruin your night."

Christian's still giving me the silent treatment, but I'm grateful, for Frankie's sake, when he orders dessert, which I hope will lighten the mood. "Good riddance," he says to Frankie. "That guy was *full of himself.*"

"You know what? You're right," she says, finally coming to her senses. "I mean, who orders two bottles of Barolo and ditches before the bill?"

"Guys named Townes, that's who," Christian says, sliding his credit card on the table.

"Some birthday," Frankie says, taking a final sip of wine.

Christian motions to the waiter, then hands him his card. "And we're going to turn it around—starting now."

Frankie smiles listlessly.

"Tell us, how was your day *before* that bonehead tried to ruin it?" he asks her.

I feel a prickly sensation on my skin; it travels from the back of my neck and down my spine.

How was your day? Four benign words, just pleasantries, really, but in the context of this moment, they're borderline profound.

"I mean," he adds, "aside from your unfortunate encounter with New York's most *ineligible* bachelor."

Frankie laughs, blotting a napkin to the edge of her mouth before recounting something that happened at work, but her voice is muffled. My heart is pounding with such force, it drowns out everything else.

"Listen," I say, coming to my senses after Frankie finishes her cake. "I hate to be a party pooper, but I'm exhausted, and I . . . need to get a new draft to my editor by tomorrow morning." I smile. "Why don't you two grab a nightcap?"

Frankie looks at me, then at Christian. "Are you sure?"

"Yeah! Don't let me spoil your evening. Go have some fun."

"Okay," Frankie finally says. "I mean, Christian, if you're up for it?"

"Sure," he says. "Anything for the birthday girl."

"Here," I say, handing my best friend an envelope from my purse. "I almost forgot—your birthday card." She begins to tear open the flap, but I shake my head. "It's just a bunch of sappy stuff. Do us all a favor and read it later, 'kay?"

"Okay," she says, nodding with a smile.

I stand up, discreetly slipping another envelope into Christian's coat pocket before I turn to leave. "Have fun tonight," I say, blowing air kisses through misty eyes. "I love you both," I whisper under my breath as I walk out the door. "I always will."

AN HOUR PASSES, THEN TWO. AT SOME POINT, I LOSE TRACK. TIME DOESN'T MAT-ter anymore, nor does my destination. I walk aimlessly, weaving through city streets until I spot Grand Central Station in the distance, like a torch in the darkness.

I'm too exhausted to walk any farther, so I slip inside the old train station and tuck into an empty bench. It seems like the appropriate place to close my eyes, to end one day and start another, in the company of other weary travelers. No matter what our destination, we're all in the same boat—lingering in the in-between place . . . saying farewell to the past and anticipating the journey ahead, wherever it may lead.

I yawn. Sleep will come soon. But before I close my eyes, I think of my best friend, home in her lonely apartment, maybe reading my card at this very moment:

Frankie,

There's something I've known for a long time, but it only recently became clear to me: It should have been you who approached Christian at that bar all those years ago, you who he fell in love with, and you who he married. He was always and forever will be meant for you.

   I have to go away for a while. Don't worry, it will all be fine. Please show Christian the love I never could. You have my blessing.

                    Love, always,
                    Lena

And Christian—perhaps he's unlocking the door right now, setting his keys on the kitchen counter. He'll find my card in his coat pocket tonight, or maybe tomorrow, but when he reads it, he'll *know*:

Christian,

I'm so sorry that I couldn't love you the way you deserved to be loved, but someone else can and will. You won't have to look far. You know who she is.

   She's your soulmate.

                    Love, always,
                    Lena

PART
SEVEN

14

When I open my eyes, a rapid-fire, jarring noise pierces the air—and my eardrums. *A jackhammer, maybe?* Whatever it is, the incessant pounding rattles every nerve in my body. I sit up in bed, taking a cautious look at the man sleeping beside me, a beam of light casting shadows on his bare, suntanned back. *Here we go again.*

I steady myself as he shifts and rolls over, letting out a yawn. *Really? The guy from the plane?* I struggle to remember his name. Dan? Dean? No. Greg? Yes, I think. We met on a flight from San Francisco to New York six or so years ago when I was upgraded to first class and seated beside him. *Greg.* I rack my brain, trying to recall the pertinent details. He was in real estate, I think. Successful and incredibly charming, from what I remember. I joined him for dinner that night at a fancy sushi place in SoHo. He pulled out my chair at the table and picked up the tab at the end, which was sizable, given that we both ordered omakase. We had fun—I think—and yet, I can't remember why I didn't see him again. Work was crazy back then. Maybe I just . . . didn't have time?

"Morning, beautiful," Greg whispers, smiling across the bed at me. With that square jaw and head of thick dark hair, he's just as attractive as I recall—a modern-day doppelgänger for Don Draper from *Mad Men*.

"Um . . . morning," I say, glancing down at my left hand. No ring, though there's an unmistakable tan line in its place. I flinch as he inches closer, grazing the small of my back under the sheets.

Seriously, at some point—soon—one of these guys is going to give me a heart attack, or, rather, I'm going to give one of them a black eye.

Fortunately, Greg stretches his chiseled arms over his head and climbs out of bed—in his boxer briefs. Suddenly I feel warm, my cheeks flushed. A bead of sweat trickles down my neck to my chest, where it makes its final descent between my breasts. *What is this place? An inferno?*

"Sorry, babe," my bedmate says, frowning. "The AC must have gone out again. Don't worry, I'll call my guy."

I nod, forcing a smile, as he turns on the ceiling fan before peering out the window for a long moment. "Won't be long until the pool's ready," he continues. "Just a bit more trenching and we'll be able to pour concrete. In a few months, we'll be sipping sangrías on flamingo floaties."

He pauses, oblivious to the fact that I *detest* sangría—and flamingo floaties. "Or maybe we just flip this place and turn a quick profit?"

Instead of waiting for my reply, Greg scrolls through his phone, face animated. "Oh, good news," he continues. "Jensen's just texted. Your ring's all fixed and ready for pickup. I'd grab it, but, honey, my schedule's jam-packed. I have a breakfast meeting with my sponsor, then a ton of Danbury Estates stuff. Mind stopping by this morning?"

Sponsor. Okay, so he's in AA.

"Uh, sure," I say, a little confused, as usual, of course.

He pulls on a pair of navy pants and white dress shirt before sitting on the edge of the bed beside me, lifting my right leg into his lap. "Foot rub before I go?"

Without waiting for my response, he begins kneading my heel. It feels good—weirdly good. "How did I get so lucky?" he muses, reaching for my second foot. "Don't worry, babe. When this deal goes through, we'll be set for life. Anything you want, it's yours."

I smile nervously as he walks to the dresser, grabbing his wallet and keys as the jackhammer continues its relentless tirade outside.

"Oh, don't forget about our meeting at eleven. Victoria Campbell. It's in the calendar. This one's pivotal." He flashes a smile. "I need your special sauce."

In the spirit of self-preservation, I nod compliantly.

"Love you," he says, kissing my cheek before heading to the door, turning back briefly as if awaiting my reply.

"Um . . ." I mutter. "Love . . . you . . . too."

I listen as Greg's footsteps fade into the ether, then let out a giant exhale and have a look around the sparsely furnished bedroom, taking in every detail. The paint is fresh, the carpet, too. A new-car smell permeates the warm air. It has that just-built-construction look—no curtains or wall art, just a few boxes in the far corner by the closet. *Okay, so we just moved in?*

I lean back against my pillow, trying to remember what Greg just said about my ring. That I'm supposed to pick it up? I reach for the phone on my bedside table, opening the shared calendar: *Pick Up Ring: 9:00*, beside Greg's appointment, *AA Breakfast*.

I cool myself off in front of a fan for a long moment, before heading to the closet, where I frown, staring at a legion of blazer-and-pants sets—in almost every color of the rainbow. They hang at attention like military officers awaiting my command. Reluctantly, I choose a navy set, pairing it with a beige silk camisole and matching navy pumps, before giving myself a long look in the bathroom mirror. My hair is a little darker than yesterday, and I notice a streak of gray at the temples. I lean in closer, shocked. *What is this?* I don't have gray hair, at least *not yet*, and what the heck is *that* on my face? I inch toward the mirror for a better look at the faded, but substantial, scar on my upper right cheek, just below my eye socket. *Yikes—what happened?* I fumble through a few drawers until I find a tube of concealer, which I dab into place.

Moderately satisfied with my camouflaging skills, I survey the bedroom a final time for any clues about this life. Greg's side of the closet tells me what I already know—he's a tailored-suit sort of guy, with plenty of polished designer loafers and even more pressed shirts. Not surprising, but something else in the closet is. I kneel to get a better look, and there, in the far corner, a safe is wedged against the wall. I tug at the handle, but the keypad is locked.

I sigh, walking across the room to Greg's nightstand. I open the top drawer and find a tube of eye cream and one of those silk sleep masks the airline gives you on international flights. I check the bottom drawer next, gulping when I find a . . . handgun lying inconspicuously beside a bottle of Advil. Spooked, I clutch my chest, sitting up straighter. Heart racing, I reach inside the drawer, grasping the handle. I've never held a gun before. Should I be worried? Is Greg . . . a criminal? I tell myself not to be ridiculous. Lots of people have guns. This is America, after all.

A little rattled, I delicately set the eerie discovery back inside the bottom drawer. I grab my phone and a beige Chanel bag hanging in the closet, then venture downstairs.

The lower floor is just as sparsely furnished, with more moving boxes stacked around the perimeter. I look inside one—pots and pans—then lift back the lid of another, where I find a collection of bubble-wrapped framed photos. I tear the plastic off an eight-by-ten from our wedding day. There we are, smiling like the two happiest people on earth—bridesmaids and groomsmen flanking us on either side. Some I recognize, others I don't, but what's most surprising is Frankie's notable absence. *Why wasn't she there?*

I set the photo on the coffee table, then venture into the kitchen, where I peer into the Sub-Zero fridge—empty, aside from a few take-out containers and a jar of ketchup. On the granite island is an assortment of brochures, folders, and various other glossy, full-color marketing materials. I open one of the packets, which is filled with sales information for what looks like a new retirement community: *The Danbury Estates: Where Retirement Meets Luxury.* The photos depict smiling people in their seventies and eighties seemingly living their best lives: playing golf, sipping wine beside a rose garden, eating gourmet food served by a chef in a big white hat. So this must be the big "deal" Greg mentioned earlier. I tuck one of the brochures in my bag, then reach for a set of keys on the kitchen island.

If I thought the bedroom was hot, I do a double-take when I step outside, where I'm immediately hit by a wall of humidity. I look right, then left, taking in the sea of houses around me—every one of them virtually the same. *What is this? The Truman Show?* A little girl, no more than eight, pedals her bike down the sidewalk, her older brother on a Razor scooter, just behind.

"Morning, Lena!"

I turn to my right, where a woman in a bathrobe with curlers in her hair is waving from her porch. She's in her late sixties, maybe older—hard to tell.

"Hot as Hades out here, isn't it?" she continues, fanning her face as I approach.

"Indeed," I reply, perspiring more by the second.

She smiles cheerfully, cinching the tie on her robe. "Oh, honey, I just wanted to say how happy Bob and I are to be investors in the Danbury Estates."

I nod, thinking of the marketing materials on the kitchen island.

"Between his bad back and my bad hip"—she pauses, clutching her side—"we just can't wait to move in. And to think that you . . . chose us . . . to come on board. Well, dear, we couldn't be more grateful. Anyway, be sure to tell that wonderful hubby of yours how grateful we are."

"Um, I will," I reply, smiling tentatively, trying my best to follow along.

"Oh," she continues, beaming, "I saw your new billboard in town!"

I stare at her.

"Front and center on North Orange." She nods, her fingers making air quotes. "DISCOVER YOUR SARASOTA PARADISE. When Bob and I drove by last night, I thought to myself, *Our neighbor is a celebrity!* I made him circle back so I could see it a second time. He said, 'Ellen, she lives next door! If you want to see her, just stop by!'" She laughs. "Well, congratulations, dear."

Dear God, I'm a real estate agent, with my face on a billboard. "Um, thanks," I say, forcing a smile. "I'll see you later, okay?"

When I press the key fob, a Mercedes SUV with Florida plates beeps back at me. I slide into the driver's seat and key Jensen's Jewelry into the navigation system.

With the AC blowing full-blast, I turn onto North Orange, immediately slamming my brakes when I notice the billboard Ellen mentioned. There I am, in a glaring magenta pantsuit—arms folded confidently across my chest, a gleaming smile plastered on my face. I pull the car to the side of the road to catch my breath. *Wow, I look like a personal injury lawyer.* Though it's painful, I will myself to take a closer look. DISCOVER YOUR SARASOTA PARADISE! the billboard reads. I'M LENA LESTER, AND I CAN HELP YOU FIND YOUR FOREVER HOME. CALL ME TODAY! It's worse than I could possibly imagine. I'm the cheesiest sort of real estate agent, with the last name Lester.

The jewelry store is just ahead, and I pull into a spot in the parking lot out front.

"Hi," I say to the woman behind the counter. "I'm here to . . . pick up my ring."

"Ah yes," she says. "I recognize you from the billboards. Derrick Lester's wife, right?" she asks, eying me curiously.

I nod, a little taken aback. *Weird, I must have gotten his name wrong.* Greg, Derrick—whatever. It was a long time ago. There's no mistaking Lester, though.

She disappears to the back room, before returning a moment later with a black velvet box. "It's all fixed up," she says, lifting the lid to reveal a stunning gold setting with an enormous diamond at the center. "You'll see that the . . . stone is now secured. You shouldn't have any more issues, with those prongs."

"Wow," I say, a little taken aback as I slip the bauble on my finger. It looks like something you'd see at a museum in London showcasing the crown jewels. "Thank you," I continue, collecting myself. "What do I owe you? I mean . . . for the repairs."

The woman shakes her head, her expression a little strained. "Your husband took care of everything."

"Okay," I say, unable to take my eyes off the enormous diamond on my hand. "Well, thanks."

"Ma'am," the woman says, giving me a long look.

"Yes?"

She pauses, eyes piercing mine, as she opens her mouth to speak, then shakes her head. "Nothing . . . it's nothing. I just . . . hope you're . . . satisfied with our repairs."

"Absolutely, yes," I reply. "Thanks again."

As if mechanically, the corners of her mouth creep upward into a smile. "You have a nice day, all right?"

BACK IN THE CAR, I STARE AT THE ROCK ON MY FINGER FOR A LONG—SWELTERING— moment before turning on the air and reaching for my phone. I search for Frankie's number, which, oddly, isn't listed in my contacts. I sigh, dialing it in manually—hers and Rosie's being the only two I know by heart.

"Hello?" Frankie says, answering on the third ring. "Who is this?" Her voice sounds different—deeper, somehow, but also clipped and impatient.

"Frankie! It's me, Lena!"

There's a long pause on the line, my heart beating faster with every second.

"Why are you calling me?"

"I . . . I'm in Florida. I'm—"

"Still with that douchebag, I take it."

I grip the steering wheel tightly. "Um . . . yeah."

"What's this about, Lena? I don't have much time."

"Oh," I continue, a little hurt. "I was just calling to . . . say hi."

"Okay, then, hi." She pauses. "Is that all?"

"Frankie, what's going on? Why are you acting like this?"

She laughs. "Are you seriously asking *me* that question?"

"Well . . . yeah?"

"Lena, it's been *six years*. You can't just snap your fingers and expect me to forget everything that happened. I mean, if you're having marital problems, I'm sorry, well, not sorry. You should have left that guy a long time ago. Listen, I've got to run." She sighs. "I wish you the best, I really do, but—"

"Frankie, I need your help. I need to know what—"

"Goodbye, Lena."

After she hangs up, I try her number again, but it goes straight to voice mail. I lean back against the edge of the car seat, deeply disturbed and more lost than ever. *What happened to us?* In what version of my life am I estranged from my best friend? She's like oxygen to me, and the thought of losing her? Well, I can barely breathe. Even if this will all vaporize in the morning, I still want to know what happened between us. I *need* to know.

I sit in the car for a few minutes more, thinking about my predicament as I slide the ring off my finger, holding it up to the light. I notice an inscription on the inside of the band. It's tiny—almost impossible to read—but I can just make out the microscopic engraving: 5683 FOREVER, it reads. *What the hell does that mean?*

When my phone buzzes, I perk up for a moment, deflating when I see Greg, er, Derrick's face on the screen. Reluctantly, I answer. "Hey."

"Hey, where are you?"

"At the jewelry shop," I say. "I . . . just picked up my ring."

"Oh good—you're not too far out. I messed up. The Victoria Campbell meeting is at ten, not eleven. I'm on my way. How soon can you get there?"

"I don't know, I'll . . . do my best."

"Thanks," he says. "I'll stall until you arrive. This client, well, she's a big one, babe. I need some of that Lena magic."

"All right," I say, sighing.

"The address is in the calendar. Hurry."

I punch the location into my GPS, just as the woman from the jewelry shop appears in the parking lot, waving her arms at me as she approaches.

"Hey," I say, rolling down my window as a blast of offensively humid air rushes in. "Did I forget something?"

She shakes her head. "I wasn't going to say anything," she begins. "I told myself I wouldn't, but I've seen your billboards. I know what a successful woman you are, and I"—she pauses, biting the edge of her lip—"well, I think you deserve to know the truth."

"What truth?"

She inhales, then exhales deeply. "Your ring," she continues. "When your husband brought it in, I gave it our normal assessment, like we do with all our clients' pieces—you know, checking the size, noting inclusions, yada, yada. Well, when I inspected yours, I . . ." She pauses, swallowing hard. "Listen, I don't know how to tell you this, Mrs. Lester, but that stone is *not* a diamond."

I look down at the ring, thoroughly confused. "Then what is it?"

She shakes her head. "Moissanite, cubic zirconia . . . possibly some other type of knockoff—I don't know. All I can tell you is that it's fake. I'm sorry. I don't know what your husband told you. I just . . . thought you deserved the truth."

I nod, taking it all in, more annoyed than anything else. Who gives someone a knockoff engagement ring? Is this the kind of thing Frankie was alluding to?

Standing beside my car, the woman purses her thin lips as she searches my face. "I really am sorry about this."

"No," I reply, regaining my composure, just like the woman on the billboard. "It's okay."

She nods. "Well, at least he did a good job with that engraving."

I pause, doing my best to follow along.

"Five six eight three," she continues. "It stands for the word *love*, right? On a keypad, anyway. It took me a minute, but when I figured it out, I had to admit . . . pretty clever." Her smile slowly fades. "Anyway, I hope this hasn't upset you."

I shake my head. "I appreciate your honesty—more than you know."

I PULL UP TO AN OLD SPANISH COLONIAL WITH CRACKED STUCCO AND A TILE roof in grave disrepair, clinging to its former glory like an old woman who was crowned prom queen in 1959.

"There you are!" Derrick says as I step out of the car, gravel crunching beneath my pumps.

Wherever we are, it's the boondocks. There isn't another house in sight—not that I'd be able to tell. With layers of overgrowth and vines creeping up the exterior, the property obviously hasn't seen a weed whacker since the first Bush administration. I shift my stance, cautiously eyeing my surroundings as if at any moment a creature might skulk out of the brush and clamp onto my ankle. *Yikes, there are alligators in Florida.*

Derrick, however, seems entirely unfazed. "Ready?" he asks, eagerly, clutching his leather briefcase as he looks up at the derelict home, eyes wide.

I shake my head. "Remind me why we're here again?"

"Lena," he whispers. "I told you. Victoria Campbell. She could be the Danbury Estates' *crown jewel.*"

Like my wedding ring? I keep my thoughts to myself as I follow him to the house, where two stone lions perch on either side of the front door. A green lizard slithers behind one, disappearing into the overgrowth as Derrick rings the doorbell.

A moment later, the hinges creak open, and a frail, older woman appears, squinting into the sunlight. At least eighty, maybe older, with unkempt wispy white hair, and obviously confused, she eyes us suspiciously.

Derrick steps in with a winning smile. "Mrs. Campbell," he says, extending his hand. "A pleasure. We spoke on the phone. I'm Derrick Lester, and this is my wife, Lena."

The woman nods blankly, her gaze shifting back and forth between me and Derrick. "It sure is hot out here!" he says, patting the back of his wrist against his brow. "Mind if we come in?"

"Are you a friend of Larry's?" she asks cautiously.

Derrick pauses, his eyes scouring family photos on the entryway wall behind her. "Well, yes, I am. A good man, Larry."

Mrs. Campbell's face lights up as if Derrick has just uttered the secret code. "Come inside, then," she says graciously, leading us to the living room, where a TV is blaring. An enormous stack of yellowing newspapers teeters on the edge of the coffee table, which is littered with wadded-up tissues and dirty plates and cups. I wince, taking in the sight of her home, but if Derrick is concerned, he doesn't let on. Instead, he opens his briefcase and places a marketing folder in her lap.

"As we discussed on the phone, we believe the Danbury Estates will be a perfect opportunity for you, ma'am," he begins. "A state-of-the-art retirement community, with all the bells and whistles, and, as one of our early, *premiere* investors, you qualify for our upgrade program." He smiles. "Mrs. Campbell, have you ever imagined yourself living in a penthouse suite?"

Her eyes get big. "A penthouse? Like in the movies?"

"Exactly," Derrick replies, pulling a sheet of paper from the packet.

"Larry loves movies," she says. "His favorite actress is Barbra Streisand. Did you see her in *Hello Dolly*?"

"A classic," Derrick replies, turning to me. "Right, Lena?"

I nod uncomfortably.

"All right," Derrick continues, directing the woman's attention back to the folder. "These are all the finishes you can choose from." He grins. "Travertine tile or granite? Jacuzzi hot tub? Walk-in closet? I know it's a lot to consider—and you can have it all—but don't worry, we have time. I'll circle back on the details. The good news is that construction is on track and clipping along well. If we can get the specifications mapped out for your penthouse before the end of the month, you should have no issues moving in by November 1—maybe even sooner. Home for the holidays, right?" He grins, turning to me. "Honey, tell her about the garden."

I pause nervously, remembering the marketing materials this morning. "Uh, the garden, it's—"

"Are there roses?" Mrs. Campbell asks. "Because I love roses. Larry always brings me two dozen on our wedding anniversary." She smiles at me. "He's very romantic."

"That's . . . sweet," I say, casting a wary look in Derrick's direction.

"And, yes, ma'am," he continues, "the Danbury Estates will have its very own rose garden. We're even procuring a sign for the entrance that reads"—he pauses, holding up his hands theatrically—"STOP AND SMELL THE ROSES."

"Well, that sounds delightful," Mrs. Campbell exclaims.

"Yes, yes," Derrick says, extracting a piece of paper from his briefcase and setting it on the table before her. "Now the easy part." He hands her a pen. "All we need is your signature, and we'll take care of the rest."

"And here I thought I'd die in this old house." She pauses, squinting at the document. "This is . . . just wonderful."

"We're happy to help," Derrick continues. "And don't forget, as a premiere investor, your return is likely to be significant."

She smiles, pleased. "Well, I guess my ship finally came in, didn't it? I can't wait to tell Larry." She looks around. "Have you seen him? He should be home by now." She cups her hands to her mouth. "Larry!" she calls. "Larry, come say hi to these nice young people!"

"It's okay," Derrick says, patting her arm. "We'll see Larry next time. I'll stop by in a few days to go over your customizations." He slips the signed contract into his briefcase, before standing up and flashing me a knowing look. "Well, Mrs. Campbell, we should be going. So much work to do, you know. I'll be in touch, okay?"

"All right, dear," she says.

OUTSIDE, DERRICK IS LIKE A TIGHT END WHO'S JUST RUN THE FOOTBALL INTO THE end zone. "Can you believe this?" he asks, almost giddy. "Lena, seriously. Do you have any idea what this property is worth?"

I shake my head, still a little stunned. Derrick, on the other hand, looks like he's about to take a victory lap. He unfastens the top button of his shirt. "Five million, at least."

I look back at the ramshackle dwelling, slightly nauseated. I feel an urge to wash my hands—or vomit. Maybe both.

"Fifteen acres." He looks around—eyes wild, plotting, planning. "That's thirty parcels—at least. Thirty homes. An entire community. Developers will be salivating."

I stare ahead; none of this is adding up. "I don't know, Derrick. Is Mrs. Campbell even in the right state of mind to make such a big decision? Also, what about Larry?"

"Babe. Larry passed away in *1999*. They didn't have children." He grins. "Told you this was a home run."

I clench my fist. "So you lied to her, then?"

"No, no," he says quickly. "Of course not. Look, if her memories of Larry give her comfort, why rock the boat?" He tucks his arm around my waist, smiling tenderly. "You have such a big heart, honey. I love that about you—always worried about others—but, listen, we just closed an enormous deal, and she's getting out of that hellhole. We're helping her; she's helping us. It's a win-win." He opens his briefcase and pulls out the signed document, along with a stack of other pages. "Babe, I've got a full plate today. Mind countersigning and sending this over to Christina at escrow?"

"Wait," I say, taken aback. "What are all of these other pages?"

"Just standard legal stuff," he says. "Be sure to send the PDF out this afternoon, okay? I want to keep this ball *rolling*."

Before I can protest, Derrick kisses my cheek and heads to his car.

15

After Derrick speeds off in his BMW, I stand beside my car, reeling. *What the hell was that?* All those promises he made to that poor woman—they can't possibly be true. He did mention that her buy-in would provide a good return, but my gut tells me something isn't right.

I eye the page Derrick handed to me, thumbing through the others—the "legal stuff." Though I know little of real estate, my years working in finance have taught me a thing or two about contracts, and it's clear that this is a deed of sale. So she just signed over her home, her property to us, in exchange for a "penthouse" in an unfinished retirement community? Yeah, this doesn't add up. I scour the fine print and, near the bottom, spot an address for an LLC, in . . . the Bahamas. *Of course.* I keep reading, and a few more pages in, there it is—the address for the Danbury Estates. According to Google Maps, it's about nine miles away. I get in the car and turn on the engine. It's time to take a little drive.

ON THE WAY, I CALL FRANKIE AGAIN, DISAPPOINTED, THOUGH NOT SURPRISED, when she doesn't pick up. She's stubborn, I know, but I can't shake the sound of her voice earlier—so cold, so foreign . . . like a stranger's. Whatever the reason for our estrangement, it must be significant. I shudder thinking about what circumstances may have led to this.

After a few miles traveling along some nondescript highway, GPS leads me to an exit, then down a winding road flanked by marshy grass—swampland on either side.

I do a double-take when I reach my destination—the supposed site of the "Danbury Estates." There's no construction site, no cranes lifting beams, and certainly no rose garden, only cicadas buzzing in the distance. I hear Derrick's voice in my head—"Home for the holidays, right?"—and cringe, thinking of poor Mrs. Campbell.

The hair on the back of my neck stands on end. This is a total scam. How many other unsuspecting people have signed away their homes to this guy, invested their life savings? I bury my head in my hands, remembering that neighbor, Ellen, on the front porch this morning. Derrick asked me to countersign the document, to send it to escrow, so I'm not exactly an innocent bystander here, but maybe something in between? It makes me sick to think that I may have played a role in his scheme today, even worse that I've known about this all along but didn't speak up. Could I be the Bonnie to his Clyde? Disgusted, I adjust the rearview mirror, eyeing the scar on my cheek—this morning's concealer wearing off in the humidity. If Derrick could con an old woman, obviously he's capable of conning me, too.

I grab my phone, keying in Frankie's number again. But this time, I text instead of call:

I'm so sorry—about everything. Frankie, I'm in trouble. I need to talk to you. You're the only one who can help. Please. I pause, remembering how we vowed to pick up the phone for each other anytime one of us texted the secret code. SOS, I type, before sending the text.

Thirty seconds later, my phone rings—Frankie. "Thank you," I say, picking up, overcome with emotion.

"Okay, I'm listening," she says, a little annoyed. "What is it?"

"Frankie . . . I . . . don't know where to begin."

"Are you okay?" she asks, her tone momentarily softening.

"No," I say. "I'm not. I'm . . . in a world of trouble. Listen, I'm . . . having some memory issues. Amnesia, possibly."

"Maybe you should see a doctor," she suggests, her tone a little dismissive.

"Maybe. But first I need you to . . . help me remember."

"Lena, we haven't spoken in years."

"Right. That's what I need to understand. Why?"

She lets out a groan. "You really want me to say it?"

"I do. Frankie, I know this is hard, but if there was ever a moment in our past when you loved me, I need you to remember that now. I need you to help me understand."

She scoffs. "Are you messing with me or just helping your asshole husband with another one of his con jobs?"

"No," I say, a little breathlessly. "I promise. I wouldn't do that to you."

"Okay, okay," she continues. "All of it—the end of our friendship— it has to do with that jerk you're married to."

"Derrick," I mutter.

"Oh, is that what he's calling himself these days?" She laughs. "Yeah. When you guys met, he seemed too good to be true. I warned you that he was love-bombing—all those trips, dinners, gifts. I was right, of course. But you wouldn't listen—even after that awful night at the bar."

"Wait, what happened at the bar?"

"You know, when you tried to break up a fight he got into—with that thug who said he owed him money. Ringing a bell now? Or maybe I need to remind you of the fourteen stitches on your cheek? I was there—I drove you to the ER."

I pause, touching the scar on my face.

"But . . . Derrick didn't hit me, did he?"

"No, but he might as well have. He put you in a dangerous situation." She sighs. "He's bad news, Lena. You refused to see it then, but you must realize now."

"I do," I say, taking a deep breath. "And you're right—you were right all along. Frankie, listen, Derrick's running some sort of scam, preying on older people. He's soliciting investments for a fancy retirement community that isn't even real."

"Not shocking at all," Frankie replies with a long sigh. "What are you going to do?"

"I don't know . . ."

"You should go to the police."

"Yeah," I say, my heart beating faster.

"Do you have any incriminating evidence on him? Something that'll get him charged, guarantee an arrest?"

"I think so," I reply, eyeing Mrs. Campbell's signed contract on the passenger seat.

"Good," Frankie says. "Lena, I know we've been through a lot—but . . . I'm *worried* about you. You need to keep yourself safe, okay? Who knows what that man is capable of?"

She still cares. "Thanks," I say, my eyes welling up with tears. "Frankie, thank you so much."

I PRESS MY FOOT TO THE PEDAL, DRIVING FAST—TOO FAST. AND YET, IF I SKIDDED out and crashed, would it even matter? I'd just wake up somewhere else, in a new life—my bumps and bruises gone. But what if I don't— what if it all goes . . . black?

This experience has been more than I can bear. I want out of this nightmare. I want it to end, but home feels far-off, and real life a mere memory that remains far from my reach. How many more days of this can I take? How many more alternate realities can I endure before my heart gives out, before I . . . do something crazy? I blink back tears as I accelerate, hurtling down the freeway at eighty-eight miles per hour, then ninety. I could end it all right now, make it all go black with one swerve to the left. I'd careen into the oncoming minivan, and—bam—this could be over. Oh, how I want it to be over. Gripping the wheel, I drift across the center line, which is when time seems to click into slow motion. Images flash through the windshield like snapshots from a scrapbook: A young mother at the wheel, pretty, smiling, with dirty blond hair tucked into a messy ponytail. Oblivious to my approach, her mouth opens and closes as if she's singing. In the backseat, two small children, both in car seats, clap their hands happily.

I press my foot on the brake pedal, swerving right and narrowly avoiding the near-collision. Yes, I want this nightmare to come to an end, but not by creating another one. I take a deep breath, wiping fresh tears from my cheeks. There must be a way out of this. There has to be. But, until I find it, no more going off the rails. I have to stay strong.

I PULL INTO THE DRIVEWAY, GRATEFUL THAT OUR CHATTY NEIGHBOR ISN'T ON THE front porch. Inside, I race upstairs, to the safe in the closet, where I punch in several combinations of numbers, with no luck. Discouraged, I take a moment to regroup and catch my breath, which is when I remember the engraving inside my ring: *5683*.

I press the digits into the keypad—voilà—and peer inside, jaw dropping when I see the guns—these ones larger—and several bundles of cash, each bound with a rubber band. I reach for the manila envelope on the top shelf and tear open the flap. Inside is a stack of . . . passports. The first two are American—both Derrick's, though one lists the name Greg. I shudder, flipping through the others—Greece, Mexico, Canada—all with the same photo, but different names.

I freeze when I hear pounding on the door below—urgent, loud. I don't remember securing the dead bolt when I came in—did I?

Hands shaking, I tuck the envelope back into the safe, securing the lock, before reaching into Derrick's nightstand for the small gun I discovered this morning—just in case. Hands shaking, I clutch it behind my back as I make my way downstairs, one step at a time, my forehead coated in sweat.

"Lester, you in there?" a man shouts from the other side of the door. His voice is deep and his accent thick.

Bracing myself, I peer through the peephole. "Who is it?" I ask, my voice shaky and high-pitched.

"It's Sal," he says. "Tell Lester to get out here. I have words for him."

"Uh, I'm sorry," I say, trembling from head to toe. "He's not . . . home right now."

"You lying to me, lady?"

"No, no! I swear . . . he's not here."

The footsteps move from the front porch to the side yard, and I panic when I hear a tap on the living room window to my left, where a large bald man is looking in at me. I scream as my body tenses. The only thing that stands between us is a couple of panes of glass.

"Lester lied to me," he shouts, pressing his hand against the window. "He owes me money, and I'm going to get it."

"Please," I say, frightened. "Derrick isn't home. I don't know anything about this."

The man laughs. "I'm no dummy, miss. I've seen those billboards around town. I know you're rolling in it." He leans down, lifting a rock from the landscaping, which he smashes against the window. I brace myself, heart racing as shards of glass fly through the air. "A little present to remember me by."

Acting on instinct, I pull out the gun—doing my best to steady my shaking hands as I secure my grip, pointing the barrel in his direction.

"Whoa, whoa, lady," he says, inching away from the window, hands in the air. "I'll go, but you tell that scumbag husband of yours that I'll be back."

I watch from the window as my would-be intruder climbs into an oversize pickup truck on the street, exhaling deeply when he drives off. Minutes pass. How many? I have no idea, but when the doorbell rings, my heart seizes. Still holding the gun, I peer through the peep-hole again, relieved to see a friendly face—Ellen, the woman next door.

"Lena?" she asks as I open the door. "Is everything okay? I heard shouting . . . glass breaking."

I set the gun down, tears streaming down my face.

"Oh, honey," she says, wrapping her arms around me. "What happened? Are you hurt?"

I shake my head, melting into her ample embrace. It feels good to be hugged—to be cared for. "A man tried to break in. He said Derrick owed him money."

"Should I have Bob call the police?"

"I'll make the call," I say, latching the dead bolt behind us. "But first, Ellen, can we talk?"

"Of course, dear," she says, eyes wide.

We step over shards of glass in the living room. "I need to tell you something," I begin, rubbing my forehead as she sits on the sofa beside me. "My husband—his business—well, it may not be . . . legit."

Ellen gasps. "What on earth do you mean, dear?"

"I mean that . . . Derrick hasn't been honest—with any of us." I take a deep breath. "Much of what I know about him . . . I just realized . . . isn't true. Anyway, whatever money you've given him, for whatever investment—it's likely a sham."

She presses her hand to her chest, taking in my words. "Dear Lord, we gave him our life savings—everything we had!"

"I'm . . . so sorry. Words aren't enough, but I promise you: I'm going to do everything in my power to make it right."

Ellen nods, obviously shell-shocked. "Lena," she continues slowly, "how long have you *known*?"

I shake my head, wondering, worrying. Maybe I became accustomed to ignoring the red flags, or, worse, just couldn't bear to face the truth. I exhale deeply. "I didn't know, but it's not an excuse—I should have—and, for that, I feel complicit."

"No," she says, reaching for my hand. "You're a good person, dear. You just got wrapped up with a bad man."

I pry a shard of glass from the edge of the sofa, longing for her words to be true. Frankly, I'm ashamed of this version of myself: the Realtor on billboards with her pantsuits and bright smile. But if you peel back the layers, a darker picture emerges, one I want nothing to do with.

Ellen and I sit in silence for a few minutes, each of us processing the ugly facts that have just come to light. In these past days, I've trudged through the depths of loss, felt the warmth of family, friendship, and forgiveness, but also the chill of betrayal and shame. I've seen the consequences of ignoring my instincts and felt the power that comes from learning to trust myself again. I've come face-to-face with love—sometimes just little glimmers, other times all-out flames that, if properly stoked, might even burn for a lifetime.

I was so broken, so lost, when I arrived at Rosie's house seven days ago. Has it really been only a week? It feels like a lifetime. A life sentence. I may still be broken, and more lost than ever, but there's a force building inside of me that wasn't there before, a force I can only describe as *knowing*. I know now that there's more to life than winning in the corporate world and following what I thought was the prescription for the perfect life: follow the plan, advance to the next level, win the prize. Look where that got me.

"I'm . . . so sorry," I say to Ellen, searching her face, overcome with emotion. I can't stop thinking about how I got entangled in this mess. Who we choose to partner with, to love, carries such weight. While it doesn't define us, it does change us, whether we like it or not. And yet, the fact remains: we get to choose—I get to choose. And I know one thing for certain, a truth that courses through my veins right now: *I do not choose this.*

Ellen nods, her expression solemn. "Bob's younger brother is an attorney. We'll talk to him."

I swallow hard. "I wish I—"

"One thing at a time," she interjects with a calming smile. "Now, are you going to make the call, or shall I?"

I nod, reaching for my phone, staring at the screen for a long moment before punching in the numbers.

"This is 911, what's your emergency?"

I take a deep breath. "Hi, my name is Lena, and I'd like to report a crime."

PART
EIGHT

16

When I wake the next morning, my mind goes straight to the terrible scene from last night: police interviews, Derrick's arrest, Ellen breaking the unsettling news to her husband, whose face immediately turned white. I didn't feel safe staying at the house, so I checked into a nearby Holiday Inn, falling asleep as soon as my head hit the pillow.

As I look around the room, I'm both relieved to be free from yesterday's nightmare and hopeful I haven't been transported into another one. Fortunately, I'm alone—for the moment, at least. The large bedroom is attached to a sitting area beside a balcony, and the décor is curiously tropical with palm-print art on the walls and an enormous conch shell on the coffee table. It looks more like a hotel than a home, and, as evidenced by the Four Seasons Hualalai room service menu on the bedside table, my hunch is confirmed. So I've gone from a roadside Holiday Inn to a five-star resort. Nice upgrade, if you could call it that. But the bigger question is: What am I doing here, and *who* am I with?

I glance at the ring on my left hand—gold, with a large rectangular diamond solitaire. It looks familiar, but then again, so do most radiant-cut rings in that classic, cookie-cutter, Tiffany sort of way. But, no, I've definitely seen this one before.

I freeze when the door clicks open, the hair on the back of my neck standing on end. *Kevin?*

"Morning, sleepyhead," he says, holding two coffee cups. "I got your latte."

Waves of shock course through me as I think back to that night at Le Rêve in San Francisco. Only a week has passed since I arrived at Rosie's house, an emotional mess over the breakup, which now feels like a century ago. Besides, I've had more important things to deal with. But now this? I'm married to Kevin, like none of it even happened?

I take a sip as he sits on the edge of the bed beside me. "It was hard to tell in the dark when we got in last night, but this place is gorgeous," he continues, smoothing his perfectly coiffed hair—thick and dark, always combed in place, not a strand askew. "I went out for a walk at sunrise, then hit the gym. Oh, and I booked us a cabana by the pool. It wasn't cheap, but I figured if there was ever a time to splurge, it's on our honeymoon."

Our honeymoon. I freeze, processing the words he's just uttered. So, in this version of reality Kevin proposed, and here we are, living happily ever after. It's what I wanted before all of this started—at least, what I *thought* I wanted.

"I keep getting texts from people saying how much they loved our wedding," he continues. "It really was special, wasn't it?"

"Um, yeah," I mutter as he lifts a pink garment from the floor (mine, obviously), which he neatly folds and tucks into a dresser drawer.

"My messy, messy wife," he says playfully.

As I gulp my coffee, he adjusts the collar of his pressed blue linen shirt, smiling into a nearby mirror, his perfectly white teeth gleaming. "All right, my bride," he continues. "I'm going to head down to the cabana. Why don't you get ready, then meet me by the pool?"

I nod as Kevin gives me a quick kiss, slips on his Ray-Ban aviators, then heads out the door. I venture to the bathroom and take a long look at myself in the mirror. My tan skin (a spray tan, no doubt) is a sharp contrast against my white silk lace-trimmed nightie. Honeymoon attire, I guess. I'm thinner than usual, and toned, too. I cringe, wondering if I'd subjected myself to months of pre-wedding CrossFit. I *hate* CrossFit. My hair is longer, and also Barbie-blond, curled in those Instagram-perfect, zigzaggy waves that I've never had the patience or interest to master.

I run a brush through the ends, and a clump of hair falls out and lands on the floor beside my freshly pedicured toes (bubblegum-pink). Fortunately, I don't appear to be a cancer patient. It's just a hair extension. Me? Hair extensions? I'm equally surprised by the massive amount of skin care and makeup products splayed out on the counter, as if I've barged my own personal Sephora across the Pacific. Has marriage to Kevin made me mental, or just someone who's trying *way* too hard?

I can't even begin to imagine how long it takes me (*this* me) to get ready, nor do I have the slightest clue where to start, so I reduce my fourteen-hundred-step get-ready process to two: sunscreen and lip balm. No need to go full glam for a day at the pool, I reason.

In the dresser, I find a bikini and matching sarong, then slide my feet into a pair of Gucci sandals. I spot my phone charging on the entryway console beside a card that reads: *Welcome Mr. and Mrs. Canfield.* Lena Canfield. I used to turn the name over in my mind on repeat, relishing the mere thought of being Kevin's wife, but now it hits a different note—somehow less marital bliss and more, well, cloistering, like a wool sweater that scratches my skin.

I reach for a bottle of sunscreen and a book, which I toss into a woven bag, before noticing a gift on the coffee table: a Scrabble box, tied with a white bow, next to a bottle of pinot grigio. I tear open the card:

To the beautiful bride and handsome groom,
    Wishing you both a happy life of love and laughter—and fun and games.
                    All my love,
                    Rosie

"HI," I SAY, SINKING INTO THE CABANA BESIDE KEVIN.

"Don't look now," he whispers covertly, "but Cameron Diaz is at five o'clock."

I turn to the right, where the blond actress sits at the edge of the pool, dangling her long, tan legs in the water as she laughs with the man beside her.

"Babe," Kevin whispers, shaking his head, "you're being too *obvious*."

"Oh, sorry," I reply, looking away quickly. "I don't think she saw me."

He nods, his irritation passing as he folds my rumpled towel into a perfect square, then leans his head back against the chaise. "Paradise, isn't it?"

"Yeah," I say, reaching for the sunscreen.

"No makeup today, huh?"

I shrug. "Aren't we going swimming?"

"Right, yeah," he says, studying my face. "I'm just surprised. You never leave the house without foundation."

I touch my face self-consciously. "Sorry," I say, less apologetic and more sarcastic, as I slip on my sunglasses before he has a chance to comment on my lack of mascara.

"No, no," he continues. "You just look different, but still beautiful, of course."

"Look what Rosie sent us," I say, changing the subject as I pull the Scrabble box from my bag. "Wine, too. Thoughtful, right?"

"Ah, how nice," Kevin replies.

"Should we . . . play?"

"Babe, you know games aren't really my . . . thing."

"Right," I say, a little deflated, reaching for the book in my bag as Kevin waves down a pool attendant to adjust the nearby umbrella when a stream of sunlight filters into our cabana.

"Just a little more to the left," he says to the man, who dutifully rolls the umbrella forward and back, then to the left again, per

Kevin's instructions. "Come to think of it, maybe if you push it a *bit* more to the right." He pauses, as if calculating the exact angle of the sun, and holding this poor man hostage while he deliberates.

"Kevin," I whisper, more worried about the pool attendant than a little sun on my face, "I think it's fine."

He frowns, then lets out a long sigh, ultimately deciding to adjust the cabana's curtain before handing the befuddled hotel employee a ten-dollar bill. "Thanks, man," he says. "Appreciate your help."

I don't care about the damn umbrella, I want to say, *just play a game with me!* Instead, I hold my tongue, and decide to take a plunge. Kevin follows, with towels for both of us.

"Wait," he says as I climb in, "shouldn't you put your hair up?"

I shake my head, confused.

Kevin smiles. "Hold on, I think I have a hair tie in my bag. Just a sec." He returns a moment later with a scrunchie, which I stare at for a long moment, before reluctantly twisting my hair into high bun. He's either the perfect husband, or the world's most anal.

We swim a few laps, at our own pace and in our own lanes—an apt metaphor for the marriage I've just found myself in. Sure, Kevin has always been somewhat of a perfectionist (don't even get me started on his sock drawer), but this is like perfectionism on steroids. He's uptight and rigid. What's worse is that he seems to expect that I fit into his carefully scripted regimen. Is this version of myself programmed to fall in line?

This isn't the marriage I envisioned—far from it. I can't help but notice the couple in the shallow end, about our age. They're sipping cocktails, obviously a little tipsy—she on his lap, his arms wrapped around her waist. Would Kevin ever hold me like that, or would he bristle at the thought of it?

I towel off, heading back to the cabana, where I order two margaritas, with salt on the rim. The drinks arrive just as Kevin returns, frowning. "Uh, sir? We didn't order these."

"Oh, I did," I say quickly, correcting him.

He laughs. "Honey, it's barely eleven a.m. Seriously?"

"Seriously," I say, officially annoyed. The waiter stands motion-less and wide-eyed, obviously hesitant to pick a side, but I choose mine. "Thank you, sir," I continue, ignoring Kevin. "I'll take both."

He folds his arms across his chest as I have a sip, licking a bit of smoky black volcanic salt from the rim. "What was *that* all about?"

I shrug. "I feel like having a drink. What's the big deal?"

"Okay," he says. "It's just . . . not like you, that's all." He scratches his head. "I mean, you never drink in the morning—or sleep in, for that matter—and, I have to admit, I'm a little shocked that you haven't hit the gym yet."

"The gym? No, thanks." I take another sip. "Aren't we supposed to be on vacation?"

"Totally," he replies, his good-natured expression returning. "You just seem a little . . . off today, that's all."

That's because I am *off,* I want to say. Instead, I busy myself with the lunch menu, stomach growling. "Maybe I'm just hungry."

I flag down a waiter and order fish tacos, with extra aioli and fries, before handing the menu to Kevin, which he studies momen-tarily with a critical eye.

"I'm going to pass," he finally says, holding up his hand virtu-ously. "The keto options are lacking. I think I'd rather hold out for dinner."

Anyway. I delve back into my book until lunch arrives, which looks divine. I feel Kevin's eyes on me as I dig in, wiping a bit of aioli from the corner of my mouth. "You sure you don't want a bite? This is outrageously good."

"No, no," Kevin replies, clutching his ice water like a rosary around his neck.

"Suit yourself," I say, reaching for the second margarita as he turns back to his iPad.

Sure, Kevin has always been disciplined, principled, but he was fun, wasn't he? I think back to the night we met—at a karaoke bar

in San Francisco for a mutual friend's birthday party. We somehow got paired to sing a song together—"Brandy" by the O'Jays. I
smile to myself, remembering how awkward it was, how off-key we
sounded, but also how much fun we had. Then again, Kevin never
would sing karaoke with me after that—even when I begged him to
on the night of our first anniversary. No, the more time passed, the
more buttoned-up he seemed to become. Now that we're married,
he's clearly taken that to exponential levels. I watch as he wipes his
sunglasses with a lens cloth from his bag, holding them up to the
light until every last smudge is buffed clean.

"Hey," he says a moment later, slipping on his shirt. "I need to
make some work calls. Catch up with you a little later?"

"Okay," I reply, slipping back into the pool, cocktail in hand.

"Your husband is soooooo handsome," says a woman who appears to be in her early fifties, swimming over to me. She wipes a
strand of her dark hair from her face, revealing a touch of gray at the
temples. "Are you two on your . . . *honeymoon?*"

"Thanks," I say, forcing a smile. "And, yes, guilty as charged."

"Awww, newlyweds!" She smiles nostalgically. "I'm Gina." She
points across the pool. "See the guy under the umbrella, good hair,
reading a book?"

I look over, then nod, as the man of the moment runs his hand
through his chin-length salt-and-pepper hair, oblivious to us gawking
from the pool.

"That's my husband, Grant," she says, proudly. "Damn, why do
men get better-looking as they age? I mean, I'm not complaining. I get
to be married to him, and he's amazing. But it's not fair, you know?"

I laugh, loving her immediately. "I know, it isn't fair. But for the
record, your husband does have amazing hair—and so do you!"

"You're too young to know how menopause wreaks its havoc,"
she replies, tugging at her long dark ponytail. "Honey, I may be going down, but I'm going down with a *fight*." She grins. "These are
extensions."

"Same," I say, gesturing to my messy bun, before taking the last sip of my drink. "Where are you guys from?"

"LA," Gina says. "Grant's a history professor at UCLA. I work in Hollywood."

"Oh wow."

"I know, so LA, right?" She grins. "I started my career in publishing—in New York. I always thought I'd become a book editor, something like that, but you know how things go. I ended up getting hired as a book scout, then moved to LA to work at a studio. I met Grant, and, well, the rest is history." She takes a sip of her drink. "How about you?"

"Uh," I reply, trying to remember what biographical sketch applies to the moment. "San Francisco," I finally say. "I . . . work in finance—investor relations. But I'm from the Seattle area, Bainbridge Island, if you know it."

"I do!" Gina exclaims. "There's a famous author who lives there. I was on the team that turned one of her books into a movie for Universal. Sounds like a lovely place."

"It is," I say. "I miss it."

She glances back at her husband, nose still buried in his book. "It feels like a million years since our honeymoon. Oh, the memories. We're celebrating our twenty-fifth wedding anniversary on this trip."

"Congratulations."

"Soak it all up, honey—all the newness, all the firsts. Sometimes I wish I could go back and relive the beginning of our marriage—before the kids." She pauses, laughing. "Before I needed Spanx. The early days are so special. It's the two of you against the world."

"Yeah," I say, pretending to understand.

"Let me ask you this," she adds, leaning in. "What sealed the deal for you? As in, what made you want to jump into wedded bliss? His breakfast-making skills? A mutual love of Will Ferrell? The way he treats his mother?"

I laugh. "Definitely not his breakfast-making skills."

She grins. "Then what?"

"Um, I guess it was . . . a combination of things?"

"Right," she continues. "When you know, you know."

"How about you?" I ask, tossing the ball back in her court.

Her expression turns nostalgic, eyes drifting out to the ocean, before nodding decidedly. "On our third date, he made me laugh so hard I peed my pants. Like, for real."

"Wow," I say, laughing. "Seriously?"

"Uh-huh," she continues. "Yeah, he's a professor, but Grant is fun—like *really fun*. Never a dull moment with my guy."

"I love that," I say, a little envious as I try to recall a time Kevin made me laugh, though I come up empty.

"Well," my new friend says, bobbing in the water, "I better get back to the hubs. I'm sure we'll see each other around." She grins.

"Wait, I didn't even get your name!"

"Lena," I say.

She winks. "Have *fun*!"

FUN IS HARDLY HOW I'D CHARACTERIZE MY AFTERNOON, WHICH I MOSTLY SPEND avoiding Kevin and staring at the clock, willing the minutes to pass. After a quick shower, I slip into a halter-neck maxi-sundress and head to the beach. I find an empty chaise lounge under the shade of a palm tree. Yawning, I lean back against the cushion, exhausted—mentally, anyway. I can't help but fantasize about making my escape. Maybe if I close my eyes, I'll fall asleep, and this will all drift away.

A shiver creeps down my spine when I feel a tap on my shoulder. *Kevin.*

"There you are," he says, sitting on the edge of my chaise lounge. "What are you doing down here?"

I rub my eyes. "Just relaxing."

"Right, well, while you were napping, I went on an epic hike."

His self-righteous tone grates my nerves; it takes every ounce of my strength not to clock his perfect jaw.

Fortunately, Gina, my friend from the pool, approaches, saving me from arrest.

"Look, it's Barbie and Ken!" she says, giggling as she turns to her husband. "Grant, aren't they the most adorable newlyweds you've ever seen?"

Her husband smiles, extending his hand to Kevin, then to me.

"You two coming to the luau?" Gina asks, pointing to the nearby lawn, which is studded with gaslit tiki torches.

"Nah," Kevin begins, "we're—"

"Sure," I interject. "I've always wanted to learn the hula."

"Yay," Gina squeals. "Come on, let's go together!"

"I don't know about this, Lena," Kevin whispers tentatively, as a woman in a grass skirt anoints us each with a floral lei.

Our native instructors sway their hips, encouraging us to do the same. Gina and Grant fit right in, dancing effortlessly to Hawaiian slack-key music as I attempt to follow along pathetically.

"I'm awful," I say to Gina, laughing.

"We all are," she replies. "That's the point." She glances at Kevin, who's standing alone, arms folded across his chest, brooding. "I take it he's not into the hula?"

I shrug, unable to hide my annoyance.

Gina grimaces. "Tell him to stop being an NPC and get out here!"

"NPC?"

"Oh," she replies, with a chuckle. "You clearly don't have teenage boys. NPC is video-game-speak for 'non-player character'—you know, like a person who's there, but not really there?" She laughs, continuing to talk as she moves her hips in a circular pattern, but I'm too lost in thought to make out her words. "It's become quite the meme in our house."

Kevin, a non-player character? Totally. But did Gina also, unknowingly, diagnose *me*? All those years winning at the corporate game, striving for the perfect partner, perfect life—I was hardly an active participant. I was merely playing a part, like an . . . NPC.

"Hey," Kevin says, reaching for my hand. "Our dinner reservation is in a few minutes." He smiles politely at Gina, then back at me. "We should probably cut out."

"You two have a beautiful night," she says, before Grant gives her a spin that looks professionally choreographed. I'm struck by their synchronicity, the way they flow together across the lawn: He senses her next move; she anticipates his. They know how to read each other, how to harmonize, like two beautiful instruments tuned in the same key. But Kevin and me? From the outside looking in, we're #couplegoals, I suppose, but peel back the façade and it's an entirely different story. Together, we're uncoordinated and sorely out of tune. We don't know how to dance in time. In fact, I now realize that we never did.

AT THE RESTAURANT, I PICK AT MY PLATE, DISSECTING THE BEETS FROM THE ARU- gula, swirling my fork around in circles to pass the time. If Kevin feels any tension, he doesn't let on; in fact, he expertly steers our conversation from one topic to the next, avoiding the most important subject: us.

"I got a text from Matt, today," he says in a breaking-news sort of tone, the way one might preface a story about someone's grandma who passed or a friend who got mugged. It takes a moment, but I connect the dots. Matt is . . . Kevin's high school best friend—right. "Apparently he and Natalie are expecting again," Kevin continues. "I think that makes baby number . . . four? Or is it *five*?" He rolls his eyes as if we're in lockstep about parenthood, or, rather, in our annoyance of other people's parenthood journeys.

"Can you even *imagine* having all those kids?" he continues, equal parts baffled and exhausted.

I shrug. "I don't know. I mean . . . maybe?"

"Wait," Kevin says quickly. "You're not *reconsidering* what we talked about, are you? Lena, I thought we agreed that kids were off the table."

"Well," I begin, proceeding cautiously, "I'm allowed to have second thoughts, aren't I?"

He laughs, refolding his napkin into a perfect rectangle as the smile disappears from his face like a fading sunset. "You're kidding, right?"

"No, actually. I'm not."

Kevin leans back in his chair, flinching as if I've just tossed a stick of dynamite across the table. "Diapers, strollers . . . tantrums . . ." He shakes his head. "You know I'm not that guy."

With his spotless Porsche, fancy Italian espresso machine, and a sock drawer that would make Marie Kondo swoon, no, Kevin is not that guy. While I may have once found these qualities endearing—exceptional, even—I see things differently now. Kevin is not necessarily a bad guy. He's just not my guy.

We pick at our dinners, each of us in our own private world on opposite sides of the table.

"I'm sorry," Kevin finally says, breaking the silence. "I didn't mean to—"

"It's okay," I reply, forcing a smile. "I understand."

He sighs, his pinched expression softening as his mouth opens, letting out a yawn. "That hike really wiped me out. Should we call it a night?"

I shake my head. "You go ahead. I'm going to sit outside for a bit, look at the stars. They say that you can see the constellations in Hawaii better than anywhere on earth."

Kevin shrugs, yawning again.

"Don't wait up," I say as he rises to his feet, giving me an obligatory kiss on the cheek.

"WHAT CAN I GET STARTED FOR YOU, MISS?" THE BARTENDER ASKS AS I SLIDE INTO a stool at the little tiki bar by the beach.

"I don't know," I say with a sigh. "Maybe some kind of potion to fix my life?"

"One of those days, huh?"

I nod. "White wine usually does the trick."

"Sauvignon blanc?"

"Perfect," I say as he uncorks a bottle, giving me a generous pour, just as Gina approaches, waving.

"Hey! I thought that was you!" She slips into the stool beside me, eying my shoulders. "Uh-oh, looks like someone got a little too much sun today."

I nod, wincing at the sight of my arms. "Yeah, probably should have reapplied my sunscreen—oops."

"Grant's the same way. SPF is his best friend. Without it, the man turns into a lobster." She laughs. "Anyway, he's at the front desk booking a snorkeling trip for us tomorrow, which is, honestly, the last thing I want to do, but sometimes you take one for the team, you know?" She grins, looking around. "Where's the hubs?"

"Kevin turned in early," I reply indifferently, but there's no fooling Gina, who raises an eyebrow.

"Everything all right in paradise?" she asks, ordering herself a Negroni.

Tears sting my eyes as I search her face, my mouth opening, but no words come out.

"Come here," she says, leaning in to embrace me as I begin to weep. "What happened, sweetie?"

I want to tell her everything about my predicament: Kevin, how lonely I am, how lost I feel. I want to say it all, but I don't.

"Lena?" she says, clutching my shoulders. "What can I do to help?"

"It's just been a . . . really hard week," I say, dabbing a napkin to my tearstained cheeks. "It's a bit too complicated to explain."

"Try me," she says, taking a sip of her drink.

"Nah," I say, pulling myself together. "How about I tell you a story instead—an idea for one of your movies."

She leans in. "Shoot."

"So, there's this woman," I begin. "She's never really known true love. Sure, there were plenty of opportunities—first dates, relationships, what-ifs—but nothing ever stuck. Maybe it's because of her childhood, her mother's relationship drama and subsequent death, or the fact that she had trouble trusting her gut and opening herself up to new possibilities. But then she goes home to visit her aunt, falls asleep, and the next morning she wakes up in Paris, married to a Frenchman she met at a wedding a decade prior. The following day, it's a farmer in Pennsylvania from years ago; after that, her high school boyfriend; then an Irish guy she met on a train in Switzerland after college. With each day comes a different reality, a different relationship from her past that she has the chance to experience as if she'd chosen it, as if she'd said yes."

"Not bad," she says, intrigued. "So, it's a rom-com, then?"

"More like a horror film," I reply sarcastically.

Gina laughs. "What would you call the movie?"

I smile, thinking of Spencer, that night on Bainbridge Island. *"Insignificant Others."*

"I dig that," Gina replies, glancing at her phone. "Maybe I can help you find an agent. You've got to be really careful with agents."

"Thanks," I say, taking another sip.

"Shoot," she says, looking down at her phone. "It's Grant. He needs my ID for the rental car tomorrow." She hugs me again. "No more tears, all right?"

"All right," I promise.

"And, sweetie, whatever you're going through, you'll get through it. I know you will."

I let out a long sigh. "Well, I've got to get through this night first. Honestly, I'd pay a small fortune to get my hands on a sleeping pill."

"Oh, you want an Ambien?" She opens her purse. "It's the only way I can survive a long flight—completely knocked out."

I nod. "Yes, *please.*"

She hands me a little white pill, which I immediately wash down with a sip of wine. "This will send you off to dreamland. In the morning, it'll all be better."

I hope so.

She winks. "See you tomorrow at the pool?"

I nod. "Yeah . . . tomorrow."

I TOSS MY SANDALS ON A ROCK, THEN SINK MY BARE FEET INTO THE WARM SAND, letting the wind have its way with my hair—to hell with the extensions.

Thanks to the Ambien, my eyelids grow heavier with each step. When I spot a chaise lounge ahead, I lie down, covering my legs with a discarded towel. The beach is empty—just me and the night sky speckled with stars, which keep me company like old friends—the kind that stay long after everyone's left the party to help clean up and load the dishwasher.

"Please," I whisper, chin trembling as I set my glass in the sand. "I want to go home. Please let me go home."

I can barely keep my eyes open. Sleep hovers, ready to pounce, and with one last yawn, I let it . . . take me away.

PART
NINE

17

What's that sound? I can't quite place the shrill, high-pitched cry, but I think it's coming from . . . under the covers? I peel back the sheets and retrieve what looks like some sort of . . . walkie-talkie? Whatever it is, it's broadcasting a noise that makes my skin crawl.

I look to my left, peering over the enormous pile of pillows at the center of the king-size bed—a barricade?—and see the muscular arm of a man sleeping beside me. He shifts, groaning. "What time is it?" he mutters, obviously annoyed, as if I'm the sole perpetrator of his disturbed sleep.

"Um, six thirty-two a.m.," I reply, eying the alarm clock on my bedside table. I brush my hair from my face, noticing the ring on my hand—gold with a large princess-cut diamond that's encircled in more diamonds.

He yawns. "Can you get her this morning, *please*? I have that big meeting today. Remember?"

My heart beats faster as the crying intensifies. "Uh . . . okay," I say, as he presses a pillow over his head, presumably to block out the noise—or me?

I'm too stunned—horrified?—by the grating noise to think of much else, like where I am or who I'm with. Instead, I climb out of bed like a zombie, tiptoeing through the door and down the hallway as the wailing intensifies. When I get to the third door on my right the sound reaches a fever pitch. Cautiously, I turn the doorknob, peering inside as my knees almost give out. Just ahead, clutching the railing of a white crib, is a little girl—a baby—in pink pajamas, with curly dark ringlets cascading around her face. When she notices me, her brown eyes light up and the crying turns to happy babbling.

I can't move or speak. Instead, I stand in the doorway as I take in the sight. In Ireland, I became a stepmom, and today? Could this be a child of my own? The mere thought is both moving and dizzying, especially after my experience on the farm with Nathan. I think back to the scar on my abdomen, and yet, here is this precious child. *My* child?

Pink wooden letters on the opposite wall spell out her name: SABRINA. "*Sabrina*," I whisper in awe. She has my forehead—my nose! For the first time in my life, I understand the concept of love at first sight.

Blinking back tears, I approach her crib, as she coos with delight, holding her arms out to me. But I pause, suddenly filled with worry. I don't know anything about babies.

Sabrina makes a grunting sound as she points to the floor, where a little brown teddy bear has obviously fallen through the crib slats. I hand it to her, which elicits more happy sounds. What am I supposed to do next? *Maybe she'll teach me?* Sabrina flaps her arms, reaching for me, obviously wanting to be picked up. I take a deep breath, reaching into the crib slowly, methodically, as if I'm extracting a bomb on the verge of explosion. I place my hands beneath each of her arms and lift her up into the air, holding her out in front of me, arms stiffly extended, which is when I notice a wet spot on her pajamas. Oh no. No, no. Her diaper leaked!

She giggles as I scour the room, contemplating my next move. I spot a changing table by the window—I mean, I think that's what it is—with a stack of disposable diapers on the shelf below. *Here goes nothing.*

"Okay, Sabrina," I say, feigning confidence, but truthfully I'm a nervous wreck, "we're going to change your diaper!" I gently lay her on the table, but she immediately rolls to her side, wiggling back into a crawling position and nearly falling over the edge.

"No, no! Be careful!"

She giggles, inching to the edge again as if this is a funny game.

Fortunately, I'm able to wrangle her back into place, this time keeping one hand on her belly, while the other fumbles for a diaper.

"There," I say, once I've finally managed to unzip her pajamas. Sabrina seems to find this all wildly amusing as I remove her soaked diaper, which must weigh as much as she does. I pause for a beat, Sabrina naked and wriggling from my grasp on the changing table. Wait, don't I need, um, baby wipes? Yes, I decide. Okay, so *where are the wipes*? I hold her in place on the changing table again as I search the shelf below. *Nothing.* "Okay," I mutter, lifting her up again in the same stiff fashion as before, but this time she's nude and we're staring at each other in face-off fashion. "Baby wipes," I say, looking into her big brown eyes. "Can you help me find baby wipes?"

Sabrina giggles again as I set her on the floor and search the room once more. I pick out a clean outfit from her dresser, but when I look down to lift her up again, she's *gone.*

"Sabrina!" I cry, panicked, before I catch a glimpse of her bare bottom as she crawls out of the doorway. I run ahead, surprised by her speed as I chase down the hall after her to the living room, where she pulls herself up to stand at the edge of the coffee table, right next to a pack of baby wipes, which she pats with her chubby hand.

"There they are," I say, relieved, but also in awe. "You were trying to show me, weren't you?"

She coos as a stream of liquid trickles down her legs to the fancy-looking Persian rug below. "Oh no! No, no, no . . ." I freeze again, triaging the situation. "Okay," I say, taking a deep breath. "It's okay. We just need to get this . . . diaper on you."

Sabrina babbles as I lay her on the sofa, making an awkward first pass with the wipes. After three failed attempts with the diaper, I finally succeed, though the final presentation appears a little lopsided. Getting her dressed is an altogether different challenge, however. While I do manage to slide her shirt over her head, the pants are a no-go—too much wiggling. "Well, I guess we're not doing pants today," I finally say, letting out a defeated sigh.

While Sabrina busies herself with a toy, I take in my surroundings, admiring the mid-century modern home and its airy, light-filled open floor plan. The well-appointed kitchen has all the bells and whistles, including black granite countertops and a double-decker wine fridge. Outside the adjoining dining room, palm trees line the edge of a rectangular-shaped infinity pool wedged against the hillside. I peer out the sliding glass door, taking in the expansive city view, which is immediately familiar. This is Los Angeles, for sure—I squint to make out the skyline—but the view is . . . Burbank, possibly—no, Universal City. Ten years ago, when Frankie had a brief stint in LA, I flew down to visit her. I laugh, remembering how we ended up at a random Halloween party in . . . Studio City, I think. The view is nearly identical.

I recall something else from that night—*a man*. He was tall, Black, ridiculously good-looking—even in that costume. I laugh to myself, remembering the horror and hilarity of how he'd shown up as one half of a peanut-butter-and-jelly sandwich. He was the jelly; his date—the peanut butter—stood him up. I, on the other hand, went in full Gatsby attire, wearing a flapper dress borrowed from Frankie. He and I danced. We laughed. He'd asked me to have dinner with him the following weekend, but I had to fly home a few days later, nor was I interested in a long-distance relationship.

Marcus. His name was Marcus.

I eye the entryway table ahead, with its collection of framed photos—mostly of Sabrina, but also of us. There we are, Marcus and I, on our wedding day. I lift the frame, studying the photo, astounded.

I rack my brain, trying to remember what we talked about the night we met. He was a talent agent, I think. No, he worked in sports—soccer? Yes! He was a *sports agent*, also funny, intelligent—a gentleman, for sure.

My heart does a little backflip looking at the photos of Sabrina that document her journey from infancy to her first birthday, where she hovers over a cupcake with one candle on top. She can't be much older than one now. A fresh one.

I sigh, taking it all in as my mind clips at lightning speed. So, in some alternate reality, Marcus and I worked out, and the result was this beautiful cherub . . . who appears to be nowhere in sight.

Her teddy bear and a few toys are on the rug where she was sitting only a moment ago, but she's disappeared. "Sabrina?" I call, panicked, and race down the hallway toward the bedroom where I woke up.

I find her there, crawling at the speed of light, about to enter the room, babbling at Marcus, who's just stepped out of the shower. Towel around his waist and an electric toothbrush in his mouth, he grins at Sabrina. She squeals with joy when he lifts her onto the bed, immediately rolling around in the duvet cover like it's covered in six inches of fresh snow.

"Thanks for handling wake-up duty today." He turns to the sink to rinse his mouth. "Has she said her first word yet?"

"Uh, no," I say, faltering. "I mean, not that I've heard."

"All right. Anyway, I've got a crazy day ahead," Marcus continues, dropping his towel to the floor and revealing every inch of his chiseled physique. It's hard to look away as he dresses, but I will myself to avert my eyes as I sit on the bed beside Sabrina, my body the barrier from her falling over the ledge. "If I can sign Lorenzo Castranova, it would be a real coup."

"Oh?" I say, attempting to follow along.

"I've got Diego, Rafael, and Paolo. But Lorenzo would be the crown jewel." He slides his strong arms into a sports coat, then kisses Sabrina on the top of her head before looking at me from the doorway, his expression somewhat indifferent. "Well, wish me luck."

"Luck," I say, trying to catch his eye, but he's looking down, scrolling through his phone.

"Sabrina has music class today, right?" he asks, turning back once more.

"Uh, yeah," I say, thoroughly confused.

"'Kay," he replies. "Have fun."

I listen as his footsteps clip along the hardwood floors, down the hallway, before the front door closes with a thud. *Am I just imagining things, or was that . . . weird?* True, I barely know him, but by anyone's standards Marcus seemed distant—cold, even. I remember the pile of pillows between us on the bed, noting the fact that he didn't kiss me goodbye, or even try. *Maybe he's a workaholic? Maybe we had a fight last night?*

I sigh, then jolt forward, reaching for Sabrina's leg, before she tumbles over the edge. "All right, Houdini," I say, pulling her into my arms. "Should we find you some breakfast?"

We head to the kitchen, where I strap her into a high chair, then proceed to stare into the fridge completely paralyzed. What does one feed a baby? Certainly nothing she could choke on (which could be *everything*), and nothing allergenic (which also could be *everything*). I finally settle on a banana, which I find in the fruit basket on the counter, peeling it before placing it in her little hands.

"Banana," I say.

Sabrina giggles, then tosses it on the floor.

"No, no, *eat* banana," I continue, picking it up, washing it under the faucet, and coaxing her to take a bite, but she grimaces and covers her mouth.

"All right, so you don't like bananas. That's okay." I scour the kitchen again, looking for baby food—looking for anything—and finally notice a strange-looking appliance on the counter beside a book titled *Organic Baby Food Essentials*. *Wow. I'm not one of those granola moms, am I?* I thumb through the book, with dozens of pages marked with sticky notes. *Yeah, I am.*

"Well," I say with a sigh. "How about some milk, then?" I pour Sabrina a glass, holding the edge to her lips, relieved when she takes a sip, then another, before wriggling and arching her back, disinterested. When I set her down, she speed-crawls back to her toys in the living room. It's only been an hour, and I'm already exhausted. How do people do this?

I pick up the cell phone on the coffee table—mine, I can only assume—and unlock it with Face ID. Marcus mentioned a music class today, so I eye the calendar and see that "Mommy and Me Music" begins at 9 a.m. If we're going to go, it's time to get ready—and soon.

After a fifteen-minute struggle, I finally win the battle with Sabrina's pants. From the closet in my bedroom, I select a slouchy, lightweight sweater and leggings, then take a quick look at myself in the bedroom mirror. My cheeks are fuller than normal, my hips a little wider—baby weight, probably, *fun*—and I can't help but notice the dark circles under my eyes, evidence of lack of sleep, no doubt.

"Okay, cutie," I say, sliding my feet into a pair of black Uggs, then lifting Sabrina in my arms. "Should we go on a little adventure?"

She smiles, babbling incoherently as I reach for the keys by the door and walk out to the street, trying to guess which car is mine. A man in front of the house next door waves. Holding a little girl in his arms, he's about my age, attractive, with tan skin and thick dark hair that he brushes from his eyes nonchalantly. He looks like the dad-next-store version of Enrique Iglesias.

"Morning," he says, grinning, walking toward me, coffee cup in hand.

"Uh, good morning," I reply a little nervously.

"Ready for class?"

"Oh," I say. "You mean the music class, right?"

He laughs. "That would be the one. I'll admit, I can think of a thousand things I'd rather do than sit in a circle with a bunch of parents while our babies bang drums and shake maracas, but"—he shrugs—"Charlotte loves it."

"Yeah," I say, following along. "Sabrina, too." I smile, eyeing my keys nervously, noting the Land Rover logo on the fob. "Well, I better get going."

"Oh," he replies, glancing at his watch a little wounded. "You're heading over early? I thought we planned to drive together."

"Uh," I begin. "Yeah, but I . . . need to stop at Starbucks first. It was an early morning—you know."

"All too well," he says, laughing, before our eyes meet again. "Still on for lunch today, right?"

"Um, yeah?"

"Good," he says, pleased. "I'll cook. The girls can play before naptime."

"Before naptime," I repeat. "Right."

"Okay, then," he says with a big smile, running a hand through his wavy hair. "See you soon."

So, I'm besties with the hot stay-at-home dad next door? I wonder what Marcus thinks of all of this as I unlock the Land Rover and stare inside at Sabrina's car seat, which looks like some sort of alien life-form. I mean, it might as well be. What the heck am I supposed to do with all these straps and buckles? Sabrina seems amused as I fumble with the various clasps—none of which seem to line up with the others. "At least one of us finds this funny," I say, wondering why anyone would invent an adult-proof baby seat. I mean, are they trying to drive us crazy? I think so.

When I've finally secured Sabrina in place, I climb into my seat, a little stunned. *Wow, I'm a mom. I actually created this little human, and I'm responsible for keeping her alive.* The magnitude of it all nearly takes my breath away. I exhale deeply and consult the GPS system for the nearest Starbucks. I need coffee—ASAP. Fortunately, there's one a mile away, and I start driving, down the winding road along the hillside, glancing back in the rearview mirror every few moments to check on Sabrina. We pass a million joggers, which I swerve to avoid, and even more people with dogs, including one woman pushing hers in a stroller, and another with a miniature poodle in a baby carrier strapped to her body.

I pull into the Starbucks parking lot, disappointed that there's no drive-through, which means I'm going to have to do this whole car seat thing all over again. But, for caffeine? It's worth it, I decide, extricating Sabrina from the seat and lifting her into my arms.

"Your baby is *adorable*," the woman behind the counter says, waving at Sabrina, who burrows her face into my chest, before peeking out a moment later, smiling shyly.

"Thank you," I say, as the man in line behind us begins playing peek-a-boo with her. In his expensive-looking suit, with that CEO look, he doesn't strike me as the type of person who interacts with other people's tiny humans in line at Starbucks, but then again, babies do bring out strange things in us. I mean, look at me.

"What can we get started for you today?"

"I'll take a triple-shot almond-milk latte."

She furrows her brow. "*Almond* milk?"

I shrug. "Oh, have you run out?"

"Well, no," she says. "But surely you've heard that it takes a *gallon* of water to produce a single almond?" She nods righteously. "Oat milk is a much better option, I mean, for the planet."

"Oh," I say, a little taken aback by the preachy barista. "That's . . . very interesting, but I'll stick with almond milk, if that's okay."

The woman nods, obviously displeased, as if my drink order may be the sole cause of climate change.

Ignoring her, I eye the pastry case, thinking of Sabrina. "Oh, I'll take a chocolate donut." I pause. "And a Frappuccino for her—but decaf, please."

The woman's eyes get big. "I'm sorry, did you just say you wanted a Frappuccino for . . . *her*?"

"Yeah—decaf," I say, inserting my card into the machine.

When our drinks are ready, I plop Sabrina into a chair at a table by the window, placing the donut on a napkin in front of her. "I bet you like chocolate, don't you?"

She stares at the sweet confection for a long moment, before timidly pressing a finger into the frosting, then dabbing it to her tongue. The corners of her mouth instantly creep up into a smile. Five minutes later, my caffeine is kicking in, and Sabrina is covered in chocolate, though I'm just happy that she ate . . . something. Oh, and the Frappuccino? A hit. In fact, she can't get enough. I ignore the glares from the other moms at a nearby table—the Frappuccino Gestapo, obviously. Give me a break, what's wrong with a little treat?

I do my best to clean Sabrina's hands and face, but a few streaks of chocolate remain. I wish I had a baby wipe. Wait, baby wipes! Diapers! In a rookie parenting move, I didn't bring any supplies. My anxiety only worsens when I look at my phone: Sabrina's music class starts in ten minutes.

Part of me wants to ditch the damn class altogether and take my daughter—*my daughter!*—to the beach and watch her play in the sand, maybe dip her feet in the surf, do this my way. But Sabrina has a schedule, and I decide to honor that.

As I struggle with the car seat again, she smears a sticky hand on my cheek. "Really?" I say, laughing as I struggle with her buckles. When she's finally secure, I type the address into my GPS, but before I put the car in gear, I decide to check in with Marcus. Something was off this morning—at least, as far as I could tell. I find his phone number in my contacts and try his cell, but after two rings, it goes to voice mail. A few seconds later, he follows up with one of those generic Sorry, I can't talk right now texts.

I dial him again, and this time he picks up.

"Lena?"

"Hey," I say, looking back at Sabrina in the rearview mirror.

"Everything okay?"

"Yeah," I reply, taking a left turn. "I was just calling to check in. We're on our way to music class, and then I'm . . . having lunch with . . . our neighbor."

"Cool," he says, a little distracted.

I bite the edge of my lip. "So . . . you don't care, I mean, that I'm . . . having lunch with him?"

I hear rustling on the other end of the line, voices. "What are you talking about? Why would I care? Listen, Lena, I'm heading into a big meeting. Kiss Sabrina for me, okay?"

"Okay," I say, ending the call a little deflated.

We're officially five minutes late by the time I lift Sabrina from her car seat and find the entrance to the music class, which is on the third floor of an old high-school-turned-community-center. I pause in the doorway, watching the parents, seated cross-legged in a circle around their babies—all moms, minus Hot Neighbor Dad, who waves when he sees me. An older woman with waist-length gray hair and a tribal-print tunic bangs a drum in the center of the circle, leading her pupils—er, the babies—in song, except for the fact that none of them can talk, let alone sing. Apparently the parents are responsible for that part.

I have the urge to run—to get out of here, and fast—but Hot Neighbor Dad has just made space for me in the circle. I have no choice. "Okay, Sabrina," I whisper, as we lock eyes. "Whatever happens, let's be professional."

Her giggles take the edge off, especially when we sit down and the mom next to me hands me a maraca.

"Welcome, Sabrina!" the teacher sings in nursery-rhyme cadence. "Welcome, Lena. How, are, you?"

I stare ahead blankly, as Sabrina burrows her face into my sweater. Obviously, she hates this attention as much as I do. Everyone's staring at us, and my heart begins to race. Am I supposed to say something? To sing something? Thankfully, Hot Neighbor Dad nudges my hip. "*Very fine, Ms. Marianne. So happy to see you.*"

"Right," I say, my cheeks burning. "I'm sorry . . . it was a late night."

"Don't worry, dear, we'll start over again," Teacher Marianne replies warmly, banging the drum again as she repeats her greeting. "Welcome, Sabrina! Welcome, Lena. How, are, you?"

This time I don't miss a beat. "Very fine, Ms. . . . Marianne. So . . . happy to see you."

"Let's, go, play," the circle of parents chant, followed by Teacher Marianne: "Let's, go, play."

Hot Neighbor Dad is up next, and Teacher Marianne begins her greeting. "Welcome, Charlotte. Welcome, Adam. How, are, you?"

He replies with perfection, winking at me after passing the maraca to the mom at his left. By the next song, Sabrina crawls into the center of the circle, cautiously picking up a rattle, which she shakes, then shoves in her mouth.

"She's awfully mouthy, isn't she?" the mom next to me whispers, eyebrows raised. "I mean, I've just noticed, that's all." She grimaces. "Don't you worry about . . . all those *germs?*"

Great. The Mom Police strike again.

I have the urge to go to battle—to defend my daughter's . . . *mouthy ways*—but Hot Neighbor Dad, er, Adam, comes to my rescue. "It's not that unusual, Vivienne. Charlotte's the same. And, you know, research has linked early childhood oral fixation with elevated IQ levels."

"Oh," she says, wide-eyed and possibly a little embarrassed. "I . . . didn't know. I—"

"It's fine," Adam replies as Teacher Marianne begins passing the parents multicolored silk scarves.

"Everyone, it's time for the Circle of Love!" she cries as the sounds of pan flutes and chanting plays through the speakers. "Please rise to your feet and twirl your scarves as you dance around the children. Be whimsical, be free, be *love!*"

Adam and I exchange nervous glances as the other moms spin and gyrate, streaming their scarves around a dozen or so oblivious babies, several of whom appear to be looking up at the adults in utter revulsion.

"I'm sorry, do we actually pay money to be here?" I whisper, attempting to comply as I wave my scarf side to side, weakly.

"I know," Adam whispers back, clearly on the verge of cracking up. "It's painful."

When I start to laugh, he does, too, but we compose ourselves when one of the moms shoots us dirty looks. Apparently we're not being very free and whimsical.

I glance back at Sabrina and, uh-oh, there's a dark stain on the back of her pants, just at the top of her right leg. Chocolate, I hope, though my nose detects a different story. Oh. No. She . . . *pooped*? Was it the chocolate donut? The Frappuccino? Both, probably. What was I thinking?

I turn to Adam, my only "friend" in the room. "Hey, um, so . . . Sabrina just . . . had an accident, and I, well, I . . . left my bag at home."

"Oh," he replies unflappably, as if this is no big deal. "Need a diaper? Wipes?"

I nod, amazed at how easily the words *diaper* and *wipes* roll off his tongue.

He reaches into the pink camo-print bag beside him, handing me the necessary supplies. "Here, take an extra change of clothes, too. Looks like you have a blowout on your hands."

"A blowout," I repeat, terrified. I can only imagine the task that lies ahead.

Adam chuckles. "Ah, the ill-timed blowout. Don't even get me started. Last week, Charlotte had two in one day—both times up the back."

I swallow hard, his words stoking my anxiety like gasoline to a flame. Time seems to shift in slow motion as the other moms continue to dance and twirl, scarves whirling in the air as the brown stain creeps farther down Sabrina's leg.

"You all right?" Adam asks, touching my shoulder lightly.

"Yeah, yeah," I say, coming to my senses. Diaper and supplies tucked under my right arm, I make a beeline to Sabrina, scooping her up and holding her as far away from my body as possible while I sprint to the restroom.

"Okay," I say in the ladies' room, intermittently covering my nose, "this is no big deal. It's just a diaper change. Well, *that* kind of diaper change." Fortunately, there's a changing table on the wall, so I lie her down and get to work.

"Are you okay, honey?"

Sabrina grins, looking up at me lovingly.

"All right, if you're not scared, I won't be, either. We can do this." She giggles as I peel off her soiled pants, then her diaper, both of which I toss in the nearby trash can—the poor, poor trash can.

"Okay, now we . . . wipe?" I pry open the little pack and begin the process, but by the time it's empty, I'm not satisfied—not at all. She needs a bath—pronto. I think for a moment, eying the sink. "All right, cutie pie, let's give you a little rinse."

After I get the water temperature just right, Sabrina squeals and coos as I plunk her into the basin, doing my best to rinse her lower half. "This is fun, right?" I ask nervously.

She doesn't have the words to reply, but her eyes tell me *yes* as she splashes and claps her hands.

Fifteen minutes later, Sabrina is finally clean(ish), dry(ish), diapered, and dressed. I, on the other hand, deserve a medal of honor—and a nap.

"How'd it go?" Adam asks in the hallway outside, his daughter fussing in his arms.

"Oh," I say, a little surprised. "You didn't have to wait for us."

"It's no problem," he replies. "I've been there, obviously. I just wanted to make sure you had everything you needed."

"Thanks," I say, smiling awkwardly, as I notice the empty classroom. *Thank God that's over.* "Well, I guess we should get going."

"Yeah." He eyes his watch as we begin our descent down the stairs. "I'll start making lunch when we get back, okay?"

"Great," I say as we head to our separate cars in the parking lot.

He flashes me a final smile before I tuck Sabrina in her seat, and I can't help but wonder, in this version of my life, *Am I playing with fire?*

18

Back at home, I freshen up in the bathroom, with a close eye on Sabrina, who's presently unfurling a roll of toilet paper, but at least it keeps her busy as I run a brush through my thin hair and swipe on some lipstick.

While Sabrina shreds toilet paper on the floor, I look around the house, thinking about Adam—his eagerness to help, the way he looked at me in the parking lot. Is there something more going on between us than just friendly parent stuff? I tell myself I'm overthinking things. This is 2024, after all. Men and women can be friends, have lunch together, even—especially neighbors who happen to be parents of toddlers.

While there's nothing shameful about being a stay-at-home mom, I can't help but wonder if I'm happy, fulfilled, under these circumstances. Yes, being a mom is an important job—*the* most important job—and for some women, that's enough. But me? I'm not so sure. Is motherhood the core of my identity? Or am I merely treading water, secretly longing for the shore?

I peer through the final doorway along the hall, the one closest to the kitchen. It's an office, and obviously mine—the framed photo of a ferry pulling into foggy Bainbridge Island being the dead giveaway. The desk is neat and tidy, aside from the withered rose in a bud vase, bearing evidence of the space's obvious lack of use, as does the powered-off Mac monitor, which sits at attention beside a leatherbound notebook.

Holding Sabrina, I sink into the beige sherpa-fleece-covered desk chair, swiveling in a few full circles, which makes her cry with joy. *What do I do here?* Or, rather, what *did* I do—before I became a mom?

The answer, it seems, is right in front of my eyes. I notice the vintage film camera by the window, then the two framed movie posters on the side wall, one of which appears to have won an award at the Sundance Film Festival. Upon closer inspection, both feature my name: *Lena Lancaster: Director of Photography.*

I'm a cinematographer? It doesn't make sense, and yet it does. I've always been visual, always seen life through a certain lens. So I turned that into a career—and a thriving one, it seems—but then . . . gave it all up for motherhood?

I check on Sabrina and see that she's moved on to tearing pages out of a magazine, so I decide to power up the Mac and get to know myself better, at least this version of myself. Fortunately, my trusty old password—"RosieOnTheIsland99"—works like a charm, and I log in to my email, overcome with curiosity, especially when I see a message at the top with the subject line "Pending Divorce Proceedings."

I gulp, opening the email.

Dear Lena,

I hope this finds you well. Per our phone call, attached is a draft of the dissolution paperwork. Please have a look and let me know if you have any questions. Two final matters for discussion: 1. Parenting plan details for Sabrina, and 2. Division of assets (i.e., assuming you'll be vying for the house, yes, and the Land Rover?). Please have a look and then let's set up a call to hash out the remaining details. With any luck, you'll be legally separated by this time next month.

Regards,

Beth

—

Beth Remington, Esq.

The Law Offices of Taylor, McHugh & Remington

I lean back in my chair, taking it all in. Am I really so miserable, that I want a divorce? I look down at Sabrina, happily playing by my feet while I'm overcome with emotion. Does this explain Marcus's chilly demeanor today? What about Sabrina? Don't we owe it to her to . . . try? I think of my mom, her endless stream of relationships. Most of her boyfriends were forgettable at best; a few, altogether awful. But some of them? I would have been happy if they stayed awhile—or even forever. I longed for a father, but even more, I longed for a *family*—a stable one—and here I am, on the verge of repeating history. How can I do that to Sabrina?

I sigh, glancing at the clock. Adam can wait. I need to call Frankie.

"Hi," I say, pausing, unsure of what to say or where to begin.

"Hey," she says, her tone cheery and upbeat. "Sorry about all the voice mails. I know you hate voice mails."

"I do hate voice mails," I reply with a laugh. "And I didn't listen to any of them, so you're going to have to repeat yourself."

"I know you're going through a lot. I just called to let you know that I'm here for you. You're not alone."

"But, Frankie, I *am* alone—*so* alone." Sabrina crawls over and pulls herself up on my leg, immediately negating my words as she happily pats my left leg, banging it like a drum. "Well, aside from you, and Sabrina, obviously."

"Aww, my sweet girl," she says, gushing. "Tell her that Auntie Frankie misses her so much!"

I smile, touching the edge of her plump cheek.

"What's the latest . . . with Marcus? Are you guys talking? Are you working on things?"

I exhale deeply, lifting Sabrina onto my lap. "The same, I guess? And no, we're not really talking."

"Maybe give therapy another try?"

I shrug. "Maybe."

"Lene, he's a good guy. I can't help but wonder if the two of you aren't just drowning in the stress of parenthood, you know? I mean, Christian and I were at our wits' end after the twins were born."

Frankie has twins? I manage to refrain from acting surprised.

"It got really bad there for a while," she continues with a laugh. "Hey, maybe I could fly out and stay with Sabrina for a weekend, while you two have a little getaway?"

"I don't know," I say. "I mean, maybe. Thanks, Frankie. I'll think about it."

"Good," she says. "Just promise me that you won't make any rash decisions right now, okay?"

"Okay."

WITH SABRINA ON MY HIP, I STAND ON ADAM'S FRONT STOOP, STARING AT THE doorbell cautiously, thinking about the pages of text messages between the two of us that I'd found on my phone earlier. While I only skimmed them, and they seemed harmless enough, I can't shake the feeling that we're toeing a dangerous line.

I take a step back, reconsidering this lunch/playdate/whatever you might call it, when the door swings open.

"Lena!" he says, a little surprised, with his daughter strapped into a carrier against his chest.

I smile nervously as Sabrina squeals with delight, arching her back as she attempts to wriggle free. Obviously, she's been here before—perhaps many times before.

"Come on in and make yourselves at home."

I nod, heading inside the mid-century home, similar to ours but a bit more bohemian, with Turkish rugs, Ikat floor pillows, and the faint scent of incense in the air. I eye the uncorked bottle of white wine on the kitchen counter beside two empty glasses.

"Hey," Adam says, lifting Charlotte out of the carrier. "Mind holding her for a sec while I run out to the garden to snip a few sprigs of tarragon for our salad?"

"Uh, okay," I say as he plops her into my arms.

"She really loves you." He grins as his daughter reaches for my necklace and begins yanking. Fortunately, I narrowly avoid strangulation when she notices Sabrina playing with her toys on the rug and flaps her arms to be let down.

Charlotte touches Sabrina's nose, then giggles. Her platinum-blond hair is either genetic or a product of the California sun—hard to tell. I wonder about her mother. Perhaps she's a workaholic, too, like Marcus. Maybe that's why Adam and I are friends. Two stay-at-home parents, bonding over exhaustion and dirty diapers. *Hot.*

While the girls play, I stand in the kitchen awkwardly, as Adam returns with the tarragon and begins mincing it with a fancy-looking chef knife.

"VOILÀ," ADAM SAYS, SETTING A TOSSED SALAD AND A PLATTER OF PANINI SAND-wiches on the table, before running back to the kitchen for spoons and two bowls of . . . green mush.

"Broccoli and bananas—for the girls," he says, smiling. "You know—from the baby food cookbook you told me about."

Oh, that one.

Sabrina frowns, pressing her hand over her mouth. "Um, sorry," I say. "She's a little . . . anti-banana these days."

"Oh," Adam replies, a little wounded. "Didn't she like them yesterday?"

Yesterday. So, this is a daily thing, he and I?

"Yeah," I say, thinking fast. "You know toddlers. One day it's bananas, the next . . . Frappuccinos."

Adam looks a little confused, but I don't elaborate, opting for a
bite of my panini instead. I offer Sabrina a piece of fresh mozzarella
that's fallen onto my plate, which she immediately gobbles up. I don't
blame her. Given the choice between green mush and table scraps,
I'd also choose the latter.

After lunch, he pours us each a glass of wine. "Glad you two en-
joyed it," he says, pleased.

"Well," I say, pushing my empty plate aside. "Can I help with the
dishes?"

"No, let's leave them," he replies, walking to the record player, where
he queues up a vinyl—Al Green—then slides into the sofa beside me.

"You didn't touch your wine." He points to my glass.

"Well," I say nervously, "isn't it a little too early to be drinking?"

He shrugs. "Never stopped you before."

Before. Right. I glance at my wineglass, the two cherubic toddlers
cooing at our feet. My heart races when I feel Adam's hand on my
arm before he points to something cute our toddlers have just built
with the blocks on the floor.

"Ummmm," I say, inching away from him. "I . . . should probably
get Sabrina home—for her nap."

"But we've hardly had a chance to talk," Adam says in protest,
leaning closer. "Look how much fun the girls are having. Let's let
them play a little longer."

"Yeah, uh, no," I say, standing up and catching my breath.
"Sabrina . . . didn't sleep well last night. I should probably get her
back . . . for naptime."

Adam nods with a knowing smile. "Aw, she's probably teething."

"Yes, *teething*," I reply quickly, "like . . . all over the place." I have
no idea what I'm talking about, just grateful for a semi-plausible
out. I lift Sabrina into my arms, then make a beeline for the door.
"Anyway, thanks for lunch!"

"Wait, *Lena*," Adam says, following me. "Did I do something, say
something, wrong?" He scratches his head.

I close my eyes tightly, opening them again when Sabrina tugs at a strand of my hair and I wince inwardly. "No," I begin, collecting myself. "But, Adam, whatever's going on between us, well, it has to stop."

He stares ahead, obviously confused.

"I'm sorry," I say, turning to the door, but he follows, undeterred, touching my shoulder when I step outside.

"Hold up, Lena, I—"

"I have to go," I say, darting outside as a silver BMW pulls up along the curb. A tall man in a suit steps out, waving as he walks toward us.

"Hi, honey," he says, kissing Adam on the lips. "LAX was a nightmare. It took an hour to get my bag." He peers into the doorway. "Is Charlotte still awake?" His face lights up as she crawls into the doorway, beaming up at both men.

"I saw your text," Adam says, scooping Charlotte into his arms, "so I kept her up a little longer."

The other man nods gratefully, slipping out of his suit jacket and loosening his tie before turning to me. "Thanks for being such a friend to Adam while the merger goes through. All this travel's been brutal." He shakes his head with an exhausted sigh, before turning to Charlotte, eyes brightening. "I swear, this little angel of ours changes every time I come home. Look at her—she's grown an inch!"

"Maybe more like a millimeter," Adam adds, smiling proudly.

"Well," I say as Sabrina begins to fuss, "I guess it's naptime for this one, too." I turn to Adam, both relieved and fifteen shades of embarrassed for my read on the situation. "Thanks for lunch, and for . . . all your help today."

"Anytime," he replies, blowing the two of us a kiss.

OUT OF BREATH, I UNLOCK THE FRONT DOOR AND CALL MARCUS.

"Lena?" he says, a little surprised. "Wait." He pauses, his voice tinged with panic. "Is Sabrina okay?"

"Yeah," I say quickly. "She's fine."

He sighs. "Thank God."

"I'm sorry," I begin tentatively. "I know you're busy, but we . . . need to talk. Listen, can I ask you something?"

"Okay?" He sounds worried, as if we've had this conversation before and it didn't go well. "What?"

I swallow hard. "What's wrong with *us*?"

"Seriously, Lena? You're really bringing this up right now?"

"Well, yeah."

He sighs.

I bite the edge of my lip so hard that I taste blood on my tongue. "Please," I say, awaiting his reply—his side of the story. *Clearly, I'm not having an affair with Enrique Iglesias next door—thank God—so what's going on? How could two people create such a beautiful child and become estranged so quickly?*

"Listen, how about we talk when I get home, okay?" he says.

"When?"

"Well, I have that dinner thing, remember?"

I exhale, disappointed.

He pauses. "Okay, if you really want me to come home early, I will."

"Yes," I say. "I really do."

"All right, then, I'll . . . be there."

I smile to myself. "I mean, I don't know what we'll eat, but I'll figure something out."

He laughs. "And by that you mean takeout."

"Exactly."

I see his smile in my mind—Mr. Jelly, still looking for his Ms. Peanut Butter. "Okay, I'll cut out of here in a few hours and try to be home by six, okay?"

"Perfect."

"HI," MARCUS SAYS FROM THE DOORWAY, HIS EXPRESSION TENTATIVE, AS IF OUR earlier conversation may have been an enigma, and me a mirage.

"Hi," I say, looking up at him as Sabrina crawls over, tugging at her daddy's pants before he lifts her into his arms.

I gather plates and utensils and start unloading our delivery Thai food, setting containers on the table as Marcus plunks Sabrina into her high chair.

"Would you like to feed her tonight?" I ask.

"Really?" He shakes his head, clearly shocked. "You never want me to."

"Well, I want you to now," I say, secretly relieved to hand off the baton, especially when he locates a secret stash of homemade baby food in the fridge, returning to the table with a spoon and bib. *A bib would have come in handy today.*

"You're so good with her." I watch as he feeds Sabrina, competently using the edge of the spoon to scrape the excess puree from her chin after each bite.

"Thanks." He looks away when our eyes meet. "I wish you'd let me help you more. Every time I try, you shut me out."

I realize how wrong I was about Marcus this morning. I thought he was a cold workaholic, but maybe he's just a loving father and husband who's been pushed away far too many times—by me.

We make small talk through dinner—a start—while Sabrina finishes an entire jar of baby food, along with scraps from our plates.

"All right, princess," Marcus says, lifting her from her high chair as I clear our plates. "Time for your bath." He turns to me. "How about you rest, and let me take care of bedtime?"

I smile. "The sexiest words in the English language."

He kisses Sabrina's cheek, then carries her down the hall.

After I load the dishwasher, I peer into the bathroom, watching as Marcus sits beside the tub, lovingly lathering Sabrina's hair and orchestrating an elaborate game comprised of a plastic boat and blue whale. She splashes in the bubbles as he does all the voices. "Don't you get me, Mr. Whale," he says as Sabrina squeals with delight. He's an excellent father—and man. So, what compelled me to isolate the way I have? Why did I push him away?

After she's in her pajamas, I follow him to the nursery, listening in the doorway as he reads her a bedtime story, watching as he settles her into the crib with her teddy bear. When she pulls herself up to stand, I approach, kissing her soft cheek and breathing in the sweet smell of baby shampoo, before Marcus lowers her into bed again, but not for long. She sits up, coos, then says, as clear as day, "Dada."

He looks at me, astonished. "Did you just hear that?"

I smile, nodding.

"That's right, baby," he says, beaming. "You just said, 'Dada.'"

"Dada," Sabrina says again, her little mouth forming the word proudly before she yawns, burrowing her head against her beloved bear as we tiptoe out the door.

"HEY," MARCUS SAYS IN THE KITCHEN, OPENING A BOTTLE OF WINE. "I'M GOING TO change and grab the baby monitor. Want to meet me outside?"

I nod, then pour us each a glass, and a few minutes later, he returns in a T-shirt and lounge shorts—monitor in hand. We sink into the double chaise lounge by the pool, watching the city lights twinkling in the distance as nearby palms sway in the warm evening breeze.

"Can we pick up where we left off on the phone earlier?" I ask, looking up at him.

"Let's," he replies with a long sigh.

"Okay, for starters," I begin, cutting right to the chase, "this morning you seemed so . . . closed off, and I just wondered if—"

"Closed off?" he scoffs, taking a sip of wine. "I could say the same thing about you." He leans back against the chaise, staring out into the night before turning back to me again. "Babe, you know *you've* been . . . off since Sabrina was born. At first I thought it was just postpartum stuff, but it's been *thirteen months*. I just . . . can't seem to break down your walls. I don't know how anymore. You don't want to talk, don't want to do anything with me. You keep a barricade of pillows between us in the bedroom, for Christ's sake. I've tried, you know I have, but, Lena"—he pauses, letting out a long sigh thick with pent-up frustration—"you have to try, too."

I gulp, his words sinking in. "I'm sorry," I say. "I can only imagine how you must be feeling. I don't know what to say, just that I want things to be better—for us, for Sabrina. I . . . want to try, Marcus."

"So do I," he replies, his voice tender. "Just hearing you say that, Lena, it . . ." He pauses, his voice cracking under the weight of emotion. "Well, it means the world to me. Baby, I've missed you so much." He clears his throat, nestling closer. "I'm sorry, too. I know I haven't exactly been the perfect husband. I work too much, and I could be a better listener." He smiles. "Plus, you know, I watch too much ESPN on the weekends, and I never bring you breakfast in bed anymore."

I laugh. "I *hate* breakfast in bed."

Marcus threads his fingers in mine as I rest my head on his shoulder.

"Have you put any more thought into hiring a nanny?" he asks cautiously. "I know it's been a sore subject, but I know your work means so much to you, and Sabrina's getting older. You could start slow, ease back in—just a few days a week."

I smile, looking up at him. "You're right," I say. "It might be time."

"I mean, it's not about money, of course. I've got us covered. I just want you to be happy." His eyes flash as he turns to me again. "Oh, I almost forgot to tell you. Guess who signed Lorenzo today?"

"Shut up, really?"

"Signed, sealed, delivered."

"Congratulations!"

We sit together for a while, holding hands, draped in the warm night air. It's perfect . . . until we hear a noise on the walkie-talkie, er, monitor: first a pint-size cough, followed by fussing, then full-blown crying.

"You stay," Marcus insists. "I'll go check on her."

He returns a few minutes later, with Sabrina in his arms. "She feels warm. Might be a fever."

"Oh no," I say, jumping to my feet and instinctively holding the back of my hand to her forehead, the way my mom used to do when I was little. "She does feel warm."

Marcus confirms her fever with a thermometer in the kitchen. "Ninety-nine-point-nine," he says, worried. "I'll give her some Tylenol and keep her with me in the guest room tonight so you can rest."

"Are you sure?"

"Absolutely. You've been on all day. It's time for Daddy to take a shift."

I search Marcus's face. "Thanks for sticking with me—through it all."

"I'll always stick with you, babe."

"Like peanut butter and jelly," I add, touching the edge of his face.

He laughs, giving me a quick kiss before carrying Sabrina down the hallway.

I head to my office and sit in front of my computer, opening my email inbox to find the message from the attorney I read this morning. I click on the reply button and begin typing:

Dear Beth,

This may come as a surprise, but I've changed my mind. Divorce is off the table. Marcus and I have decided to work things out for our daughter. Needless to say, I won't be needing your services anymore. I'm sure you can understand.

Thanks for everything,
Lena

After pressing send, I peer into the guest bedroom, where Sabrina is sleeping peacefully, cuddled up beside her daddy, who's also fast asleep. The sight nearly slays me.

I know life isn't perfect, and especially not love. In fact, it's messy and broody and fraught with feelings. But connection is the glue. Marcus and I lost it, somehow, but tonight we started finding our way back to it again tonight. I'm proud of that, even if it'll all slip away, for me, at least, when the sun rises tomorrow morning.

After all these days jumping from one reality to the next, I'm starting to wonder if my longtime view of love might be fatally flawed. While I'd hardly subscribe to Kevin's conveyor-belt theory, the idea of finding "the one" feels more like a fantasy as real as leprechauns and unicorns. Maybe love is less about fate and fairy dust and more about grit and intention? Maybe it's as simple as being *the one* for the one you love?

Tiptoeing across the room, I slide into the queen-size bed next to Sabrina, her arms extended over her head, which is exactly how my mom said I slept as a baby. Marcus on one side, me on the other, we surround her like a cocoon. Family, connectedness, love, showing up for each other even when it's hard—now that I've had this experience, maybe this is how it ends? Yes, maybe this wild ride will grind to a sudden halt in the morning, with Sabrina's sweet face smiling up at me, Marcus yawning across the bed, the two of us hashing out the morning's child-care duties. But if not, and I wake up somewhere new, I know *this—all of this*—will remain in my heart forever.

PART
TEN

19

I feel a balmy breeze on my face as I open my eyes. The room—wherever I am—is rocking, violently, side to side. *An earthquake?* Maybe I'm still in Los Angeles. My heart lurches. *Sabrina!* Panicked, I brace myself as the rocking continues and a glass of water on the nightstand slides to the right, shattering on the floor below.

My eyes dart around, taking in the small, claustrophobic room and circular window. This isn't LA. There is no Marcus, nor Sabrina in a nearby nursery. Aside from the extra pillow and rumpled sheets beside me, the bed is empty. It's much smaller than yesterday's queen or the others I've woken up in previously, almost miniature-size, in fact. Either I'm an elf, or this husband du jour likes to cuddle.

I rub my eyes, grateful when the rocking stops, though I freeze the moment I hear water splashing outside . . . *the porthole?* I peer through to the turquois-blue sea outside. *I'm on a boat—a very rocky boat.*

I glance down at the ring on my hand—a simple gold band studded with tiny diamonds, a few of which are missing. Married again, I see. I feel a pang in my heart—for Sabrina, for Marcus, for yet another life I've been ripped from—but if I've learned anything from this journey, I know I have no choice but to forge on. I quell the ache inside of me as my imagination clicks into overdrive. Who have I ended up with today? Someone I dated in college? After college? Maybe a guy I met in those overcaffeinated years in New York? I freeze, remembering the handsome Canadian from the latter era—Trent? He talked about sailing, I think, and seemed charming; that is, until I realized he lived in *his mom's basement*.

Okay, no. *No, no, no, no, no.*

Wait, why am I on a boat? Is this a vacation? A cruise? Maybe we're . . . castaways, or . . . pirates? I pause, thinking back to all the adventure novels I read as a kid. I laugh to myself, then grimace, imagining Trent in a tricorn and eye patch.

"Hello?" I say, poking my head out the door and casting a cautious glance down a surprisingly long hallway. Spools of neatly wrapped rope hang on either side. Okay, this is a *big* boat. I hear the creak of footsteps on wooden floorboards overhead as I make my way up a varnished ladder that leads to the open-air deck above. A spray of seawater hits my face as I reach the final step. I look up at two enormous white sails, taut from the wind, and gasp. Okay, I'm on a sailboat, but not just any sailboat—*this is a freaking yacht*, as in the type of vessel you see influencers posting photos from in the South of France.

I clutch the edge of the railing for balance as I stumble ahead to the boat's helm, where a man—his bare back all I can see—holds the edges of a large spoked wheel. *The captain?*

"Hi," I say, stepping closer, the wind whipping my hair against my cheeks.

"Morning," he replies, his gaze fixed ahead. "We're really clipping, aren't we?" His voice sounds familiar, and Australian, though I can't quite place it.

"Totally . . . clipping," I reply, eager for a look at his face.

"Glad you slept," he continues, eying his wristwatch. "Passengers board at one. It's going to be a full day." He cranks the wheel sharply, and I stumble, gripping the railing, as we veer right. "But everything's ready. All stations prepped." He finally turns to me, his smile unlocking my memories like a key. "We have a few hours before D-Day, want to have a little fun?"

My God, Del? The Australian I met in . . . Positano? Yes, Positano! It was the summer before Frankie started grad school. She booked a trip to the Italian Riviera, but Christian couldn't get the time off work, so I took his spot. My boss wasn't exactly thrilled, and it took some creative convincing, but the Italian Riviera with my best friend? Duh! However impromptu, though, it was a proper girls' trip, and I had zero interest in meeting anyone. Honestly, I wasn't even looking. But then came *Del*.

Frankie and I were on a morning walk, heading down the winding steep path to the village. When we got to the marina to take photos, I spotted a handsome man tying his sailboat to a slip. Of course, I did my best to impress him, and by that, I mean tripping in front of his boat on the dock.

I wince, remembering all those splinters in my left thigh. Frankie plucked most of them out later, but some were impossible to remove. *Souvenirs*, we called them. I rub the edge of my leg, wondering if a bit of Positano lingered under my skin, perhaps even now.

That day, Del was a gentleman, offering to help and pulling out a first-aid kit. On a two-month break from his captain duties on a large yacht, he had that rugged Matthew McConaughey vibe—tan skin, sun-kissed streaks in his hair, and a wild, adventurous gleam in his eyes—that made me feel weak in the knees, just as it does right now.

"How about we veer north?" Del suggests. "Maybe head over to the little swimming hole off Thirassia, you know, the one you love?"

I'm instantly charmed by his words, which sound like a page torn from a beloved novel. So, in this life I frequent swimming holes off the coast of tiny Greek islands? *Yes, please!*

"So, what do you say?"

"Okay," I reply, coming to my senses. "Sure."

Del smiles, fiddling with a dial on the dash. "All right, we'll head west, throw down anchor for a couple of hours before picking up our guests in Santorini. The winds look decent—shouldn't run into any trouble." He grins. "You and me, a little calm before the storm. Sounds perfect, right?"

I choose to ignore the word *storm*, focusing, instead, on *Santorini*. In fact, my heart begins to palpitate. *Santorini!* "Yeah," I reply, beaming as I look out at the crystal-blue water dotted with islands as far as the eye can see. Some are massive, with rocky cliffsides and endless white-sand beaches; others miniature—basically just rocks poking out of the Aegean Sea.

How many times did I tell Kevin about my dream of visiting the Greek Islands? A hundred? A thousand? Of course, he always had a *sensible* reason why it wasn't a good idea—timing, logistics, weather. But now I'm finally here. And Kevin? A distant memory.

"Sweetheart, why don't you go get changed?" Del's strong arms flex as he cranks the wheel again. "We're only a few knots away. I'm going to need your help bringing down the sails."

Help? He speaks as if I have some inkling of how to be useful on a sailboat. I may have been a lifelong ferry rider, but I have zero boating skills—as in, zilch. Seriously—I wouldn't know an *aft* from my *ass*.

I CLIMB DOWNSTAIRS TO THE LITTLE ROOM WHERE I WOKE UP, OPENING DRAWERS and compartments, with no luck. I need to find a swimsuit—towels, too, maybe? It takes a few minutes, but then I pry open a storage compartment under the bed, where I find the mother lode: my belongings. I reach for a pale blue bikini, holding it up to the light. *Do I even have the body for this?* I sigh, slipping it on, before making my way back up to the main deck, where Del is busy wrangling one of the sails.

"Thank God," he says. "The wind just picked up. I can handle the jib, but I need you to put down the anchor, and fast."

"The anchor," I say, wide-eyed, as I watch him climb up an enormous pole (the mast?) and tie various ropes in place. *Okay, if I were an anchor, where would I be?* I decide to head to the front of the boat—the cockpit?—where I look around, though nothing seems obvious. In fact, it's all foreign.

"Lena! What are you doing? We're getting close to shore. You need to get the anchor down!"

Heart racing, I run my fingers along the various levers. What am I looking for? A button? A crank? Yes, a crank. I see it now, attached to a rope, *the anchor* dangling at the edge. I start yanking, twisting it counterclockwise.

"That should be good," Del says from his perch.

Whew. I smile, looking up at him, my arm a little strained.

"Lena!" he calls out again, startling me. "Secure the line!"

I freeze, completely out of my element.

"Hurry! Tie it up. We're dragging!"

Dragging? I freeze, unsure of what to do. Fortunately, Del climbs down like Spider-Man, confidently swooping in to secure the loose rope.

"Sorry," I say, a little embarrassed as I sink into the captain's chair, rubbing my arm. "I think I got a . . . muscle cramp."

"All good, sweetheart," he says, pointing ahead to the secluded cove. The clear blue water is breathtaking. "Shall we go for a swim?" He sets his sunglasses on the dash, and I follow him to the boat's upper ledge, where he takes my hand, smiling.

My heart beats faster as I look down at the water below. "I don't know," I mutter, nervously. "That's a pretty big *jump.*"

Del laughs mockingly. "Wait, what? My wife, the water dog, is suddenly *scared*?" He grins, pulling me closer to the edge, tickling my side. I flinch, laughing, as we both fall forward, plunging into the sea.

I gasp, pulling the hair from my face, as Del takes a breath, then dives down again, coming up for air a few moments later, triumphant. "Did you see the octopus?"

Before I can remember if octopuses—octopi?—are friend or foe, Del submerges again. A few seconds later, he returns above water, holding his prey: a prehistoric-looking creature that I *do not* want to touch. Keeping my distance, I tread water as he sets the unfortunate thing on the boat's back deck, before heading in for round two, then three. "There," he says, proudly displaying his final catch. "Tonight's appetizers."

I can't help but marvel at Del's knowledge of the sea, which is clearly a language I don't speak. True, I grew up splashing around in the Puget Sound, but that's a lot different than sailing the high seas. Frankly, I've always had a deep-seated fear of the ocean—its power, mystery, and unpredictability. But my anxiety is quelled by Del's strong, capable arms as he cradles me in the clear blue water. For a moment the heaviness of my life lightens. For a moment I feel . . . weightless.

"WHY DON'T WE SHOWER AND GET CHANGED INTO OUR UNIFORMS BEFORE Santorini?" Del says as we towel off on deck. "I want to make sure we're ready when we arrive in port."

Uniforms?

"You know how demanding these posh types from the UK can be," he continues, with an exaggerated eyeroll. "We're in for *quite* a week."

"Right," I say nervously, heading downstairs to shower. In the drawer beneath the bed, I find a blue polo shirt with an embroidered logo that reads MAJESTIC CHARTERS; I slip it on, along with a pair of very unflattering khaki shorts, pulling my damp hair into a ponytail.

Del sports a matching look, with the addition of a captain's hat. We motor into the marina, and my jaw drops at Santorini's breathtaking beauty, with its pristine white stucco buildings wedged into the cliffside, sprinkled with pockets of bright pink bougainvillea flowers.

"Toss me the stern line," he says, jumping off to the dock.

"Um . . ." I pause, paralyzed with confusion. *What's a stern line?*

He points to the rope ahead, and I hurl it over the edge, stubbing my toe in the process. Obviously, I've miscalculated the distance, because it lands with a splash in the water below. Del leans over the edge to fish it out before tying up. If he's annoyed, he doesn't let on.

Back on the deck, and in full captain mode, he rubs his forehead, pacing. "All right, the galley's stocked, right?"

"Right," I reply, in a *yes-sir* tone, though I have no idea where the galley is or whether it's stocked.

I hear a loud thud and look to my right, where a man has just hoisted an enormous Louis Vuitton trunk onto the deck. I guess Del wasn't exaggerating when he said these people were posh.

"Good," Del continues in a shipshape tone. "The porters are onboarding." He turns to me. "Why don't you get the champagne popped and poured?"

"Champagne, yes," I say, jumping into action. I descend a spiral staircase at the center of the boat that leads to a chef's kitchen, which is when it hits me: *My God, I'm the "chef," aren't I?*

How did this happen? I don't cook. What are these poor people going to eat? PB&J? In a panic, I fumble for champagne glasses, which I find in a lower cabinet. I set six on a tray, then peer into the wine fridge, reaching for one of the dozen bottles of Dom Pérignon.

I struggle with the cork for a minute, but finally get the offensive thing pried off, before pouring bubbly into each glass, sneaking a sip (liquid courage, you know) before heading back to the upper deck. Miraculously, I manage to hold the tray steady, setting it down on a teak table just as our first guests arrive, and, oh, do they *arrive*.

A woman in her late forties embarks first, wearing a white caftan and Chanel slides, a Hermès silk scarf draped around her neck. She adjusts her enormous round sunglasses, fanning her face. "Darling," she says in a clipped British accent, "be a dove and fetch me a Pellegrino, will you?"

"Uh," I say, as she hands me her Birkin bag. "Sure."

"Thanks," she replies with a sigh. "And put my bag in my stateroom, will you? This blazing sun is the devil on leather."

effort effort

I nod, darting down the stairs. I have no idea where her "stateroom" is, so I throw the Birkin on the counter, then grab a chilled Pellegrino.

"Here you are," I say, handing her the bottle. An equally posh man has also just arrived, and he's busy grilling Del about our course for the week. "Would either of you care for champagne?" I ask, holding out the tray.

The woman reaches for a glass, taking a dainty sip. "Are you the crew?"

"Uh, yes. I'm Lena. And you are?"

"Victoria," she says. "My husband, Charles, is over there, speaking to the captain."

"Well," I reply, smiling awkwardly. "Welcome aboard."

"Our friends will be arriving soon," Victoria continues. "Well, family, I suppose—Pamela's my younger sister. She's here with her new husband, who's a bit of a character." She sighs. "You'll see."

"Oh," I say, a little confused.

"Dear, tell me, who's the chef on this voyage?"

I swallow hard. "Well, I am."

Her eyes widen. "Please tell me you're Le Cordon Bleu–trained."

"Definitely," I lie.

"Good," she says with a sniff. "So many of these husband-and-wife, captain-chef teams can be decidedly lacking in refinement." She fans her face, frowning as a very tall man steps on board, his face obscured by the large box he's carrying. "Speaking of the devil," Victoria whispers with an eye roll. "My *Irish* brother-in-law."

"Every voyage needs a proper supply of Irish whiskey," he says, setting the box down with a thud that rattles the bottles inside. "Well, would you look at this," he continues, eyes running the length of the boat, which is when the blood practically drains from my veins. *That face, that voice.* "I've gone from paddlin' in puddles to sailin' the high seas!"

Colm.

Suddenly my hands are clammy—no, downright sweaty. *How is this even possible?*

I remain frozen, heart pounding loudly in my chest. Victoria's mouth is opening and closing, words are, presumably, coming out of her lips, but I can't hear them—it's just *blah, blah, blah.*

Preoccupied with the vessel, Colm hasn't noticed me yet. "Is this a sailboat or a floating castle?" he quips, running his hand along the polished wooden railing. "Look at this beauty. My, she's grand."

When he turns around again, our eyes finally meet and his carefree expression morphs into pure shock.

"*Lena?*" he says, eyes wide.

20

Victoria watches us suspiciously. "I'm sorry—do you two *know each other*?"

"Uh," we both begin in unison, laughing nervously.

"It was ages ago," Colm explains, picking up the slack. "Right?"

"Yeah," I say, at a loss for words.

"We met on a train," Colm continues, "in Switzerland, I think?"

I nod, smiling. "Correct." I can only assume that he has no awareness of our reunion or that beautiful proposal in his family's pub. But it felt real—it *was* real—at least to me.

"Wow! How've you been?" he asks, searching my face as Victoria hovers.

"Uh, great," I say, choosing my words carefully. "One adventure after the next!"

He rubs his forehead nervously. "So, you work in hospitality, I take it?"

"I . . . do," I reply, glancing ahead, where Del is presently held hostage by Charles. "I'm the chef, and that's my . . . husband over there, you know, the captain." I'm pretty sure I've never uttered a more foreign sentence.

"A dynamic duo," Colm replies, wiping a bead of sweat from his brow.

Victoria sighs, helping herself to another glass of champagne. I ignore her, keeping my eyes fixed on Colm. "So . . . you're . . . *married* now?"

He nods. "Yeah, recently."

"Colm, darling," Victoria interjects, her frown melting into a saccharine smile. "What have you done with that sister of mine?"

"Oh," he begins, at a loss for words. "Pamela decided to go . . . shopping."

Pamela. The mere mention sends a chill in the air.

"Shopping?" Victoria sighs, visibly unamused. "Did you not inform your lovely wife of our imminent departure? Ah, my dear baby sister—never one to understand the virtue of *punctuality*."

Colm scratches his head, smiling nervously as he shifts his gaze from Victoria to me. "Vickie," he finally says, "I think we're both aware that Pamela *does* what Pamela *wants*."

"I suppose you're right," the elder sister replies as she lets out an exhausted sigh. "And yet, the tales of her ill-timed escapades will surely become bedtime stories for generations to come." She smirks. "Remember last month in Cannes, when Pamela insisted on stopping at Cartier right before our flight? How long did we sit on the runway, waiting for her?" She grimaces. "I must say, this is becoming rather tiresome."

Before Colm can respond to his sister-in-law's grievances, our attention is swiftly drawn to commotion on the back deck. A blond thirty-something woman captures the scene, her shrill scream piercing the air.

Hurricane Pamela has arrived.

Colm darts ahead, eyes wide. "Darling," he says, taking her hand, "are you all right?"

"I might be if there was a crew member to help me aboard," she snaps, extracting the spiky heel of one of her Louboutins out of a gap in the teak decking. She looks around the ship, frowning. "Oh, how charming, a floating *broom closet*." Colm shoots me an apologetic look as she drops her shopping bag on the deck. "Vickie, I thought you said this was a *yacht*. Perhaps you mistakenly booked the minimalist excursion?"

Victoria is clearly annoyed with her sister's tantrum, but it's no question that they're cut from the same cloth. "I know, darling," she says, handing me her empty champagne glass before adjusting her enormous sunglasses. "It *is* rather ordinary, isn't it? A shame—the photos online told a different story. Oh well, we'll survive."

"Darling," Pamela says, shooting Colm an exasperated look, "please find the crew and have them take these bags to our stateroom. I bought some Greek olive oil for Mummy, and I want it out of this heat."

Colm looks at me nervously, before nodding at his wife. "Yes, love, but first I want you to meet an old friend of mine." He shifts his stance, smiling at me. "This is Lena." He fumbles with his hands, as if he doesn't know what to do with them. "We met a million years ago, on a train through Switzerland. Her husband is the captain; the two of them run this ship."

Pamela stares ahead indifferently. "How quaint."

I feel Del's hand on my shoulder. "Lena, I'm sure our guests are dying to freshen up. Why don't we show them to their staterooms?"

"Right, yes," I say, following his lead.

"SHEESH," DEL SAYS LATER IN THE GALLEY, SETTING AN OCTOPUS ON THE COUNTER. "Might be our stuffiest group yet."

"I know," I say, eyeing the creature's nubby tentacles with trepidation.

"So, you . . . know that guy, huh?" He adjusts the brim of his hat. "The Irishman?"

"Yeah," I reply, avoiding eye contact. "Small world, right?"

"Shockingly small," he says, scratching his head. The concern in his eyes disappears when we hear glass breaking on the deck above. "I'll take care of that," he says, rolling his eyes. "Why don't you get started on this octopus, okay?"

I nod, staring at the eight-legged specimen for a long moment, before finally reaching for a cleaver and forcing myself to get to work.

I wince with each cut, completely clueless. I mean, I've had calamari, but this is an altogether different beast. Am I supposed to fry it? Bake it? *Sing* to it? I pull a cookbook down from the upper shelf, flipping to the seafood section, which is when I find a recipe for octopus ceviche. *Yes, ceviche!*

While I can't find half of the ingredients, we do have lemons, onions, and salt. What did Pamela say earlier? Yes, I'll make a *minimalist ceviche* for this *minimalist excursion*. Laughing to myself, I arrange the desiccated octopus on a serving plate, dousing it with lemon juice and salt, then onions for garnish. "Here goes nothing," I whisper, climbing the stairs to the upper deck.

I find our guests sunning themselves in lounge chairs to my right. "Care for some ceviche?" I say, clearing my throat. "The captain caught it just this morning."

Colm looks up from his phone, smiling. "Yes, please!"

I hand him a napkin as he reaches for a piece—well, a leg—taking a bite off the edge.

"You like it?" I ask nervously.

He covers his mouth, nodding, then coughing.

"Did you say this is ceviche?" Victoria asks, eying the platter cautiously as Charles helps himself.

I nod. "And locally sourced. We just pulled it out of the water this morning."

"Hmm," she says, finally reaching for a piece, which she stares at for a long moment. "Peculiar presentation."

Pamela appears pained, lying on her chaise in a geometric-print bikini, which leaves little to the imagination. "None for me," she says, grimacing. "I stopped eating *sentient creatures* a decade ago." She sighs, reaching for the bottle of body oil beside her. "Colm, darling, will you get my back, please?"

He nods, leaping to his feet—the bulge in his right cheek making it obvious that he hasn't yet swallowed his first bite.

Pamela shifts to her side as Colm begins lathering oil on her skin.

Lovingly or just dutifully? I can't tell. They're married, of course—so am I—and yet, the sight of them together makes my heart contract. Yes, the memory of our connection is fresh, but it's more than that. How could Colm be truly happy with a woman like her? I leave the platter on a table, slipping off before anyone notices I'm gone.

"LENA," DEL SAYS, CONCERNED, WHEN HE FINDS ME AT THE FRONT OF THE BOAT, wedged into a corner, knees to my chest. "What's wrong?"

"Nothing," I lie, composing myself. "I'm just, honestly . . . a little homesick."

"Ah," he says, sitting beside me. "I know this life has a way of getting to you sometimes, doesn't it?" He looks out at the sea, the enormous white sails billowing in the wind overhead. "But isn't it amazing that we get to be out here? To live like this? Just you and me and the sea." He laughs, gesturing to the back deck. "Well, and those assholes, I guess."

I grin. "Do you ever miss home?"

Del shrugs. "Land? Sometimes. That's what three hundred and thirty nautical days a year does to you, I suppose. But home?" He shakes his head. "Nah, the sea is my home—*our* home."

I've heard stories about adventurous people like Del—mountain climbers, triathletes, paragliders. They thrive on adrenaline, chasing it like a drug. So what if you summit Mount Fuji? There's always Kilimanjaro. Home isn't a single place where you lay your head down each night, but rather the journey. It's obvious that Del loves it. Do I? I have to admit, all of this is far more exhilarating than my career in investor relations. Maybe this is what I've been missing all along?

We sit in silence for a long moment, until Del reaches for my hand. "Listen, this is probably the worst time to tell you this, but I need to get it off my chest."

"What?"

He fidgets with his gold wedding band for a moment. "I know you had your heart set on visiting your aunt Rosie next month, but . . .

I screwed up. I didn't look at the calendar right. We have a charter that week, and there's no getting out of it. The group booked the trip a year ago, and somehow I didn't notice the overlap. Honey, I'm so sorry, but we're going to have to reschedule your trip home."

"Oh," I say, a little disappointed, not that it really matters—we would never take that trip anyway—but his words still sting.

"Well," Del says, eyeing the horizon. "Better get back to it. The weather forecast changed, and it doesn't look good. There's a storm brewing out there—might get nasty."

I follow his gaze to a mass of dark clouds in the sky above, threatening to blot out this glorious weather in one fell swoop. The wind has picked up, too, churning up white-capped waves all around. I shiver, feeling a raindrop hit my arm.

Exciting, maybe, but in this reality, the sea is my ball and chain. But Del, with his wild eyes gleaming? It's the freaking love of his life.

BY LATE AFTERNOON THE STORM HAS ARRIVED, AND WITH A VENGEANCE. RAIN splatters the deck, sending Pamela and Victoria scurrying from their chaise lounges to take cover, while Charles paces nervously, pelting Del with rapid-fire questions. "How many storms have you encountered in your career? Where are the life vests? How many knots is this wind blowing? Will the storm pass by cocktail hour?"

"Listen, mate," Del finally says, obviously frustrated. "I assure you, we're going to be just fine, but I do need you to let me do my job. This is going to get worse before it gets better."

Charles's eyes get big, digesting Del's words. "Right," he says, retreating belowdecks.

Del's biceps flex as he grips the wheel, veering left. "Lena," he calls to me. "Take my spot for a second, will you? I need to reduce the sails before the wind gets any stronger."

"Okay," I say, terrified, as I reluctantly take the helm. I don't know what the hell I'm doing, just that I need to *hold on*, and I do—fiercely.

Fifteen minutes later, the storm is only gaining momentum, and when Del returns to resume his position at the wheel, I'm overcome with relief.

"Nice work, sweetheart," he says. "We're bearing forty knots south. With any luck, we'll be out of the woods in three hours, maybe four."

"Four hours?" I reply, frightened as rain and seawater batter Del's face. His eyes blaze, not with fear, however, but excitement. It's clear that he was born for this. I, on the other hand, just want to run and hide.

"Listen," he says, gripping the wheel, "it might be too late, but I need you to secure what's left on the upper deck. Chairs, tables—everything. Tie down whatever you can; throw the rest below." He locks eyes with me. "Be careful, okay?"

I nod, gripping the railing as I make my way to the center of the vessel, where Pamela is screaming hysterically, huddled next to Victoria. They both look green, and when Pamela leans over, vomiting all over the deck, the sight triggers her sister, who follows suit. I look away, covering my mouth as a wave of nausea rises.

"Girls," Colm says, climbing up the stairs. "Come down, quickly!" He shepherds the two women belowdecks, before making his way up again. "Can I do anything to help?"

"Yes, please," I say, holding one of the lines to steady myself as the rain lashes down. "We need to get all this furniture secured—tie down what we can, collapse the rest and bring it down below."

"Okay," he says, swiftly mobilizing. "I'll take the left side; you get the right."

I nod, scared out of my mind, but at least we have a plan. I collapse a set of teak chairs, depositing one belowdecks, before losing my footing. I fall on my left side and slide across the deck when the boat's nose dips up into the air. When it crashes down again, the force hurls me in the opposite direction, depositing me in a pool of Pamela's vomit.

"Lena!" Colm says, crawling toward me. "Are you okay?"

"I think so," I say with a gasp, clutching a rope for dear life.

He reaches for my arm. "It's not safe up here. You need to get down below."

"But the furniture," I say, looking around as the wind plucks a chair, spinning it like a feather before it flies overboard.

"To hell with the furniture," Colm replies as we brace ourselves for another swell. It's too dangerous to scramble the twenty or so feet necessary to get to the stairwell, so we hunker down in place. "Hold on to me!" He clenches the rope with one hand and holds me close with the other. I can feel the stubble of his chin on my cheek, smell his cologne. I, on the other hand, reek of Pamela's vegan stomach acid.

"Don't let go," Colm says as a table slides across the deck, narrowly missing us. "We're going to get through this."

"Okay," I whisper, chin quivering as I cling to his arm.

It's a miracle that Del still has his hands on the wheel. "Hold steady," he shouts from the bow. "We're almost through the worst of it."

A bolt of lightning illuminates the dark sky, followed by a boom of thunder and more screams from down below. I detect Charles's voice in the hysterical symphony belowdecks, as another chair comes barreling our way. Fortunately, Colm thinks fast, shielding my face and extending his leg to blunt the impact.

I squeeze his bicep so tightly that I might be cutting off circulation. I don't have to be an expert sailor to know, full well, that at any moment we could succumb to the might of the ocean. She could pluck us into her tendrils and toss us into the abyss. Maybe that's the thrill Del keeps chasing, the fragility and awe of being at the mercy of the sea? Maybe. I, however, can't wait for this to end. I feel dizzy.

"Let's play a game," Colm suggests, attempting to lighten the mood.

"Strange suggestion for a time like this, don't you think?"

"Nah," he says, grinning. "The only way to get through a tough situation is to distract yourself."

"Fair enough," I say. "So what's the game?"

"Places."

"Uh," I say. "Maybe clue me in a little more?"

"Right," he continues. "If you could magically teleport out of this hellhole right now, where would you go?"

"You first," I say.

Colm nods. "Kinsale, Ireland. I'd have a pint, then a plate of my mum's roast chicken." He pauses, eyeing me skeptically. "What's that face for?"

"What face?"

"You're making a *face*."

"No, I'm not!"

"Yes, you are!"

"Well," I finally say, laughing, "I guess I just assumed you'd rattle off some posh location like . . . Hotel du Cap-Eden-Roc in Antibes."

"Hotel du what? Honey, yer going to need to translate that for this humble Irishman."

I grin. "It's some place I read about in *Vanity Fair*, you know, the type of hotel you and Pamela frequent."

He screens his face from the rain. "Can I tell you a secret?"

"Sure."

"I *despise* fancy, and I'm allergic to posh."

"Probably shouldn't admit that to your wife," I say, laughing. "Or Victoria Beckham."

Colm secures his grip around my waist. "I have a confession."

"What's that?"

"Pamela bought me these god-awful Louis Vuitton slides in Santorini, and I fecking hate them. I look like a clown, don't I?"

"Sorry, but yes, you do."

He frowns. "Should I toss 'em overboard? Tell her that the storm swept them away?"

"I dare you."

He chuckles, slipping the slides off his feet before hurling them into the sea, one by one. "Wow," he says, turning to me. "That was weirdly cathartic."

"Glad to be of service."

"Okay," he continues. "You next: If you could be anywhere right now, where would it be?"

"Easy," I reply. "My aunt Rosie's house, on a little island called Bainbridge in Washington State."

"Guess we're a couple of homebodies, the two of us," he says, looking up at the sky, where a patch of sunlight beams through the dark clouds. "Looks like blue skies ahead."

As if on cue, there's a momentary reprieve from the thrashing, and Colm takes the opportunity to carefully shepherd us to the ship's midsection, before we hit another swell and take cover under the bar.

"You sure you're not hurt?" he asks, draping his arm around my shoulder again.

I shake my head, brushing away a chunk of vomit from my shirt. "No, but I *can't wait* to take a shower."

Colm laughs. "Sorry about that."

"How do you think Pamela's faring?"

"She'll be fine," he replies. "Pamela may look like a shrinking violet, but don't be fooled. She comes from a long line of tough Brits with plenty of fortitude running through their blood. Keep calm and carry on, you know?"

"Right," I say, nestling my head against his shoulder as another round of seawater splashes up over the railing.

"Crazy running into you again," he continues, marveling, "and under these circumstances. It's almost like it was . . . fate."

"Yeah," I say with a raised eyebrow. "*Almost.*"

AN HOUR LATER, A SEABIRD SQUAWKS OVERHEAD, FLAPPING ITS WINGS ACROSS the horizon. The winds have subsided, and the water is calm again.

"All clear," Del says, peering under the table where Colm and I have waited out the storm. He reaches for my hand, lifting me to my feet. "You all right, sweetheart?"

"I'm okay," I say, tugging at my soiled shirt. "I just . . . need to find a shower—pronto."

"You do that," Del says before turning to Colm. "Thanks, man—for looking out for my girl."

"My pleasure, Captain," he says, giving me a final look before slipping down below.

After a hot shower and a change of clothes, I head back to the upper deck, where Del has just dropped anchor in a serene-looking bay beside an island dotted with cypress trees. "Mind keeping an eye on things while I head down to the engine room for a bit?" he asks. "Just want to be sure everything's in order."

"Sure," I say, finding a dry spot on the edge of the bow. I sit down, dangling my legs over the edge. No one seems to have an appetite, so instead of cooking dinner (if one could call it that), I watch the sun begin its slow descent. With broad strokes of orange and crimson, it's obviously showing off and in full farewell pageantry.

When I hear footsteps approaching, I look up to see Colm. "Nothing better than a sunset after a storm," he says, holding up two glasses. "A little Irish whiskey to wash away yer troubles?"

"Thanks," I say as he tucks in beside me.

He hands me a glass. "That was quite a wild ride. How ya feelin'?"

"Sufficiently traumatized," I reply with a chuckle, "but still breathing. You?"

"Same. Still standin', still smilin', and with a proper glass of whiskey in my hand." His eyes twinkle. "Guess that's all a fella can ask for."

I smile, breaking eye contact. "And Pamela?"

He rubs the stubble on his chin. "She's stable—finally—but

staying in for the night. The others, too. Let's just say, I feel a little sorry for those toilets in their staterooms."

I bite the edge of my lip. "I hope it wasn't the ceviche."

"That, combined with the swells?" Colm chuckles. "The perfect storm."

"Sorry," I say, trying not to laugh, but humor has a mind of its own, and suddenly we're both in stitches. "I have to admit something," I continue, struggling to compose myself. "I didn't go to Le Cordon Bleu. I can't cook—at all."

"Ah, you thought you fooled me, did ya?" He grins. "I knew all along."

I grimace. "Was I *that* obvious?"

"You were," he replies knowingly. "Then again, I was born with the sixth sense for detecting shenanigans."

"Ha," I say, resisting the urge to rest my head on his chest as my mind turns to Liam. *Liam!* "Uh," say, pausing, "how's . . . your son?"

Colm shakes his head. "Wait, how did you know about—"

"Pamela," I lie, nodding. "I, uh, overheard her talking about him."

"Really?" Colm scoffs. "Pamela talking about Liam? That's a pleasant surprise. She can barely remember his birthday, let alone his existence."

"Oh," I say, pausing for a long beat.

"Listen, I don't mean to throw her under the bus or anything—it's just . . . it is what it is. Some women make amazing mothers; Pamela's not one of them." He nods to himself, as if trying to justify every choice that led to this moment. "I hoped that motherhood would come naturally to her—well, stepmotherhood—but . . . no dice. She and Liam are like oil and water. She doesn't get him, and he can't stand her."

I remember how I tucked Liam into bed, how he'd asked if he could call me "Mummy." I may not be a "natural" mother, either, but I know one thing for sure: That little boy was easy to love. So was Sabrina. A surge of emotion rises in my chest, but I push it back down. "So . . . where is he? Why isn't he on this trip with us?"

Colm's expression turns pensive. "Look, like I said, Pamela comes from a very prestigious British clan. They've sent their children to the same boarding school for centuries."

Boarding school.

"It was only logical that we gave Liam the same opportunity," he continues. "I mean, with all of our travel, and my business—it actually made a lot of sense." He smiles proudly. "If ya haven't heard, I own one of London's most popular distilleries. In fact, we happen to be drinking one of my finest vintages."

He clinks his glass against mine, but I feel more unsettled than congratulatory. I stare off to a nearby island, where a seabird has just dropped a clamshell onto the rocky hillside. So Colm left that beautiful little village, said farewell to his family's cherished pub, and set off for greener pastures—aka, a prestigious, affluent life with a vapid woman in Louboutins. And he sent his son away? This isn't the character of the man I thought I knew.

"When we met," I begin cautiously, "you told me about your family's pub in Kinsale. It sounded so charming." I swallow hard. "Is your mom still running it?"

"No," he says, shaking his head solemnly. "After her stroke, I stepped in for a while, but the back-and-forth from London was a lot, and Pamela didn't see the point in me trying to keep a struggling business afloat, especially when my own company was taking off."

My heart seizes, remembering Dalton's Pub, where he proposed to me with Liam by his side.

He sighs. "I sold it. I mean, I didn't want to, but it was the logical thing to do. Mum had medical expenses piling up, and we got a decent offer from a developer who's been hounding us for decades. My brother, Declan, was adamantly opposed, but I've learned a lot from Pamela's father. In business, you can't think with your heart."

"Right," I say, my eyes drifting out to the sea. *What does Pamela's blueblood father know about an Irish pub beloved for generations?*

"Hey," Colm says, touching my arm. "Why the broody face? You don't like the whiskey?"

I shake my head, forcing a smile. "The whiskey's . . . fine," I say, choosing my words carefully. "Listen, I know we met a thousand years ago, and only for a moment, but I guess I'm just a little surprised how things turned out for you. I mean . . ." I pause, unsure of how to continue or even if I should. "Well, it doesn't matter. Congrats on all your success."

He shakes his head, contemplative. "What were you just about to say? Go ahead, be blunt."

"Well," I begin slowly, "Pamela is the *last* person I'd imagine you ending up with."

"Fair play," he says, nodding. "I'm not gonna lie, Pamela is, well . . ."

I grimace. "Pamela?"

Colm chuckles before his expression turns pensive again, his eyes distant. "I met her at a party in London, the two of us about as different as a pebble and a gemstone. But somehow, I made her laugh, and, you see, she hadn't laughed in a great while." He pauses. "We went on a few dates after that, and when she told me her father was interested in funding my business, it seemed too good to be true, but then the wire came—straight into my bank account." He rubs his forehead. "It was a windfall for me, and it couldn't have come at a better time. Without that funding, we would have folded. She saved me, and, well, I guess I felt that I had to do right by her."

"And by that you mean marry her," I add.

He nods.

"So, you did right by her and wrong by your son?"

"Ah, Lena," he says, leaning back onto his elbows. "So black-and-white. Life's a bit more complicated, don't you think?"

I shake my head, struggling to understand. "Is it?"

Colm tops off each of our glasses as he gathers his thoughts. "Success is a funny thing. You spend your whole life chasing it, but when you catch it, then what? Are you really any happier?" He shrugs. "I'm not sure if I am. But I will say that having wealth makes life a whole lot easier."

I tuck my knees to my chest, overcome with disappointment—and sympathy—for Colm. This version of his life breaks my heart as much as it makes me mad, and yet, who am I to judge? Earlier this week, I was married to a con man who was ripping off retirees.

All I know is that when we were together, Colm led with his heart, and the result was something beautiful in Kinsale. Yes, while I can still see glimpses of that version of him, they're only faint whispers of the man I fell for—in another life. Above all, today has cast a magnifying glass on his character—what he's capable of, and what he's not. I thought he was strong, and maybe he is, in a sense. But Colm has no anchor. He's just a feather drifting in the breeze, the direction of his path subject to the next gust.

"Well," I finally say, taking another gulp of his prizewinning whiskey before pulling myself up to stand. "I should probably turn in."

"Wait, Lena," he says, rising to his feet. "Before you go . . . can I just ask you something?"

"Sure."

He looks around, making sure no one's in sight—or earshot. "That night we met, on the train . . . I gave you my phone number, remember?"

I nod.

"I've always been curious . . . why didn't you call?"

"I wanted to," I say. "I mean, I intended to—but when I got to my hostel, the scrap of paper in my pocket was gone. I guess it slipped out."

"Oh," Colm says, his expression thick with regret. "But why didn't you try to look me up? On Facebook, or something. You knew my last name—I told you—but I never knew yours."

I pause, collecting my thoughts. "It was so long ago," I say, our eyes meeting for a long moment. "Part of me wonders what our lives might look like if I did, but at the end of the day, we only get one life."

Colm nods solemnly. "So, what you're saying is we weren't—"

"Meant to be," I reply, before he can finish.

He looks down, hands clutching the lacquered railing. "And this is? Out at sea with your Aussie captain, tending to fussy people like us week after week?"

"I wouldn't call you fussy, Colm. But the others in your party? Uh-huh."

He laughs. "Guilty by association, I guess."

"Honestly, I'm just trying to figure it all out, like you are. Doing my best with the hand I've been dealt."

"Right," he says with a long sigh. "Speaking of, I should probably go check on the missus." He grins—that same Colm grin that will be forever cemented in my heart. "Lena, it's been amazing to see you again." I can't help but notice a tinge of loneliness in his eyes as he searches my face.

"Yeah," I say with a genuine smile. "You, too."

THE SUN DIPS BELOW THE HORIZON. WHILE DEL CHARTS TOMORROW'S COURSE on the map, I make my way down to my bedroom. Yawning, I ignore my growling stomach as my head hits the pillow, where I glance through the porthole window, taking one last look outside before it all fades away. Under the moonlight, a sparkle of phosphorescence catches my eye. I marvel as plumes of green and blue light dance under the water's edge. It's far from supernatural, just phytoplankton giving off light in response to the shifting tides. Rosie explained the phenomenon when I was in seventh grade, shortly after my mother's death, and I guess, somehow, those moments fused together in my brain. I can't see phosphorescence without thinking of *her*—without thinking of home.

I'm thousands of miles away, of course, in the middle of the Aegean Sea, but home feels closer than ever, somehow—like it's almost within reach. Is it because the fog is finally lifting, allowing me to see my life, and myself, in new ways? I'm not sure, only that I feel a sense of knowing—about what matters and what doesn't, what I thought I wanted in life and what I really *need*.

For now, one of those things is sleep. Heart heavy, I curl into a ball. *Please, let me go home. I want my life back. I can hardly take much more.*

PART
ELEVEN

21

When I wake, the first thing I hear is rain splattering against the window—but not a porthole window, thank God, a real one. There's also a new man lying beside me—no surprise—and I immediately extricate myself from his limbs. Grateful to be on land? Yes. But the saga continues. I brace myself for today's iteration, which begins in some ritzy high-rise condo with a modern painting on the wall and a shirtless man lying face down on his pillow.

I tiptoe to the closet to dress, then sneak into the living room. The familiar view from the window heartens me: the Smith Tower, my favorite building in Seattle. *Seattle!* I may be stuck, but at least I'm *back*, with Bainbridge Island just a ferry's ride away. I know what I need to do.

I head for the door, pausing in the kitchen when I notice a man's wallet on the honed marble countertop beside an empty wine bottle and two glasses—one with lipstick on the rim. I eye his ID: Robert Fenway. Green eyes, six-foot-two, 195 pounds. Organ donor. My type, at least. Now to place him. *Who are you, Mr. Fenway?* I struggle for a minute, but then something about his smile hits me: the lack of *braces*.

Robbie? I think back to my crush at age fourteen, each of us in braces and that near-miss kiss. I picture his lips, puckered up, as I pry the American Express card out of his wallet along with a few hundred-dollar bills and some twenties.

"Lena?" he calls from the bedroom. My pulse races as I dash for the door, slipping into the elevator in the hallway.

Outside, the rain hits my cheeks as I make my way down Pike Street, picking up my pace when I see a ferry pulling into Elliott Bay. I shudder, thinking back to yesterday's ordeal on the sailboat, the storm, Colm. I have the urge to fall to my knees and kiss the ground, but I don't stop; in fact, I pick up my pace, speed-walking through the familiar streets of my adolescence—this grungy old beautiful city—until I arrive at the ferry dock, where I pay my fare for the next crossing. Finally, I'm going *home*.

"ROSIE?" I SAY, CAUTIOUSLY PEERING THROUGH THE FRONT DOOR. MY HEART skips a beat at the sight of the framed photos on the entryway wall as I slip off my shoes and sink my feet into the old wool runner with ragged tassels. *Thank God, I'm back.*

I hear music playing inside—1950s jazz—and footsteps in the living room as I walk through the kitchen and around the corner, my jaw dropping when I see my aunt dancing with a man beside the fireplace.

I clear my throat.

"Oh, hello, dear," Rosie says. "What a nice surprise. I didn't hear you come in." She looks up at the man beside her, who appears equally as startled. "This is Jim, my friend and dance partner. Jim, this is my niece, Lena."

Since when does Rosie dance—in the living room—at eleven o'clock in the morning?

"Hi," I say to Jim, with his bow tie and his thinning gray hair neatly combed. He has the vibe of a retired geometry professor who leads a Boy Scout troop on the weekends.

"Pleased to meet you," he replies, adjusting the pale pink rosebud in his lapel.

Rosie beams. "Jim is the finest dancer on the island."

"Second only to you, my dear," he counters.

"And he's a master gardener, too! That's how we met." She looks at Jim. "Tell Lena about your work at the Bainbridge Botanical Gardens."

"Well," he begins, in an *awe-shucks* tone. "It's a labor of love, I guess. I've been volunteering there for a few decades. There's nothing quite like putting a seed in the soil and watching it grow."

Retired-people shenanigans.

"Well, I should probably let you two catch up," he says, kissing Rosie's cheek as she waves him away like a bossy schoolgirl—one with a secret crush.

"Who was *that*?" I ask after Rosie's seventy-something Casanova makes his exit.

"I told you," she replies, smiling confidently. "My dance partner. Jim's an absolute pro at the western swing—eastern, too." She smiles, taking a pill from a prescription bottle, which she washes down with a glass of water. "Why didn't you call, sweetie?" she asks. "I would have made lunch."

"Sorry," I say. "There's been . . . a lot going on. Look, can we talk for a minute?"

"SO?" ROSIE ASKS, SITTING ON THE SOFA BESIDE ME. "IS EVERYTHING ALL RIGHT with you and Rob?"

Robbie. Braces Robbie. "Um, yeah, everything's fine, but listen, can I stay here tonight?"

"Of course, dear. Your old bedroom is—"

"Actually, I mean the guesthouse."

Rosie eyes me curiously. "The guesthouse?"

I reach for her hand, and in fits and starts explain what's been happening to me—the men, the circumstances, all of the twists and turns. She's quiet for a long while, folding and refolding her hands in her lap. "So what you're saying is that nothing for you . . . is real?"

I shake my head as a surge of emotion rises in my chest. "This isn't my life."

Rosie squeezes my hand, her expression strong and sure, signaling to me that, no matter what, it's all going to be okay.

"Well, I, for one, wouldn't mind waking up next to a handsome Frenchman."

I laugh. "Not *this* Frenchman. Sebastian was . . . complicated—and that's putting it lightly."

"What about Marcus?" she asks. "He sounds nice. And that sweet baby girl . . ."

"Sabrina," I say, with a lump in my throat. "Her name is Sabrina."

Rosie holds her hand to her heart. "And that Irishman?" She raises an eyebrow. "I've always loved an Irish accent."

I look out the window to the beach, where a flock of pesky Canadian geese startles and flies off. "Colm might have had my heart, but he lost it."

Rosie shrugs. "Maybe in real life he's—"

I shake my head. "Not in real life, not in any life—just no."

"Well," she continues. "So many eligible bachelors, it's almost too much for this old heart of mine to process."

"To be fair," I add, "some of them were a bit more *ineligible* than others."

Rosie takes off her glasses and turns to me, her expression curious. "How do you feel about it all?"

"Like I have a major case of whiplash," I reply. "It scared the hell out of me to see how different my life could look, but it's also opened my eyes."

"How?"

"Well," I continue, "like realizing that I could be a mother—and a good one."

Rosie nods.

"And that I've been on autopilot for so long that I've failed to notice the scenery along the way—experience the good things that come when you go off course. To think that I was sitting in this chair ten days ago, heartbroken that Kevin didn't propose, and now I'm actually, well, relieved."

"Kevin?"

"Kevin Shmevin."

Rosie laughs.

"Listen, all this time, I've been trying to figure out how it happened—how it works. I mean, why the guesthouse? Is it your crystals? Space-time continuum stuff? Something else?"

"Something else, indeed," she replies, nodding. "What, exactly? I'm not sure. All I know is that little corner of the island out there is special. I've always felt it." Rosie folds her hands in her lap, deep in contemplation. "So this all began when you fell asleep in the guest-house, correct?"

I nod, looking out the window where the little cottage sits at attention on the edge of the rocky hillside. It's more weathered than ever, but fortunately, this time, not bulldozed to the ground.

"Then, tonight, that's where you should be."

THE AFTERNOON FLIES BY, AND I SOAK UP EVERY MINUTE IN ROSIE'S COMPANY. After dinner, I pour us each a glass of wine and we sit in the living room by the fire.

"I can't wait to talk to you about all of this in the morning," she says, squeezing my hand reassuringly, as if our science experiment is predestined to go off without a hitch. But the truth is, neither of us knows for sure. All we can do is hope.

We linger for a long while, sharing memories until we're both yawning.

"Is it time?" she finally asks.

I nod, taking a deep breath as I follow her to the kitchen, where she pulls out a tarnished brass key from a lower drawer, placing it in my hand.

"I'm going to miss you," I say, memorizing her face.

"Enough of that talk! We'll see each other in the morning." She grins, reaching for a book on the counter, flashing me the cover: *Fifty Shades of Grey*. "I picked this one up at the library the other day—might be a bit scandalous for an old lady like me, but, hey, you only live once, right?"

I blink back tears. "I have a feeling you're going to like it."

Rosie smiles, handing me a quilt and fresh sheets before kissing my cheek. "Good night, dear child."

"Good night," I say as she heads toward her bedroom.

THE WIND PICKS UP AS I CROSS THE LAWN TO THE GUESTHOUSE AND, SHIVERING, unlock the door. Inside it's just as I left it, but maybe with a few more cobwebs. As I lie down on the bed, I ponder the road that led me here, the people I encountered along the way, some more endearing than others, and all the alternate lives I experienced. For better or for worse, all those memories are with me now, some more appealing than others. But the cumulative experience makes me realize that I'm capable of doing more with my life, though maybe not working as a ceviche chef in the Mediterranean or a real estate agent in Florida.

Each day has been like a Choose Your Own Adventure novel, with some choices exhilarating, others downright scary. But they all taught me to value the actual life I've been given, even if it's flawed and not going according to plan. For too long, I've been operating from a script, checking all the boxes. Changing course from that feels scary, even a little rogue, but there's a sense of freedom that comes with going off-script, and I'm finally ready to embrace it. I lie still for a long moment, watching the stars through the window and listening to the waves crash against the shore. I'm home, yes, but not really—*not yet*. Tomorrow can't come soon enough. I'm ready.

PART
TWELVE

22

A stiff mattress coil creaks beneath me as I shift, pulling the blanket up higher on my neck when a cool draft of air hits my skin. I rub my eyes, the blur of sleep slowly fading as the room comes into focus. I'm in *the guesthouse*. There's no strange man beside me. I look down at my ringless finger and feel a sensation of giddiness that spreads through my body like a fever. *It worked! It really worked!* Leaping out of bed, I glance at myself in the bathroom mirror, never happier seeing the sight of my boring, stick-straight lob.

My phone buzzes on the nightstand. It's Frankie. *Frankie!*

"Hiiiiiiiiiii!" I cry into the phone, practically kissing the screen.

"I take it we're sufficiently caffeinated this morning." Her sarcasm has never sounded sweeter. "So, how're you feeling?"

"Fabulous! Frankie, I'm home! I'm finally home!"

"Uh, yeah, I know. Lena? Are you . . . okay?"

"Yes! In fact, I've never been better!"

"Well, good, because you were a hysterical mess yesterday."

"I love you so much, Frankie! And I love that you and Christian love each other!"

"Dude," she replies. "What's with all the love?"

I chuckle. "I'll explain later. I've got to find Rosie!"

I RACE ACROSS THE LAWN, GRINNING FROM EAR TO EAR. MY CHILDHOOD HOME has never looked more beautiful, even under this gray sky with rain splattering my face. I open my mouth to catch a drop on my tongue, overcome with relief to be home—to *really* be home. Back to my life.

"Rosie?" I call from the entryway, kicking off my boots.

In the kitchen, she looks up from the stove where she's flipping a pancake. "Oh, hi, honey," she says, smiling. "You slept past nine. I'm glad. You needed the rest."

I wrap my arms around her, squeezing her so tightly she nearly drops the spatula.

"Kevin's called a few times," she says, her voice tentative as she searches my face.

"Kevin?"

"Yeah, I think he's worried about you." She pauses, her expression shifting into a smile. "It sounds like he wants to patch things up."

I shake my head. "Rosie, I don't want to patch things up."

"But yesterday, you were so—"

"Listen," I continue, taking a deep breath, "can we talk?"

Together, we sink into the pair of chairs by the fireplace. "I don't even know where to start."

"How about from the beginning?"

As I had yesterday, I tell Rosie about my experience—the seemingly endless stream of new realities, the different men and divergent lives, all the highs and lows. She listens intently, as if they're bonus chapters from *Fifty Shades of Grey*, and once I've finished, she nods, her eyes filled with compassion, understanding. But if she knows the secrets of the guesthouse, she keeps them to herself.

"So what now?"

"I don't know," I say, smiling to myself. "And that's the best part."

"This doesn't sound like the Lena from yesterday."

I nod. "I thought I had everything all figured out, but I was so wrong. And Kevin, well, he's so wrong for me. I was just too stuck in my own head to see it."

So you're not going to call him back?"

I shake my head. "Rosie, I hate hiking."

She laughs.

"I've always hated hiking."

I pause when I notice a familiar painting hanging on the living room wall that hadn't been there before—the still life of the ceramic pitcher beside two ripe pears that had previously been shuttered away in my mom's old bedroom for decades.

"I figured it was time we displayed some of her art," Rosie says, tracking my gaze, her voice thick with emotion. "No sense keeping such beauty locked away. She really did have a gift for making the ordinary seem extraordinary, didn't she?"

I nod. "I thought a lot about her while I was gone. I realized that there's more of her in me than I ever knew. All these years, I guess I've been afraid to face those similarities."

"Oh, honey," Rosie says, shifting in her chair to look into my eyes. "Yes, I see many reflections of your mother in you. That's the legacy of family. She was as brilliant as she was flawed. But you are your own soul. Never, even for a second, think that your path is predestined to follow in anyone else's footsteps. You get to choose the good, reject the bad." She smiles. "You're already doing that."

"You think so?"

"I know so."

I tuck my knees to my chest, pressing my head back against the chair. "I wonder what she'd be like right now, if she were here."

"Me, too," Rosie says, nodding. "Even in the finality of death, you never stop looking for them. Do you know how many mornings I've walked into the kitchen, certain that I could hear Bill sitting at the breakfast table, crunching away at his Raisin Bran?"

I smile.

She takes a steadying breath. "Yes, I keep looking for him—your mom, too—because I know if I pay close enough attention, I'll find them in the most unexpected places."

"Even at the breakfast table," I add, my eyes misty.

Rosie stands and stretches her arms. "How about we take our

minds off all this and head over to Pike Place this afternoon? I need to pick up some more honey—and a million other things. Are you in?"

"In," I reply.

"Good. Let me finish up some projects in the garden first, but let's plan on leaving shortly after noon."

While Rosie heads outside to tend to her hydrangeas, I think, not for the first time, how lonely she must be here on her own, missing Bill. I smile to myself, remembering her septuagenarian dance partner yesterday: Jim, with his bow tie and that pink rosebud on his lapel. Where did he say he volunteered, again? The Bainbridge Botanical Gardens? *Yes*. I was a child the last time I visited, though I know it's not far. I reach for my phone and do a quick search on Google Maps, surprised to discover that it's even closer than I expected—just a half mile up the shore. What if he's there right now? I reach for my coat, slipping out the back door.

"HELLO?" I SAY TO A FIGURE IN THE DISTANCE, HOVERING OVER A GARDEN BED.

A woman looks up in the misty air, garden trowel in hand. "I'm sorry, but we're only open to the public on weekends."

"Oh right," I say quickly. "I was just looking for Jim."

"Jim?" She stares at me, confused, as she shakes dirt from her gloves.

"Yeah, he . . . volunteers here, doesn't he? Tall, older guy, balding a little. Likes to dance?"

"Oooooooh," she finally says, as if I've just given her the secret handshake. "You mean the Colonel!"

"Um, the *Colonel*?"

"Yeah, the Colonel of the vegetable garden."

"Right," I say, struggling to keep a straight face. "Yeah."

"We all have posts here," she continues, her tone very official. "I'm the Queen of Herbs. Fred's the Duke of Delphiniums. Mary's the Countess of—"

"Let me guess," I interject. "Cauliflower?"

"Kale, actually," she replies, her tone strict and serious. "We have fourteen heirloom varieties." I think of Barb and Babbs. They'd be in kale heaven.

"Wow," I say, "but, about Jim, er, the Colonel—do you know where I might find him?"

"Yeah," she says, pointing down a gravel path. "He's right around the corner, getting the carrot seeds in the ground."

"Thanks," I say, darting ahead, spotting a man holding a shovel beside a pile of fresh, black soil.

"Jim?"

He looks up, a little confused.

"I'm sorry," I say quickly. "Should I call you Colonel?"

He chuckles. "Jim's just fine. I take it you've met Mary."

"The Queen of Herbs? Yes." I grin. "Listen, I'm a neighbor." I point to the south. "And I'm here to ask for an *unusual* favor."

"CAN YOU FEEL THAT *ENERGY*?" ROSIE BEAMS AS WE STEP ONTO THE COBBLE-stones of Pike Street. I take a deep breath, breathing in the Market's unique collage of scents—seafood, fresh-baked bread, smoky meat grilling in a nearby Persian restaurant.

"There's nothing on earth like it," she continues, walking ahead.

I follow her through the crowd as she stops at her favorite stalls, purchasing a bouquet of flowers, loads of vegetables and fruits, and three jars of honey. If that wasn't enough, she places an order for another case, some upcoming special edition.

"Do we need anything else before we go?" she asks as we meander, treasures teeming out of her woven basket.

"Yeah," I say, eying the staircase to the Market's lower floor. "Maybe a coffee."

Together, we descend the stairs, freshly roasted coffee beans wafting in the air. Café Vita is just ahead, and standing in the window . . . Spencer.

I freeze, squeezing Rosie's arm as I take in the sight.

"That's him, isn't it?" she says. "The old friend you told me about?"

"Spencer, yes."

Rosie nods. "He's quite the dreamboat." She watches my expression shift as a beautiful blond woman approaches and gives him a long embrace. He holds her face in his hands for an elongated moment, before turning when someone taps him on the shoulder. The woman stands beside him, flipping her long flaxen hair the way I used to in junior high.

"Lena?" Rosie says, sensing my unease. "Do you want to go in and say hi, or . . ."

"No," I say quickly. "Let's go. Now."

THE DOORBELL RINGS AT SEVEN SHARP; ROSIE LOOKS UP FROM HER BOOK, ANnoyed.

"I wasn't expecting a package." She frowns. "It's probably that neighbor boy who comes down here every other week selling candy bars for his baseball team. In my day, we didn't bother people after dinner!"

"I'll get it," I say, ignoring her grumpy rant as I smile slyly, peering through the side window, where Jim stands outside the door—in a suit with a fresh rosebud tucked into his lapel. *Perfect.*

"I hope I'm not late," he says a little awkwardly, holding a supermarket bouquet of pale pink roses.

"Right on time," I say, lowering my voice to a whisper. "I probably should have warned you that my aunt knows nothing about this, and also . . . *she's really stubborn.*"

"Well, I know a thing or two about stubborn women," he says, adjusting his sleeve. "I was married to one for forty years. It's like I've always said: 'Expect the best, prepare for the worst.'" He grins. "I think we're going to have a nice time."

"But maybe plan your escape route just in case," I suggest as we walk into the living room, each of us bracing ourselves—especially me.

"Who was at the door?" Rosie asks, flipping the page of her novel—the next book in the *Fifty Shades* series, I see.

"A guest," I say. "For you."

She looks confused and a little embarrassed as she tucks her book into her seat cushion—concealing the evidence.

"Rosie," I begin, "this is Jim. He's an excellent dancer, and I invited him over to see if you'd like to dance."

"Hi, there," Jim says, handing her the bouquet.

Rosie shakes her head. I can't tell if she's annoyed or amused—or both. "Dance? Lena, what's gotten into you?"

"Have you ever been swing dancing?" Jim asks, making an earnest attempt to lighten the mood.

"Well, yes," Rosie replies, a little cautiously. "But that was before this old hip of mine stopped cooperating."

"I'll take that hip and raise you a shoulder," he says, patting his left rotator cuff. "How about we flex our old muscles and give it another go?"

Rosie shifts in her seat, clearly flustered. For a moment I regret this whole idea, but then she smiles at Jim, her resolve weakening, before turning back to me. "Lena, you might have warned me that a handsome gentleman was coming over. I would have put on some lipstick."

"You're perfect the way you are," Jim interjects, offering Rosie his hand, her cheeks immediately flushing.

"Should I put on a record?" I ask as he pushes the coffee table aside.

"Yes," Rosie replies immediately, pointing to the old turntable. "Benny Goodman."

"Ah, I see you have excellent taste in music," Jim says as I sort through her records. "But what about your dancing skills?"

"I was about to ask the same of yours," she spars back, her words both playful and razor-sharp as I take the album out of its sleeve and set the needle in place.

As the music starts, the old vinyl scratchy and filled with patina, Rosie clutches Jim's shoulders, and I watch from the kitchen as he leads her around the room gently.

"Is that all you've got?" she chides before he dips her so low, her hair nearly grazes the floor.

"Better?" he asks, with a wide, confident smile as he lifts her upright again.

"I'd say so," she exclaims, a little breathlessly.

And just like that, Rosie is smiling again. They laugh hysterically as he spins her this way and that to the soundtrack of vintage jazz. The clarinet, the trumpet, the beautiful simplicity of two steps forward, one step back. Would they have found each other again without my intervention? Passed each other on the beach, or crossed paths at the supermarket, perhaps in the cereal aisle? Maybe. Maybe not. Yes, I orchestrated this moment, but it feels good to see something redemptive emerge from my harrowing journey—a little green sprout growing out of the darkness and into the light. I may have planted the seed, but it's Rosie's to nurture.

23

TWO WEEKS LATER

Bleary-eyed, I reach over to the nightstand to silence my phone's alarm. It's been fourteen days since I woke up in the guesthouse. Now I'm back in my old childhood bedroom, where a poster of Justin Timberlake with platinum-blond highlights is still pinned to the wall.

My world, it seems, has done a backflip. All the things I thought I wanted before this wild experience have faded into the background, leaving space for the here and now: an orange-hued sunrise over the Puget Sound, a mug of Rosie's chamomile tea with honey, the crunch of pebbles under my feet on the beach at low tide. Though I'm home, I'm still reeling—still trying to make sense of the highs and lows of all those alternate lives. And while I may always wrestle with the hows and the whys, perhaps for the rest of my life, my time "out there" left me with a sense of clarity: what matters and what doesn't.

Above all, however, I realize I was given an impossibly rare gift: the chance to see how life might have turned out had I chosen one path or another. That changes a person, and it certainly changed me. This experience has taught me many things, but most importantly, that our choices matter, more than we know. Life can often feel so one-foot-in-front-of-the-other, so prescriptive: Must be successful. Must find the perfect mate. Must check all the boxes. I did that, attempted to, anyway, but I lost myself along the way. I was so fixated on the finish line that I neglected to see all the beautiful moments along the way. I understand now that we're writing our stories every minute of every day, and all of it counts: Letting a tired grandma cut in front of you in the grocery store checkout line; showing up to a friend's birthday party, even when you'd rather stay home with takeout and Netflix; smiling at a fellow passenger on the train; finding the courage to apply for the job of your dreams, or quit the one that's draining your soul. All these decisions, big and little, add up to become the story of your life.

As for mine, I'm still figuring it all out. For starters, I decided to take a leave of absence from work. My boss, Christina, was more than a little miffed when I gave her the news, but I remained firm. "I haven't taken a vacation in five years," I told her over the phone. What I didn't express, however, is my growing uncertainty about spending the rest of my career "driving value" for soulless companies and their vapid executive teams.

"You could start a cupcake company," Frankie suggested over the phone a few days ago.

I nixed the idea immediately. "There isn't a market for inedible cupcakes."

"Maybe pick up writing? Try your hand at a screenplay?"

True, I do have plenty of material, and I was a bestselling novelist—in another life. Perhaps I could even look up Gina, the woman I met in Hawaii. She wouldn't remember me, of course, but I could pitch her my story, the one she resonated with on the beach that night. Maybe.

"Oh, I know!" Frankie added. "You could get in touch with your artistic side—maybe finish some of your mom's old paintings!"

When Frankie came to visit, we lugged my mother's assortment of easels and canvases to Rosie's living room. I even ordered some brushes and tubes of acrylic paint on Amazon. But each time I sat down to begin, my hands felt leaden.

AFTER ANOTHER FRUSTRATING GO OF IT, I LET OUT A DEEP SIGH AND PUT DOWN
my paintbrush, just as the phone in the kitchen rings.

"Get that, dear, will you?" Rosie calls from her bedroom.

"Hello?" I say, picking up.

"Rosie?" a woman asks.

"No, this is her niece," I say. "Can I help you with something?"

"This is Kelly from Firefly Honey in Pike Place. Your aunt ordered a case of our special-edition release, and we have it here for
her." She pauses. "If she could swing by and grab it, that would be
great—and the sooner, the better. Like today, even. We're running
out of space."

"Okay," I say. "Sorry. I'll let her know."

"Great, thanks."

"Who was that?" Rosie asks, walking into the kitchen.

"The honey people," I say. "Your order is ready for pickup at the
Market. They want you to swing by today."

Her eyes light up. "The *blackberry honey*?"

I shrug. "I don't know. She didn't specify."

"Sweetie, can you get it for me? Jim's coming over after lunch,"
she says, her eyes bright, "and we're practicing a *new move*."

"Of course," I say, grinning widely.

AS I MAKE MY WAY OFF THE FERRY IN SEATTLE, SEAGULLS SQUAWK AND FLAP
their wings overhead. The Market isn't far—just a short walk up from
Alaskan Way—and fortunately, the sun's out. I pass the infamous
"gum wall" as I make my ascent up Post Alley, smiling as I recall
that night after prom when Mike and I went out for ice cream then
deposited two wads of bubble gum along the brick façade just below
the Market's entrance—a Seattle right of passage, as gross as it is.

It's an unusually warm spring day, and Pike Street is thick with
tourists, many of them stopping to take photos under the famous
PUBLIC MARKET sign. Others watch in awe as fishmongers toss an
enormous salmon back and forth in theatrical fashion. I walk to the

flower stand ahead, where I select a bunch of tightly packed pale pink peonies—Rosie's favorite—before picking up the honey. I load the jars into my bag, then head for the exit, pausing momentarily at the edge of the staircase that leads to Café Vita, when my phone buzzes: Frankie.

"Hey," I say, setting my heavy bag on the cobblestone walkway beneath my feet. "I thought you were flying to Iceland today." She and Christian had been planning the trip for the last year. He wanted to see a real volcano and she dreamed of soaking in the Blue Lagoon.

"Yeah, we just landed in Reykjavik," she begins, her tone exasperated. "You wouldn't believe what just happened."

"What?"

"The airline tagged my bag wrong at JFK, and apparently it's on its way to Paris as we speak." She sighs.

"Oh no!"

"Oh yes. And don't even say it."

"Say what?"

"That thing everyone says about how you can tell the true character of a person when their luggage is lost. I'm furious. I could have throttled the airline employee just now. She just looked at me and shrugged, like, *Too bad, lady.* Anyway, Christian's at the customer service counter trying to sort it all out, but it looks like I'll be wearing the same outfit for the next five days."

I feel bad for her, but have to stifle a laugh when I imagine my jet-lagged and probably hangry best friend facing off with the unsuspecting employee at baggage claim.

"Try to shake it off," I suggest. "Maybe you can stop somewhere and grab some extra clothes." I smile to myself, remembering what Spencer said that day on Bainbridge Island. "You're just having a Helpless Traveler moment. Christian will be the Competent Traveler."

"Lena, what the hell are you talking about?"

"It's a line from a book," I say, laughing to myself. "Anyway, don't let this ruin your vacation. It's just a bag."

"Yeah," Frankie replies with a long sigh. "You're right."

"Okay, send photos and be nice to the airline employees. Love you!"

I tuck my phone in my bag, and with Spencer's words echoing in my mind, I proceed down the staircase to Café Vita. My heart beats faster as I step inside, taking a spot at the end of the line.

The café is the same, but different—in the best of ways: new marble countertops and a larger pastry case brimming with tasty-looking selections. I think about what Spencer told me, about his vision for the café: the changes he wanted to make and the things he vowed to keep the same. I immediately smile when I see the old wing chairs—tattered and worn, but still holding court by the window. I can't help but wonder if this is all his doing—his dream, actualized.

At the counter, a tattooed woman with a nose ring and blunt bangs greets me with a smile. "What're we feelin' like today?"

"Uh, a chai latte, please," I say, "with almond milk." I peer over her shoulder to the espresso machine. "Hey," I continue, a little tentatively. "Is Spencer here, by chance?"

She shakes her head. "The big boss flew out to New York this morning."

"The big boss?"

"Yeah, Spencer," she says. "You know, the owner."

"Oh yeah . . . right," I reply.

She hands me my drink. "You might have heard that we're expanding to Brooklyn. He'll probably be out there for a while, setting up the new roasting plant." She points to a rack of bagged coffee beans beside me. "Have you tried our anniversary blend?"

I shake my head.

"Get it while you can, because we'll be sold out by the weekend, if not sooner." She smiles. "And don't forget that for every bag sold, we give ten percent to farmers in South America."

I grin, filled with pride. Spencer did it—and exactly how he planned. "I'll take four."

She eyes me curiously as I tuck the beans into my already heavy bag. "You a friend of Spencer's or something?"

"Yeah," I say, smiling. "An *old* friend."

I wander up the stairs a little aimlessly, carrying the weight of my thoughts—and Rosie's enormous order of honey. I smile to myself, thinking of Spencer, how he'd comforted me that day on Bainbridge Island, the way he held me so tenderly. It was so natural, it was like we . . . fit, and yet, it was the first time I saw him through that lens, the first time I considered anything out of the bounds of friendship. Maybe I'll see him again, maybe not. But now I have a ferry to catch.

Picking up my pace, I pass a group of slow-moving tourists as I make my way to the exit, stopping suddenly when I *think* I hear my name in the distance.

"Lena?" a man's voice calls again from somewhere in the crowd.

I turn around, eyes darting right and left until I spot a familiar face a few yards away. "Spencer?" I freeze in place as annoyed strangers zigzag past me. He's the same—that boy-next-door smile, those kind blue eyes—but changed, somehow, more polished, more professional, as he walks toward me in a navy sports coat, leather satchel slung over his shoulder.

"Wow," he says, obviously stunned. "Lena! I can't believe this! I thought it was you, but I wasn't sure. How long as it been? Ten years, maybe more?"

No, just a couple weeks, I want to say. *Twenty-two days, to be exact.* "Yeah, something like that," I say instead.

"Did you move back to Seattle?"

I shake my head. "I live in San Francisco, but I'm in town for a little while, visiting my aunt on Bainbridge Island. It's nice to take a little time off work—clear my head, you know?"

"Tell me about it," he says. "I don't think I've taken a single day off since I took over the café three years ago."

"Congratulations," I say, a fluttery feeling rising in my chest. "I, uh, was just there . . . stopped by to . . . say hi. One of the baristas said you were in New York." I search his face.

"My flight got canceled," he replies with a shrug. "Apparently there's a hurricane brewing in the Atlantic."

I set my overloaded bag down beside me, never more grateful to hear of a hurricane than at this moment.

"Funny bumping into you after all this time," he continues, beaming as a ray of sunlight hits his left cheek.

"Yeah," I say a little breathlessly. "Funny."

He scratches his head. "This is going to sound crazy, but I'm having a total déjà vu moment right now—like this has all happened before."

"Same," I say, more than a little stunned.

He eyes my bag. "So you're just doing a little shopping, then?"

"Oh, I'm here on very important business. I had to pick up my aunt's special order of honey."

"Honey."

"Yeah, want some? We now have a lifetime supply."

Spencer grins, lifting my heavy bag over his shoulder, which makes my heart contract. "When do you head back—to San Francisco?"

"I don't know. I'm still figuring all of that out. I took a leave of absence from my job. It's complicated. They want me back, but I'm not sure I want to go back."

Spencer eyes me curiously, and I can't help but notice his gaze shift to my ring finger. "So, I take it you're not married, then?"

I shake my head. "I certainly hope not."

"No *significant other*?"

"Only a bunch of *insignificant* ones," I reply, recalling the woman I spotted him embracing when I was last at the Market. "Listen," I continue, squirming a little. "I have a confession to make."

"Oh?"

"I was at the Market with my aunt last month, and I saw you, with your *girlfriend*."

He grins. "Spying on me, I see."

"No, no," I fire back, a little embarrassed. "I was just . . . passing by and happened to notice you in the window."

"And this woman you *saw* me with," he continues, "was she tall? Blond?"

"Uh, yeah."

"Any other identifying details?"

"Well, she flipped her hair like this." I make an exaggerated gesture with my hand.

"You were *so* spying."

My cheeks flush. "I was not!"

He laughs. "That was my *sister*, Anne. She was in town that week, visiting from Pittsburgh."

"Oh," I say, a little mortified, though the corners of my mouth begin creeping up into a smile—without my permission.

"Yeah, I'm a party of one."

I look up at Spencer, inwardly debating whether or not to make my move, but then my eyes meet his. "Maybe we could be a party of two," I say suddenly, pulling the trigger. "Well, for dinner tonight, that is, if you're free."

"Yes," he replies. "I mean, no. I mean . . ." He pauses. "I *don't* have plans, and I'd *love* to have dinner with you. Have you ever been to Matt's?"

I shake my head.

"Well, you're in for a treat. Best oysters on the half shell in the city. Afterward, we could head down to the café, play a little Rummikub for old times' sake? If you can believe it, that old box is still under the counter."

"Sounds perfect," I reply. "I mean, if you want to get your butt kicked."

He laughs. "Well, I think we both know who the Rummikub champ is, and her name is not Lena."

"We'll see about that," I fire back.

A shiver creeps down the back of my neck as we weave through the Market, my mother's words echoing in my mind. She was right, so right: The most beautiful things in life are almost always right in front of our eyes. It just took me thirty-five years and a ten-day roller-coaster ride to figure that out.

"Should we get you a refill of that chai?" Spencer asks.

"You *remember*," I say, looking up at him, happily surprised.

"How could I forget?" His eyes scour mine as if he's peering into my soul.

I smile, my mind—and heart—reeling. *It was him.* In a suit or an apron, in this version of life or another, it was *always him*.

As we walk toward the staircase that leads to Café Vita, my heel catches on a cobblestone. When I lurch forward, Spencer swoops in to blunt my fall, grabbing my hand, which I hold on to.

I don't let go. In fact, this time, I don't think I ever will.

ACKNOWLEDGMENTS

This book wouldn't be a book had it not been for my dear friend and partner in crime, the movie producer Chris Goldberg. Our friendship spanning more than a decade paved the way, of course, but also his brilliant mind helped. I still remember reading an email from him with the title "Insignificant Others." "Would you be interested in collaborating?" he asked. My answer was an immediate "yes" (when you know, you know), and we spent the following months putting our heads together on the story. While the novel is written in my voice, there is so much of Chris in these pages: his humor, eye for story, stealthy ability to stop me from overcomplicating things, which I'm prone to do. Chris, I loved writing this book with you, and I love being your friend. Now, go take your vitamins, please.

To my amazing literary agents, Elisabeth Weed and Jenny Meyer (and D. J. Kim and Heidi Gall), I owe any and all success in my career to you—for believing in my stories and in me. I'm eternally grateful for our partnership and friendship.

Big thanks, also, to my intrepidly wise editor at William Morrow, Liz Stein, who loved this book from the very beginning, when it was only a handful of pages and a rough outline. Your brilliant ideas and thoughtful notes helped us create a story we're all so proud of. Liz, you're a rock star, as are your colleagues at Morrow, including Jen McGuire, Ellie Anderson, and the larger team behind the scenes who deserve my heartfelt gratitude.

I'd like to also thank my friends Aimée O'Carroll and Nabil Benali, who supported me with research and technical questions, as well as bestselling authors Emily Giffin and Nita Prose, who took time out of their busy schedules to read early copies and lend their support. (Emily, sorry about giving you COVID!)

To my friends at CAA, notably my agent Michelle Weiner and the Hollywood dream team, Ilda Diffley, Cat Vasko, and superwoman Sofia Stern: Thank you for falling in love with this novel as much as we've fallen in love with you. That week in Los Angeles remains one of my favorite professional experiences to date. Friends for life: on or off the red carpet!

To my three boys, who listened to me tell them about this book (over and over again) in car rides to and from school. Carson, Russell, and Colby, the only thing I love more than being an author is being your mom (and bonus mom to Josiah, Evie, and Petra—adore you three!).

Sarah Gelman, Natalie Quick, Lauren Vogt, Lisa Curran, Claire Bidwell Smith, Mimi Jung, Tess Andersen, Mariana Emsenhuber, Linda Duffus, and too many more to mention: Love is great, but female friends are everything. Thank you for being my *significant* tribe.

Last but not least, to Viviana and Brandon: Vivi, you are the yin to Chris's yang, a beautiful soul and dear friend. Thank you for all the ways you supported him (and me) while we worked on this project. And, Big B, my husband and the most significant love of my life: When I think about all the steps that led to you, it makes me appreciate every single one (even the hard times). I love you with all my heart.

ABOUT THE AUTHOR

Sarah Jio is a journalist and a *New York Times*, *USA Today*, and number one internationally bestselling author of eleven novels published with Penguin, Random House, and HarperCollins. Sarah's novels have been translated and published in more than thirty countries worldwide. In addition to being a longtime columnist for *Glamour* magazine, she has contributed to dozens of magazines and other news media, including the *New York Times*; *Real Simple*; *O, the Oprah Magazine*; *Parents*; *Marie Claire*; *Seventeen*; *Redbook*; and *Woman's Day*, as well as CNN, NPR, and many other outlets. Jio lives in Seattle with her husband, the record label executive Brandon Ebel; three sons; three stepchildren; and two puppies.